A HERO IN THE MAKING!

A piercing cry cut through him from above.

Through snow-thick lashes he peered up to see a weird and fantastic shape, black and be-winged, beating against the stars.

He could not see it clearly—a moving blackness, blotting out the starlight—its eyes like golden fire, brighter than any star, and moonlight glittering on beak and outstretched claws.

It fell like a thunderbolt from above, swept by him like a whirlwind, and swung down upon the white bear-thing with a scream of fury.

The mountains shook as the two came together, and the stars were blotted out.

Ragged black wings beat with cyclone force. Shaggy white jaws roared and crunched. Scythe-sharp black claws caught at the white breast and tore it asunder. The white thing moaned, and toppled, and came apart in chunks of broken snow.

The black shape whirled about and glared at the boy for the space of a single heartbeat.

And black eyes stared deep into his golden ones.

Then the wings spread and caught the wind and it was gone. Thongor lay gasping in the snow, the sword fallen from his nerveless hand.

Agony lanced through him as circulation returned to his half-frozen body. Hot blood went pumping through numb flesh; he shook his head dully, trying to waken his sluggish, frozen brain.

He had attained manhood, after all.

YOUNG THONGOR

LIN CARTER

WITH ADDITIONAL MATERIAL
BY ROBERT M. PRICE

EDITED AND WITH A FOREWORD
BY ADRIAN COLE

WILDSIDE PRESS

I am indebted to
Robert Price and Morgan Holmes
for their invaluable advice and assistance
in aiding me to compile this collection.
—Adrian Cole

"Diombar's Song of the Last Battle" first appeared in *Dreams from R'lyeh*, 1975 (Arkham House). "Black Hawk of Valkarth" first appeared in *Fantastic Stories*, September 1974; © Ultimate Publishing Company Inc. "The City in the Jewel" first appeared in *Fantastic Stories*, December 1975; © Ultimate Publishing Company Inc. "Demon of the Snows" first appeared in *The Year's Best Fantasy Stories*, Volume 6, 1980, edited by Lin Carter (DAW Books Inc.) "The Creature in the Crypt," based on a title by Lin Carter, is published in this form for the first time. "Silver Shadows" by Robert M. Price first appeared in *Crypt of Cthulhu*, no. 99—Lammas 1998. "Mind Lords of Lemuria" by Robert M. Price is an original tale, published here for the first time. "Keeper of the Emerald Flame" first appeared in *The Mighty Swordsmen*, 1970, edited by Hans Stefan Santesson (Lancer Books Inc.) "Black Moonlight" first appeared in *Fantastic Stories*, November 1976; © Ultimate Publishing Company Inc. "Thieves of Zangabal" first appeared in *The Mighty Barbarians*, 1969, edited by Hans Stefan Santesson (Lancer Books Inc.)

CONTENTS

FOREWORD

It would be difficult to identify the first Barbarian ever to wield a sword and tangle with sorcerers, monsters and other burly ruffians of similar ilk. His fantastic adventures would not necessarily have been recorded anywhere, but would almost certainly have been part of a rich tradition of oral story telling, around campfires, long before cities were conceived and the birth of what we, rather arrogantly, call civilization. The heroic tradition did eventually pass to the written word, creating immortal warriors whose names yet conjure up visions of splendid deeds and valor beyond the call of duty: Gilgamesh, Ulysses, Hercules, Beowulf, Sinbad, Cuchulainn, Viracocha, to name but a few.

Thongor, Lin Carter's most notable heroic Barbarian, first saw print in 1965 in *The Wizard of Lemuria*[1] and at once it could be seen that he undoubtedly had his ancestral roots in many of these ageless champions. Lin Carter, who was himself a champion of the heroic fantasy genre and an avid, omnivorous reader of its numerous branches, was more than a little familiar with the archetypal Barbarian. Thongor, however, has two very distinct roots, both of which Carter himself would have been the first to acknowledge.

These are Conan the Cimmerian, Robert E. Howard's *nonpareil* muscle-bound superman of an imaginary history set around 10,000 B.C. and John Carter, Edgar Rice Burroughs's superlative swordsman of Barsoom, or Mars. They are two entirely different characters, adventuring in very dissimilar worlds, though sharing certain common traits, not least of which is their appetite for action, their fearlessness in the face of impossible odds and the kind of determination to succeed that once built spectacular, world-spanning empires. Lin Carter drew heavily and unashamedly on these two robust fictional heavyweights when he put his own Barbarian together. The result is an unusual fusion, an affectionate tribute to two of the lasting champions of fantastic fiction.

---

1   *The Wizard of Lemuria*, first published by Ace Books (NY) 1965, revised and reprinted by Berkeley (NY) as *Thongor and the Wizard of Lemuria* in 1970.

Thongor himself is "...*cast very much in the mold of Conan...*"[2] apart from the occasional show of somewhat rough-hewn gallantry (as with Conan himself) he could hardly be mistaken for the gentlemanly John Carter, although he behaves and speaks very much like Burroughs' greatest creation, Tarzan, on occasion. In the tales that comprise Young Thongor, the Cimmerian's influence is particularly strong, while in the novels that follow on from this collection, John Carter and the characters of his world come more into focus as inspirations for the ensemble of Lemuria.

This prediluvian continent, while evidently prehistoric and pulsing with appropriate monsters, conjures up regular comparisons with Barsoom, which seems to be even more its blueprint than the Hyborian world of Conan. It is a compliment to Carter's energy and enthusiasm for his creation that the confusion of two such worlds and potential for anachronism and resulting dissonant clashes never actually materialize. In a bizarre kind of way, Thongor's saga works and works well.

As for the Barbarian's name, Lin Carter chose it quite deliberately and has said, "... *'Thongor' has grim weight to it, solidity, and the ring of clashing steel. The character is obviously a fighting-man; you can sense that from the sound of his name alone...*"[3]

And what of Lost Lemuria itself? In some ways it has been the poor relative of Atlantis, down through the ages. Initially it appears to have been a quasi-scientific explanation for there being lemurs in Africa and India, in the form of a geological bridge that spanned the ocean between two continents. The continental drift theory put paid to that, but Madame Blavatsky and her redoubtable Theosophists clung to the belief that Lemuria did actually exist and that it was the home of very curious inhabitants indeed. Lin Carter, much read in such lore, was familiar with all this, of course.

Rather than utilise the more familiar territory of Atlantis (as found in Howard's King Kull stories) Carter opted for the lesser-known alternative. Howard referred, albeit briefly, to Lemuria in his 'prehistory', which prefaces the Conan saga, *The Hyborian Age*.[4] Carter, who worked with Sprague de Camp on a number

2   From Lin Carter's own introduction to the Thongor stories in Lost Worlds, published by DAW Books (NY) 1980.
3   *Imaginary Worlds*, published by Ballantine (NY) 1970
4   *The Hyborian Age* was originally published in book form in

of Conan and Kull pastiches, was thoroughly *au fait* with this material and put it to good use in the Thongor epic. Hence Thongor's Lemuria still has strong links to the age of dinosaurs and its own history is steeped in conflict with reptile-beings, more saurian than human. Just as King Kull had to deal with lizard men who stubbornly refused to sink down into the swamps of oblivion, so does Lemuria have its Dragon Kings and their spawn. Add to this the half-forgotten technology of a former age, *à la* Barsoom, together with denizens who could have stepped straight from the dead sea-bottoms of that war-like world, and you have a colorful mix of culture, biology and history.

Quite apart from the Hyborian/Barsoomian connection, Lin Carter also drew heavily on the pulp tradition for the Thongor saga, a tradition that goes back through many of the writers and magazines that he promoted so ardently and successfully in his work as an editor. And he did not confine himself simply to the heroic elements of pulp, but drew on such diverse sources as H.P. Lovecraft, Lord Dunsany, A. Merritt and Clark Ashton Smith, to name but a few. The devout fan of pulp fiction will quickly recognise these elements in the Thongor saga and indeed, part of the fun of reading the work is in checking out the sources! One example from this volume is the story, "The City in the Jewel," in which Thongor finds himself in an enclosed world more in keeping with Dunsany than Howard, a direct contrast to some of the other stories.

Magic vies with technology, too. There are crumbling citadels, reeking with old sorceries and demonic powers, juxtapositioned with decadent super-science straight out of Edmond Hamilton or Van Vogt.[5] This Lemuria is a *potpourri* of pulp ingredients, wildly improbable, scornful of boundaries, reminiscent of the old Saturday morning movie serials, with their fabled "cliff-hangers." Burroughs used this technique to perfection in his own plots, and in Thongor we see the same style at work, so much so in places that one would almost expect Tarzan himself to swing out from the jungle to add weight to Thongor's cause.

Skull-Face and Others by Robert E Howard, Arkham House (Sauk City), 1946 and part one was reprinted in *Conan*, Lancer Books (NY) in 1967, edited by Lin Carter and L. Sprague de Camp.

5   Edmond Hamilton's *The Star Kings*, 1949 and A.E. Van Vogt's *The Book of Ptath*, 1953 in *Unknown Worlds*.

With the boom in heroic fantasy and sword and sorcery that came in the sixties, Thongor was by no means the only muscular barbarian to batter his way pell-mell through a catalogue of adventures. Conan spearheaded the advance, of course, but there was also Brak the Barbarian, creation of John Jakes, whose world and exploits therein mirrored those of Conan and Thongor and which were no less dynamic. An entire sub-genre sprang up, with an odd preponderance of "K" warriors—Kothar, Kyrik, Kandar, Kavin and Lin Carter's own Kellory.[6] Many of these fitted into a standard set of rules, with villains, monsters and beautiful maidens who were interchangeable and who could have comfortably slipped across from one series to another, like a wandering troupe of actors, taking the stage as and when required.

Yet the success of this itinerant band of heroes opened the way for other, more ambitious characters, still toiling away within the genre, but thrusting its boundaries ever wider into more imaginative and exotic terrain. Cugel the Clever, Jack Vance's lovable villain from the revived Dying Earth series, Karl Edward Wagner's turbulent, passionate Kane saga (Wagner himself wrote a couple of fabulous Howard pastiche novels), Fritz Leiber's highly polished and amusing Fafhrd and the Grey Mouser stories and Michael Moorcock's brooding, sombre Elric and Eternal Champion novels—all wonderful examples of the development of the genre. It is a less active genre these days, but it still has its wonders, the most outstanding example of which is surely the superb Nifft the Lean series from Michael Shea.

Lin Carter first enjoyed success with Thongor, but his zealous enthusiasm could never have been confined to one character and he was soon to produce a whole wave of sagas, each of them no less heavily influenced by writers like Burroughs, Howard, Vance and others. Burroughs very obviously remained the main source of this inspiration, directly or indirectly. The Callisto series is, for some critics, too close to Burroughs and Barsoom for comfort, whereas

---

6   The five Kothar novels (Belmont/Tower, NY, 1969-1970) and four Kyrik novels (Leisure Books, NY, 1975-1976) are from the busy pen of Gardner Fox, Kandar's only novel (Paperback Library, NY, 1969) from Ken Bulmer, Kavin's two novels (Lancer, NY, 1969 and 1972) from David Mason and Kellory from Lin Carter himself (Doubleday, NY, 1984).

the Green Star series, with its homage to Amtor (Venus) introduces enough variety to hold its own with Thongor. Another writer that Lin Carter greatly admired and praised was Leigh Brackett, whose own Martian stories were inspired by Barsoom. She created a Mars of her own, an evocative variation on the original theme (as did C. L. Moore with some of her outstanding Northwest Smith yarns) and Lin Carter pastiched their work with his own Mars quartet, although he drew, as always, on several other celebrated sources for his mixture. The first three of this series, *The Man Who Loved Mars, The Valley Where Time Stood Still* and *The City Outside the World*, are considered by many to be among his best works.

Young Thongor brings together for the first time the short stories that Lin Carter wrote about Thongor, published between 1974 and 1980. He had intended to write more Thongor material, referring to "*...the first and second volumes of the completed saga, which I plan to call Thongor of Lost Lemuria and Thongor in the Land of Peril...*"[7] but other projects occupied him up until his death in 1988 so that he never fulfilled that ambition. Like one of his idols, Robert E Howard, Lin Carter left a number of notes and plots among his papers and, perhaps ironically, we have used these to round out this book, which we hope will serve as an appetizer for the rest of the saga.

During his heyday in the 70s, Thongor featured in a comic book series, albeit a brief 8-issue run,[8] and there was even some serious discussion about a film.[9] The latter, though, never got made, which

---

7   *Imaginary Worlds*, published by Ballantine (NY) 1970.

8   Thongor was the main feature in Marvel's *Creatures on the Loose*, issues 22 through 29, March 1973 to May 1974. Issues 22 and 23 saw an adaptation of *Thieves of Zangabal*, with a script by George Alec Effinger that was true to Carter's original and with artwork by Val Mayerik. Issues 24 to 29 ran the complete *The Wizard of Lemuria*, again scripted by Effinger and with excellent art by Vincente Alcazar, who worked at various times on some of the more prestigious Conan comics.

9   Milton Subotsky, who co-produced with Max Rosenberg movies such as *At the Earth's Core* and *The Land That Time Forgot*, both from the work of Edgar Rice Burroughs, wrote to me for some information about Thongor in the 1970s. This was for a potential Thongor movie he was considering for Amicus Productions, so there were at least some basic plans on the drawing table! Movie rights to the Thongor books were licensed by a different production company in 2001, so hope for a

may be as well, as sword and sorcery never translated to the big screen very well in those days!

Robert Price, joint executor of the Lin Carter estate, himself a worthy scribe and editor, has written "Silver Shadows" from a title Lin coined for a Thongor tale he never got around to writing and has written "The Creature in the Crypt" from an abandoned Thonor synopsis. There is an even deeper irony here, for this story was published by Lin Carter as "The Thing in the Crypt," a Conan yarn and part of the *Conan* volume,[10] although it actually began life as a plot for the Thongor saga! And to round out the collection, Robert Price has written "Mind Lords of Lemuria," a stirring yarn that captures both Carter's style and not a little of the mighty Valkarthan's panache. It also more than hints at the bizarre deep past of Lemuria, linking it to the Mythos cycles in a way that I am certain Lin Carter would heartily have approved of.

What follows, then, is the beginning, an appetizer for even greater exploits, a feast of heroic fantasy on the grand scale.

—ADRIAN COLE

---

film version lives on.

10   *Conan*, published by Lancer (NY) 1967, edited by Lin Carter and Sprague de Camp.

The following originally appeared as part of the introduction to Thongor and the Dragon City, *which is now chronologically the third volume in the series about the Valkarthan warrior. A section of it is reprinted here as a fitting opening to Thongor's saga, setting the stage for the dramatic adventures that unfold.*

LEMURIA

Half a million years ago the first and most glorious civilization arose on the Lost Continent of Lemuria amidst the blue vastness of the Pacific.

This was the middle of the Pleistocene epoch, a division of geological time which began *circa* one million BC and extended to about 25,000 BC. The continents of Eurasia, Africa and the Americas were very different then. Mammoth and mastodon and sabretooth tiger fought for the mastery of the earth, while tall, stalwart Cro-Magnon man and his hulking, ape-like predecessor, Neanderthal man, fled from the remorseless advance of the towering glaciers. The age of the mighty reptiles was long over: it had ended with the birth of the Cenezoic Era seventy five million years ago.

But amidst the steaming jungles and fetid swamps and thundering volcanoes of primal Lemuria, the colossal saurians yet lived. They had come close to dominating the earth itself, and they would have trampled the first, small, timid mammals into the quaking slime.

But the Nineteen Gods Who Watch The World intervened. Seldom does The Unknown One permit the Nineteen Gods to influence the flow of time—only in moments of cosmic peril may they take action on the physical plane. But the future history of the planet trembled in the balance, and the unwritten chronicles of age upon age hovered in the mists of the Might-Have-Been. Thus the Nineteen Gods were permitted to act, and Man arose upon the earth to challenge the might of the Dragon Kings in war.

It is written in the age-old pages of *The Lemurian Chronicles* that this war lasted for one thousand years.

Man triumphed, the Dragons fell, and the Age of Men began. But, from beyond the Universe itself, the dark forces of Chaos and

Old Night schemed and plotted against the Lords of Creation. Evil cults of demon-worshippers arose in primal Lemuria: dark druids sworn to the service of Chaos, who subtly undermined the nine young cities of the World's West. King was pitted against king, and city against city, in ruinous wars. Soon the bright torch of that first civilization would be crushed out, and Man would descend into the red murk of howling savagery…

DIOMBAR'S SONG OF THE LAST BATTLE

1.

With dawn we rode from Nemedis
*   in all her pomp and pride.*
The white road thundered beneath our tread
*   and the white sea at our side.*
The wild waves broke on the naked rocks
*   and returned to break once more*
Where the grim black walls of the Dragon Keep
*   loomed on the grim black shore.*

2.

The foam-maned lions of the sea
*   drove madly against the strand.*
On a desolate stretch of wet black rock,
*   the heroes took their stand.*
Above, against a storm-torn sky
*   of whirling crimson smoke,*
The jagged walls of the Keep rose sheer
*   from the rocks where white waves broke.*

3

And Thungarth, son of Jaidor, urged
*   his mount to the grim black gate*
That rose above him like a cliff,
*   death-cold and dark as fate.*
Ah, he was young as morning,
*   a hero to behold;*
His mighty thews like ruddy bronze,
*   his mane like ruddy gold.*

4

The challenge was his alone to claim,
*   by clan-law and blood-right,*
For the Dragon Kings had slain his sire
*   in treachery by night.*
He set his war horn to his lips—
*   the thunder of its cry*
Aroused the Dragon warriors forth
*   to conquer or to die.*

5.

And from the ebon citadel
*   the Dragon Warriors came,*
And they were mailed in adamant,
*   and armed with evil flame.*
The heroes rode against them
*   and strove with sword and shield*
To fight and fall—if fall they must
*   —to die, but never yield!*

6.

And Khorbane fell, and proud Konnar,
*   and gallant Yggrim too;*
Yet still we strove with the Dragon Kings
*   and the great war trumpets blew.*
And for every hero of Phondath's breed
*   who upon that black shore fell*
We sent a dozen Dragons down
*   the scarlet throat of hell!*

7.

From wild red dawn to wild red dawn
*   we held our iron line*
And fought till the blades broke in our hands
*   and the sea ran red as wine.*
With arrow, spear and mighty mace,
*   we broke the Dragon's pride,*
Thigh-deep in the roaring sea we fought,
*   and crimson ran the tide.*

8.

But we were armed with simple steel,
*   and they with sorcery;*
And step by step they thrust us back
*   into the hungry sea.*
And Thungarth saw that he must use
*   that Sword the Gods had made*
Although he knew it meant his doom
*   to lift that dreadful blade.*

9.

As one by one his brothers fell,
*   he raised the Star Sword high!*
He sang the runes to the Lords of Light
—and thunder broke the sky!
Red lightning flashed—drums of thunder crashed—
*   a rain of fire fell*
To sweep the last of the Dragon Kings down
*   to the smoking pits of hell!*

10.

But the Lord of the Dragons was old and wise
    and a mighty mage was he.
He loosed a bolt of flaming death—
    his warriors laughed to see
The Star Sword broke in Thungarth's hand!
    and now what hope for Men?
The scaly might of the hissing horde,
    they were upon him then...

11.

But he beat them back with the broken blade,
    there, caught in the roaring tide.
And one by one they fell before
    young Thungarth in his pride.
But the Dragon Lord, with a great black spear,
    he drove them forth once more,
They closed again with Thungarth there
    while the wild waves ran with gore.

12.

Yet once again he beat them back
    with a fragment of the Sword;
They broke and fell before him then,
    and he faced their mighty Lord.
The great black spear was sharp and long,
    his Sword but a shard of steel;
The Dragon Lord was fresh and strong,
    but Thungarth would not yield.

13.

He battled there with the broken blade,
*   half-drowned in the roaring tide;*
The great black spear drank deep as it sank
*   in Thungarth's naked side.*
But ere the Son of Jaidor fell,
*   or ere his strength could wane,*
The Broken Sword of Nemedis
*   had clove the Dragon's brain.*

14.

Thunder rolled in the crimson sky.
*   the War Maids rode the storm*
To bear the soul of Thungarth home
*   to the Halls of Father Gorm.*
The Age of the Dragon ended there
*   where the seas with scarlet ran:*
Though the cost was high, the prize was great,
*   and the Age of Men began.*

It is almost five thousand years since the Thousand-Year War was fought between Man and Dragon Kings, when the reptiles, long time rulers of Lemuria, were vanquished at the culminating battle at Grimstrand Firth. It is a new age, a time of growth, of savage kingdoms, yet beset by turmoil, a world ripe for adventure, conquest and the winning of fabulous fortunes. A hard world for a boy scarce turned fifteen.

It is the year 6997 of the Kingdoms of Man...

BLACK HAWK
OF VALKARTH

1

Blood on the Snow

The flames of sunset died to glowing coals in the crimson west. Slowly, the brooding skies darkened overhead, and the first few stars glared down upon a scene of terrible carnage.

It was a great valley in the land of Valkarth in the Northlands, beyond the Mountains of Mommur, where the cold black waves of Zharanga Tethrabaal the Great Northern Ocean lashed a bleak and rock-strewn coast.

Although it was late spring, snow lay thick upon the valley. It was trampled and torn, and here and there bestrewn with motionless black shapes. These were the bodies of men and women and children, clad in furs and leather harness, clasping broken weapons in stiff, dead hands. In their hundreds they lay sprawled and scattered amid the trampled snow, and against its dirty grey their blood was crimson.

The battle had begun at the birth of the day and with day's end it, too, had ended. All the long, weary day the warriors and hunters and chieftains of the Black Hawk nation had stood knee-deep in the snows and fought with iron blade and wooden club and stone axe against the enemies that had crept upon them in the night. One by one they had fallen, and now no single man lived or moved upon the gore-drenched snows of Valkarth. They had not died easily, but they had died; and very many of their foes lay beside them in the black sleep of death.

The valley was like a charnel-pit. And the stars looked down, wonderingly.

They had been a mighty people. The men were tall, strong-thewed, with thick black manes and virile, golden eyes. The women were deep-breasted, their unshorn hair worn in heavy braids, their strong white bodies clad in belted furs against the bite of wintry winds. They had fought beside their men, the women of the Black Hawk clan, or back-to-back, and they, too, had heaped their dead before them. In the end they had gone down fighting; and their young, too, children scarce old enough to walk, had died with bloody knives clenched in their small fists.

Life in the bleak Northlands of Lost Lemuria was one unend ing struggle against grim Nature, ferocious beasts, and no less savage men. The weaklings and the cowards died young: this nation had been strong, and it had died hard; but in the end it had died.

By one great rock a tall and stalwart warrior had taken his last stand. He had set his back against that rock and with his great sword he had hewn and hewn until the snowy slope before him was buried beneath the corpses of those who had come up against him. They had cut him down with arrows at the last, no longer daring to come within the reach of that terrible blade; at that, it had taken five arrows to kill him. He lay now with his broad shoulders still flat against the rock, his square-jawed face grim in death as in life, snow and blood daubed on his thick grey mane and beard. The wife of his youth lay beside him, a bear-spear still held in her cold hands, her head resting lightly against his shoulder. They had cut her down with an axe, and two of her tall sons and her young daughter lay near.

The name of the dead warrior had been Thumithar; he had been a chieftain of the clan, of direct descent in the male line from the hero Valkh—Valkh the Black Hawk, Valkh of Nemedis, the seventh of the sons of Thungarth of the first Kingdoms of Man. The war bards of the tribe, the old, fierce-eyed sagamen, told it had been Valkh who had founded the Black Hawk nation in time's grey dawn. And the great broadsword that lay still clasped in the dead fingers of Thumithar was none other than Sarkozan itself, the very Sword of Valkh.

He had been a wise chieftain, had Thumithar, just and strong. And a great war-leader, and a mighty hunter.

He would hunt no more, would Thumithar, with his tall sons at his side.

* * * *

In that grim panorama of death, one indeed yet lived. He was a scrawny boy, scarce fifteen, naked save for a ragged clout and a cloak of furs slung about bare shoulders. They were broad, those shoulders, but stooped with weariness now, and they bore a burden of sorrow, heavy for one so young to bear.

Blood was bright on the brown hide of his deep chest, and some of it was the blood of the foemen he had fought and slain, but much of it was his own. He limped through the bloody snow, dragging one foot behind him, and, now and again, he paused to look at this dead face and that one. He knew many of them, the dead faces; but he did not find the one he was looking for.

At last he came up to the place where the grey-maned warrior had taken his last stand, and the limping boy flinched at the sight of that dead face in the starlight. And the serene face of the woman that lay beside the dead man wrung a sharp cry from the white lips of the boy.

He crumpled into the snow before them on his knees and he hid his face in his hands. Tears leaked slowly through the blood-encrusted fingers, and he wept there at last—he who had not wept before.

His name was Thongor.

2

The Cairn in the Valley

After a time the boy climbed wearily to his feet and stood staring at the ruin of his world. In repose, he had the same grim-jawed face as his father, the same heavy, unshorn mane—save his was yet untouched with grey. His eyes glared golden like the eyes of lions, under scowling black brows. He had long, rangy legs, and strong arms seamed with scars, some of which were raw wounds.

In the crush and swirl of battle, he had been swept away from his father and his mother and his brothers. All day he had fought alone, with the tigerish fury of a young berserker, and many of the enemy had fallen before his murderous wrath. When his old sword broke in his hands, he had fought on with the stub, then with rocks clawed up from the snowy ground—finally, with his bare fingers and his strong white teeth.

He had taken a deep wound on the breast, and lesser wounds on thigh and shoulder and brow. He was splattered with blood from head to foot, although he had stemmed the bleeding with snow until the wounds were numb.

The Snow Bear warriors had clubbed him down and beaten him to earth and left him for dead. That was their only mistake.

For he had not died.

He had slowly climbed back from the Shadowlands into the realm of the living again, to find night fallen and the battle over and the terrible valley silent with its dead. Slowly, dragging his injured foot behind him, he had searched among the fallen until at last he had found that which he sought. And now he knew what he must do.

He cleared away a patch of earth, clawing back the snow, and he laid out the bodies of his mother and father beside the bodies of his older brothers and his younger sister.

He set their weapons beside them. All but the great sword of his father, the mighty broadsword Sarkozan; that he took, for he would need it.

He kissed their cold lips one last time in farewell.

Then he began to pile the stones upon them.

There must be many stones, else the beasts would feed upon them in the night. Although he was bone-weary, and sick with loss of blood, he dragged the great stones one by one upon them, heaping up a tall cairn until it stood higher than a grown man. Then, and only then, did he rest; and by then he was shaking with exhaustion.

It would stand for the rest of time, that cairn, to mark the place where Thumithar of the Valklings had fallen. Or until the mighty continent itself, riven asunder with earthquake, was drowned beneath the cold waves of the sea.

He sang the warrior's song over them, his clear young voice sharp and strong and strange to hear in that deathly silence.

* * * *

The black sky lit with cold glory as the great golden Moon of old Lemuria rose up over the edges of the world to flood the bleak land of Valkarth with her light. In the cold flame of the moonlight, he saw that the cairn was high and strong. The white bears would not claw it asunder, nor the grey wolves, to feast on what lay beneath.

At the thought, his jaws tightened and his lips clamped together. For the white bear of the Northlands was the totem beast of the enemy clan who had worked this day's red ruin, even as the black hawk of the skies was his own tribal totem.

He hated the mighty *ulth*, the white bear of the snow countries, and had often hunted him down the bleak hills of this wintry land. And now he had another reason for that hatred.

The cairn was done; and he was finished here.

But there was one last task the dead had set upon him.

And its name was Vengeance.

3

Horror on the Heights

He gathered up his gear and was ready to depart. From the dead, he took what he needed, nor did it bother him to plunder them. They were the men of his race, and the blood that lay strewn upon the snows about them, that same blood ran hot and fierce in his own veins. They would not begrudge him what he needed of them. Nor would they need it any longer.

From one he took the black leather trappings that were warriors' harness, the leather yoke studded with discs of brass that fitted about the throat to protect the shoulders, the affair of buckled straps and the great brass ring that shielded the midsection from the flat of a blade, the iron-studded girdle worn low about the hips, the heavy boots, the broad-bladed dagger and the twin leather bottles, one filled with water and one with wine. His sword he slid into its worn old scabbard, which he clipped to a baldric and slung it across his chest so that the scabbard hung high between his shoulders.

He was not truly of age to don warriors' harness, for he had not yet undergone initiation into the rights of manhood by the old shaman of his nation. Nor would he now, for the garrulous old tosspot lay dead across the vale, having slain a dozen Snow Bear warriors with a two-handed axe before they had cut him down. Had not this day befallen, Thongor would with summer have gone up into the high mountains, there to dwell alone amid the heights, drinking the water of melted snow and eating only what he could slay with his bare hands; there would he have dwelt for forty days until the vision of his totem came to him and he learned his secret name.

Now that would never be. But manhood was upon him without the old rites.

Vengeance is for men. It is not a task for boys.

* * * *

Half the night was worn away. He crossed the valley and climbed the hills, ignoring the pain in his injured foot. Strong red wine had warmed his numb flesh and it drove new strength and vigor through his tired frame. The cold, thin air of the heights cleared his throbbing head and the exertion of the ascent made the blood tingle in his veins.

There would be time enough to rest, later, when the deed was done.

If he lived…

The Moon was high in the heavens now; the night sky was black as death and the stars blazed like diamonds strewn on dark velvet. He thought of nothing as he climbed, neither of the dead he had left behind him in the valley, nor of those he went to kill, but merely of setting his foot upon first one rock and then upon a higher one until at last he came to the crest and the wide world fell away beneath him to every side and the stars seemed very near.

Here a saddle-shaped depression sloped between twin hill-crests, thick with virgin snow. It had fallen here, perhaps, when the world was young and fresh and the Gods still went among men to teach them the nine crafts and the seven arts.

He began to wade through the snow between the twin peaks. With each step he stirred snows that had lain for a thousand years, and the crystals swirled up before him like ancient ghosts awakened by the step of a rash intruder into places better left undisturbed.

His nape-hairs prickled and the flesh of his forearms crept. He had a sense that something was aware of his coming, that something—*roused*.

The cold breath of fear blew along his nerves, and it was colder than any snow. One hand went to his breast where a fetish of white stone lay over his heart, suspended about his neck on a thong. He muttered aloud the name of Gorm, his god.

And terror woke, roaring!

Was it a sudden gust of wind which raised the snow before him in a whirling cloud—a cloud that shaped itself into a mighty, towering form—a phantom-thing of numb snow that reared up before him on legs like tree-trunks, hunched shoulders massive and monstrous, huge paws raised to crush and tear, dripping jaws agape, red eyes of madness glaring into his?

He fell into a fighting stance and the great blade was alive and singing in his hand, starlight glittering on the blue steel, acid-etched sigils blazing with eerie fires.

The thing came lumbering towards him. And he knew no steel could slay it, for it did not really live.

4

Vengeance in the Night

The gigantic, white, hulking monster was almost upon the boy now. He knew it for an *ulth*, a snow bear, but twice the girth and height of any *ulth* ever seen by mortal eyes before.

He knew also that it was a ghost-thing, that demon of the snows. For there poured from it a freezing cold, inhuman and magical. The sheen of perspiration on his bronze limbs froze like a thin sheath of glass upon his body. The icy breath of those fanged jaws panted in his face and he felt it go dead and numb as if he wore a mask of snow.

A red haze thickened before his eyes, blinding him. Each breath he drew was like fire stabbing in his lungs, cold fire, black yet burning. He fought against the cold that coiled about him, swung Sarkozan high, glittering against the stars, and hewed and cut at the ghost-bear. But from each stroke he took hurt, for a wave of stunning cold went through him as the steel blade touched the lumbering monster of snow.

He fought on, knowing death was near; flesh could not long endure such cold. His heart was a frozen thing in his breast; his very blood congealed in his veins; he could no longer breathe, for to draw in each breath was as painful as a blade of ice driven deep into his lungs. But he fought on, and would fight until he fell.

A piercing cry cut through him from above.

Through snow-thick lashes he peered up to see a weird and fantastic shape, black and be-winged, beating against the stars.

He could not see it clearly—a moving blackness, blotting out the starlight—its eyes like golden fire, brighter than any star, and moonlight glittering on beak and outstretched claws.

It fell like a thunderbolt from above, swept by him like a whirlwind, and swung down upon the white bear-thing with a scream of fury.

The mountains shook as the two came together, and the stars were blotted out.

Ragged black wings beat with cyclone force. Shaggy white jaws roared and crunched. Scythe-sharp black claws caught at the white breast and tore it asunder. The white thing moaned, and toppled, and came apart in chunks of broken snow.

The black shape whirled about and glared at the boy for the space of a single heartbeat.

And black eyes stared deep into his golden ones.

Then the black wings spread and caught the wind and it was gone. Thongor lay gasping in the snow, the sword fallen from his nerveless hand.

Agony lanced through him as circulation returned to his half-frozen body. Hot blood went pumping through numb flesh; he shook his head dully, trying to waken his sluggish, frozen brain.

He had attained manhood, after all.

He had gone up on the heights alone, and there the vision had come to him, and he had seen his totem-beast, and learned his True Name.

And he was blest above all the warriors of his tribe since time began: for the beast of his vision was the Black Hawk of Valkarth itself, the symbol of his race. And he knew then that his destiny would be stranger and more wondrous and more terrible than that of other men.

And he had seen a prophecy, too.

He had seen the Black Hawk fight and slay the Snow Bear. The ghost-beasts had fought there on the windy heights near to the blazing stars, and from that fight the Black Hawk had borne away the victory.

He drank down cold wine and rested for a time.

Then he went on, to make the prophecy come true.

* * * *

It was the month of Garang in late spring, and the thaws had begun. The great snow that lay thick upon the heights and that cumbered the steep slope of the cliffs was rotten and lay loose, water trickling here and there. When he crossed over to the other side of the ridge he could look down on the valley where the tents of the Snow Bear tribe stood out black against the snow, which reddened, now, to the first shafts of dawn.

They were weary after the long battle, the Snow Bear warriors—those of them that had survived. They had killed and killed and come away with the Black Hawk treasure of mammoth-ivory and red gold and with those of the Black Hawk women and girl-children who had not been fortunate enough to die beside their men.

They had feasted long, drunk deep, and caroused lustily and late, the victorious Snow Bear warriors. And now they slept heavily, gorged on meat and blood and wine and womanflesh.

From that sleep they would not awaken.

For a long moment the boy stood, arms folded against his breast, looking down on the camp.

His face was grim and expressionless, like a mask cast in hard bronze. He was a boy in years, but the iron of manhood had entered his soul. He knew what he must do; the spirits of the dead called to him in the windy silence, and he hearkened, and bent to the task.

With the great sword he began to cut the snow away.

It was not hard to do; the growing warmth of a Northlands spring had done half the job for him. The broken masses of snow began to roll down the steep, high slopes; as they came whirling down, they broke more snow loose, and each mass became a greater mass, until at last a mountain of heavy snow poured like a ponderous white river down the cliffs to collide in thunder on the floor of the valley below.

They had put up their tents close under those cliffs, the Snow Bear warriors, to block away the wind. Now it was snow that came down upon them, not wind, and by the time the avalanche came thundering down upon the tents it weighed many tons.

It crushed them into the earth, smothered them and their treasure and the ruined, broken, empty-eyed women they had taken captive; and in that thundering white fury not one lived.

The tribes of Valkarth have a simple faith.

Only those brave warriors who face the foe, and fight, and fall in battle, only their bold spirits are borne by the War Maids to the Hall of Heroes, to feast eternity away before the throne of Father Gorm.

And what of they that die by accident in gross and drunken slumber? The shamans shrug and do not say. But they do not die the death of men, the death of warriors; the Hall of Heroes does not open to such as they. Their miserable souls slink cringing through the grey mists and cold shadows of the Underworld forever.

The vengeance of Thongor was completed.

5

Red Dawn

Morning lit the east and the stars fled, one by one, before the red shafts of dawn.

When Thongor had made certain that not a single foe had survived the avalanche, he turned away and set his face to the sun.

The task was accomplished and he had lived.

Where, now, would he go? To a valley of corpses and an empty hut, whose walls would ring no more to his father's joyous laughter and his mother's quiet, crooning songs?

Not there; he could not go back.

But where, then? No other tribe would take him in, for life in the Northlands was a grim, bleak struggle for existence, and every mouth that was fed meant that another must go hungry.

His people were extinct; there was nowhere for him to go.

And then it was that a verse from the old warriors' song he had sung over his father's grave for a dirge returned to him. And he thought of the Southlands, of the Dakshina, the lush jungle-countries that lay beside the warm waters of the Gulf, beyond the Mountains of Mommur to the south.

There, bright young cities glittered in the bold sun, with green gardens, and laughing girls. There, fiery kings and princes contended in mighty wars, and kingdoms lay ripe and ready for the taking. He thought of gold and gems, of fruit warm from the sun, of whirling battles on the green plains, of dark-eyed, barbaric women...

And he set the great broad sword back in its scabbard, and drank deep of the red wine, watching dawn rise up over the edges of the world to fill the land with light; and he set his face towards the south, that last of the Black Hawk warriors.

And he passed from sight, down the hill-slope, striding with long steps towards the place where the great range of purple mountains marched across the world from west to east.

His heart lifted within him, for the night was over. And as he strode from view, he lifted his voice and sang again that warriors' song...

> *Out there, beyond the setting sun,*
> *Are kingdoms waiting to be won!*
> *And crowns, and women, gold and wine—*
> *Courage! And hold the battleline!*

For over two years, the youthful Thongor wanders the vastness of the Lemurian Northlands. Here the tribesmen are clannish, suspicious of strangers and a swift death is promised to anyone straying into their jealously protected domains. Thongor lives on his wits, often forced into using his fighting skills to survive, developing them, hardening himself until he has become a dangerous, fierce warrior, lion-like and elusive.

Not yet seventeen, he moves ever southward, away from the lands of his birth, into the huge range of the Mountains of Mommur.

THE CITY IN THE JEWEL

1

As the Sun Died

The fierce tropic sun of old Lemuria had long since passed the zenith of day. Now it descended the dome of heaven to perish in its pyre of crimson vapors that lit the dim west with flame. In all this desolate land of jagged, jumbled rock, nothing lived, nor moved, but shadows.

The level shafts of flaming light struck across the vast tableland of the plateau and drew long ink-black shadows from the circle of standing stones amidst the waste.

Seven they were, and twice taller than a man: tapering columns of dark volcanic stone, rough-hewn, coarsely porous. They stood in a circle on the plain of broken rock, and the red rays of the sinking sun drew long tapering shadows from them. Seven long black narrow shadows…like the fingers of a monstrous groping hand.

Glyphs were deep-cut in the ringed monoliths. Ages of slow time had all but worn them smooth. Yet still were they faintly legible, were there any eye to read them in this shadowy land of stone and silence.

That which stood amidst the circle of standing stones caught the red rays of sunset and flashed with gem-like brilliance. It was a vast, rugged mass of crystal, cloudy, misted: a huge gem of green and sparkling silver, so large that the arms of a full-grown man could scarce encompass it.

Into nine hundred uneven geometric facets was the glimmering crystal cut. Each facet was engraved with a curious sigil; each sigil was subtly alike each other, yet no two were precisely the same.

As the sun died in thunderous glory on the western horizon, the faceted stone caught the last beams and burst ablaze with sparkling splendor. Amidst the shimmering radiance, the strange sigils glowed weirdly, as if sentient. Like watchful eyes, cold, alert, intent, they peered through the purpling shadows.

No man alive on earth in all that distant age could read those carved signs on the monstrous jewel, nor spell the sense of those deep-carved and age-worn glyphs upon the seven monoliths.

But something pulsed amidst the dazzling radiance of the stone and as it lay bathed fully in the sunset flames.

Power!

Vast, awesome, magical.

And...*deadly.*

2

When Dragons Hunt

For five hours now the boy had fled for his life, and now he had reached the very end of his strength. His numb legs would move no farther and he fell, gasping for breath, in the coarse rubble that bestrewed the plateau. His lungs were afire, his raw throat ached and thirst was like a raging torment within him. But he could flee no more.

Against the blaze of sunset, the dragons circled. Black, horrid shapes with snaky necks and ragged, bat-like wings. They had caught the hot scent of manflesh shortly past midday and they had hunted him lazily down the high mountain pass that cleft all this mighty range, the Mountains of Mommur, and across this bleak and desolate tableland, until they had worn him to the point of exhaustion.

Now they swung casually, wings booming like sales on the quickening breeze, cold ferocity flaring in the mindless reptilian eyes that shone through the gathering dusk like yellow coals.

Sprawled panting amidst the broken stones, the boy glared up at them, his strange gold eyes blazing lion-like through tangled black locks. He did not fear them and would fight them to the last with every ounce of strength in his bronzed and brawny form. But he was doomed, and he knew it.

His savage people, tribesmen of the cold north, had a saying. *When dragons hunt, the boldest warriors hide.*

He was young, not yet seventeen, and nearly naked, his brown hide bare save for high-laced sandals and a rag of cloth twisted about his loins. His breast and strong arms, back, belly and shoulders were scored with old scars and white with road dust, for he had come far—halfway across the world it seemed, from that gore-drenched battlefield whereon all his people had died save he alone. Down from the wintry tundras of the frozen Northlands had he come, alone and on foot, battling savage beasts and even more savage men, and the scars of many battles marked him.

Strapped in a worn old scabbard across his broad young shoulders, a great Valkarthan broadsword lay. It was his only weapon: and it was useless against the winged death that hovered, indolently flapping, against the sky of darkening crimson. Had he but a bow he could likely have struck down the flying horrors that had playfully, cat-like, lazily hunted him all afternoon down the bleak mountains to this desolate plateau.

Here, in a brief scarlet flare of agony, he would die. And here his bare white bones would lie bleaching to powder under the Lemurian skies forever.

But he knew no fear, this bronzed boy who lay helpless, panting, exhausted.

3

Where Horror Dares Not Pass

Suddenly a cold hand went gliding across his hot thigh. He jerked about, nape prickling with primal night-fears, one capable fist seizing the hilt of the two-handed broadsword. Then he relaxed, chest heaving. It was a cold, black shadow that had crept across his flesh, dark and stealthy. A long, tapering shadow, like a pointing finger.

Curious, the boy raised himself on one arm and peered about to see the source of that shadow. He threw his tangled black mane back from his face and stared with amazement. Stared at the ring of dark columns that encircled a lone cube of black stone like a rude altar. And stared at that which glittered and flashed there.

He was looking directly into the sunset, but that roiling mass of crimson flame was less brilliant than the immense and sparkling jewel that stood amidst the monoliths.

Cold wind swept over him in a gush.

Fetid, hot breath blew, stinking, in his face. He flinched—ducked—as one of the scaly horrors of the upper sky swung low, snapping yellowed fangs at his flesh. The dragons were bolder, now. Or, perhaps, hungrier.

He staggered to his feet, levering himself erect with one hand braced against a broken boulder. He would meet death face to face, standing on his two feet like a man, he thought grimly.

They swung about far above, the twin, bat-winged horrors, circling for the kill. He glared about for a place to stand, a tall stone to set his shoulders against, and suddenly he thought of that circle of smooth lava pillars. The monoliths were set close together: the bat-winged horrors would not be able to come at him from above or behind it if he set his shoulders against one of those pillars; they could only come at him from in front, and then they would face the glittering, razor scythe of that mighty broadsword with which he and his forefathers had fought against many a foe. Perhaps he had a chance after all.

Staggering a little, his aching legs still numb with bone-weary exhaustion, he headed for the ring of standing stones and the sparkling enigma they guarded and enclosed. He drew the great sword, Sarkozan. He set his back against the rough cold stone and took his stand. He threw back his head and shouted a challenge to the winged predators of the sky.

They swerved and came hurtling down at him, those flapping black shapes. He could see the flaring coals of their burning eyes and the immense grinning jaws lined with yellowed fangs, the long snaky necks stretched hungrily for him, clawed bird-feet spread to cling and rip—

Ignoring the ache of weariness in chest and arms and shoulders, the boy swung up the great sword as the flying dragons flashed for him—and swerved aside!

Puzzled, the boy's strange gold eyes narrowed thoughtfully. He watched through tousled black locks as the flying reptiles curved in their flight, veered away, and flapped off hesitantly, to rush down at him again.

Again they came swooping down. And again they veered to one side at the last moment.

It was strange. It was more than strange, it was a little frightening. It was as if those horrid dragons of the sky—*feared* the circle of standing stones!

Propped against the rough pillar, leaning weary arms on the cross-hilt of the great sword, Thongor watched as the sunset died to smoldering coals. The skies darkened as night rose on black wings up over the edges of the earth to shroud the great continent in shadow.

The dragons hovered and circled, and, at length, flapped away and were lost in the gathering darkness. Then the boy turned to explore this peculiar ring of monoliths, where even the fanged predators of the sky dared not come near. This circle of stones, which mailed, mighty dragons dared not pass.

4

The City in the Jewel

Thongor examined the seven stone pillars. They were of cold dead rock, dark, volcanic, rough and porous to the touch. With curious fingers the young barbarian traced the strange heiroglyphs inscribed upon them. He could make nothing of the curious symbols, but, then, as for that, he could neither read nor write. He had no way of guessing that those inscriptions were in a long-dead tongue whose last living speaker had perished from the earth untold aeons before…

He next approached the low altar.

It was a six-sided cube of black rock and it bore no carvings. On its top, the great gem flashed and twinkled. Never before had the boy seen a mass of crystal so immense. He bent over it curiously, and the cold shifting lights that moved within bathed his features in a restless glow.

His was a strong young face, square of jaw and broad of brow and cheekbone. Scowling black brows curved over lion-like eyes. Sun and wind had burnt his face to the hue of old leather; there was strength in that face, and intelligence, and breeding. Though how a half-naked wild boy from the savage wilderness of the wintry Northlands had come by that breeding, none could say.

He was curious about the carved sigils, which adorned the glassy surface of each of the odd-angled facets, and he stretched out his hand to trace them—

And jerked back numb, tingling fingers with a muted cry. A cold, electric shock stabbed at him as his outstretched fingers touched the slick, glassy surface—a weird, thrilling force.

Frowning, puzzled, he bent over the glittering, flashing gem and peered deep into it.

Deep and deep…through the angled mirrors of the many facets…down through twinkling mists of dim green and sparkling silver dust…to the strange pulsing core of the monstrous gem, where cold phosphorescent fires coiled and glared.

But something happened. The crystal *changed*.

The mists thinned—faded—evaporated.

Had the touch of his fingers closed a contact between the boy and the forces that slumbered, locked deep within the mystery jewel? Had his nearness triggered some dormant, age-old spell—some mystic sorcery whose secret was traced in the weird sigils that had been hewn into the facets of the gem?

Sparkling mists coiled—cleared—whipped away.

Suddenly the clouded green crystal was clouded no more. Now it was clear and pellucid as glass…and the boy's eyes widened in amazement as he stared down upon that which was now clearly visible in the very core of the gigantic gem. He stared down upon…

A city! A city there in the heart of the jewel.

It was exquisite, elfin. Tiny, delicate minarets and needle-pointing spires of dainty glistening ivory. Swelling bells of domes, twinkling with goblin lights. Delicious little houses, peak-roofed and gabled, with stained-glass windows no bigger than his thumbnail.

A faerie princedom in the frozen heart of a gem!

Breathless with awe and wonder, the savage boy stared down at little, crooked streets cobbled as if with cowrie shells; at curved flights of alabaster stairs a finger joint in width; at elfin gardens of miniature trees where tiny brooks meandered like shimmering strips of blue satin ribbon.

All of exquisite ivory it was, walls fretted like lace, thread-thin, lit with tiny silver lamps like acorn shells. He stared down at courts tiled with malachite; at walls of rosy coral, towers of glistening jade, slender arcades of delicate marble pilasters, beams of ebony, scrolled carvings over windows, balconies, balustrades—so tiny it hurt the eye to search their detailed work.

It was an elfin mirage—a goblin vision—a glimpse into a strange miniature world of marvel.

And gone in the flicker of a lash!

In a breath, the city blurred—faded—and was gone. The huge gem clouded again with swirling mists of jade shot through with dazzling coils of silver sparkles. The boy frowned in bafflement and stepped away from the squat cube of black stone and the glittering globe of mystery it bore.

Had it been a dream—a vision—an enchantment? Whatever it was, it was gone.

5

Dreams in Jade and Silver

The boy growled a wordless oath and fingered a small idol of white stone that hung about his throat suspended on a leather thong: his tribal fetish, a crude thing, like a bearded face crowned with a circle of stars. His scalp prickled with superstitious awe. Wild young barbarian that he was, yet to visit cities, a fighter from birth, reared in a harsh land of ignorant savages where every phenomenon of nature was an inexplicable wonder, he instinctively hated and feared magic and dark wizardry.

And that weird gem, that glyph-inscribed circle of ominous dark stones, *stank* of wizardry.

He stood warily, like a young animal at bay, before the twinkling stone. Its inner fires were quiescent now, calm, dully glittering.

And yet he feared it and the unknown forces that had fashioned it, and which perhaps lurked within it.

Should he quit this strange place that even the dragons feared? Should he dare the grim dangers of the night beyond, the prowling predators, great black shapes that crept through the broken waste of stone, hunting hot flesh?

Sunset had died to faintly glowing coals by now; the plateau was deep in darkness; the sky a mass of turgid vapours, hiding the few faint stars that had dared to emerge at the sun's death. To venture forth from this curiously protected place into the unknown dangers of the plateau might be foolhardy.

Soon the great golden Moon of old Lemuria would rise over the edges of the world to flood all the land in light; then he could traverse the rocky tableland in relative safety. He would still be prey to all the roaming monsters of the dark, but at least he could see them and protect himself against their attack with the great sword that he still clasped in his hand.

Perhaps the wisest thing to do was to wait here behind this ring of standing stones which, for some reason, the beasts seemed to fear. Wait here for the moonrise, and then set forth upon his long journey to the Dakshina, to the lush and jungle-clad Southlands, with their golden cities and mighty kings. There lay his goal and his destiny. He would wait for the moon.

But he was still bone-weary from being hunted down the mountain passes by the twin dragon-hunters. He would rest here, stretch out his aching limbs, ignore the thirst that raged within his throat like a flame, the hunger that growled in his empty belly. He lay down on the smooth rock, between the black cube of the altar and the soaring pylons.

And, of course, he slept…

Strange dreams filled his brain with curious visions.

It seemed that as he lay there in the darkness a cold radiance bloomed within the enormous mass of crystal; a weird luminance of mingled jade and silver that pulsed like a living heart—a heart of throbbing light!

Waves of green and silvery glare swept over his sleeping body, and from somewhere within the huge pulsing core of light that the magic gem had become, a far, faint voice called to him in a language he did not understand.

But the message in those words he understood all too well.

The voice lured, sang, beckoned. It was siren-like; it called to him irresistibly. It sang of marvels and wonders, of impossibly beautiful things, of unguessable mysteries…and he yearned to obey that mystic summons.

Like chiming silver bells, the voice spun a net of magic about his sleeping mind…and drew him…drew him, on and on…

And in that strange, haunted dream it seemed to the boy that he opened his eyes and rose lithely to his feet, for all that he still slept. Step by step, entranced, wide-eyed, but still deep in slumber, he approached the great jewel.

It was ablaze now, a throbbing sphere of radiance. An aura of crackling power stood out around it like a huge glittering gateway—and through that gateway the tiny elfin city could be seen clearly now, yet it was somehow no longer small, but large…large enough for him to enter and to walk those crooked winding streets, to stroll those cool enchanted gardens, to quaff chilled, sparkling wine in those ivory palaces…

Step by step he strode up to the burning gate and came awake in a ringing silence.

6

Through the Crystal

Shock sluiced over him like a cold, unexpected shower. In his sleep he had, in truth, risen and approached the great gem and now he stood frozen, his extended hands only inches from the glistening crystal, which was, even as in his dream, ablaze with whirling lights and a beating aura of throbbing force.

Rage flamed in the heart of the boy savage. This vile witchery aroused his wrath. His scowling brows contorted. His lips drew back in a challenging snarl, baring white, wolf-like teeth. A deep menacing growl rumbled in his chest.

"*Gorm!*"

Growling aloud the name of his primal god, the youth reached forward deliberately and seized hold of the huge sparkling crystal, as if challenging it to work its secret wizardries.

An icy tingling ran through him as he touched the chill, slick crystal. An electric shock that numbed him as it flickered along his nerves. Waves of cold dazzle buffeted his mind, dulled his sight. He staggered on numb limbs—he fell—

Into the crystal.

It was as if in the instant he fell forward the hard sparkling surface melted into a glittering mist that swirled about him in icy coils but offered no resistance to his warm flesh. He fell forward and down and through the crystal…and hurtled into the dark throat of a spinning vortex of swirling jade and silver motes of light.

Strangely he felt neither surprise nor fear. It was like some weird occurrence within a dream—too fantastic and improbable to be real, and hence nothing for him to fear, since it could not really be happening.

He fell through the whirling vortex of moted light and now, it seemed, he fell slower and slower, as if the vaporous spangles of jade and silver radiance beat up and somehow sustained his weight.

In the next instant he struck a sloping surface with stunning force and went rolling down an incline. Crisp, dew-wet, emerald grass slid across his limbs and he came to rest in a mass of drowsy flowers under an amber sky of dim, luminous vapours.

Dazed and uncomprehending, he stared about him wide-eyed at clumps of strange feathery trees that loomed up against the topaz twilight…trees without leaves, whose slick, black boughs bore fantastic peacock-plumes of metallic green and gold and lapis.

Beyond them, weird, impossibly slender animals of snowy white grazed the dewy sward. Earth, he knew, had never bred those strange yet lovely creatures with their silken hides and long, thick gold manes. If not Earth, then—where was he?

Then a vagrant glitter caught his gaze and drew it beyond the feathery trees and the grazing unicorns…to the exquisite, soaring minarets and swelling domes of a faerie city that lifted in the haze of distance.

The city in the jewel!

This was no dream, but strange reality.

As real as the fantastically clothed, bird-headed warriors who stood ringed about him—distilled from emptiness in a twinkling—as real as the spear-blades of cold blue steel levelled at his naked breast.

7

The Man with No Face

They took from him the great broadsword and its scabbard and baldric, and they bound his wrists behind his back with tinkling brass chains, or chains of what looked like ruddy, glistening brass, and all the while he stared at them with wonder.

At first he thought they had in very truth the heads of birds; later he determined that they wore curious, avian headdresses or helmets. They were very lifelike: plumed at the crest, with sleek, gleaming feathers down over the face, glittering soulless eyes, and cruel, hooked beaks. Birdlike, too, the fantastic costumes they wore: robes and cloaks of woven plumage; hooked gauntlets affixed to their hands like the claws of winged predators. Even their tunics were woven of the soft breast-feathers of hawks.

The bird-warriors moved like automatons, without a sound, stiffly. They said utterly nothing to him, not deigning to reply to his questions. Neither did they handle him with rough, uncaring manner…it was as if someone had commanded them to seize him, disarm him, and render him helpless, but taking all the while the greatest possible care to see that he was not harmed.

It was bizarre. Thongor put it away for further thought: just another of many mysteries. Then he was led through the glittering streets into the impossible city.

Dawn—pearly, nacreous, rosy-pale—lit the strange, amber skies as he was led captive into the weirdly beautiful city. But it was like no dawn that ever Thongor had seen on Earth, for there was no sun, no orb of fiery light, but merely a gradual brightening of the vaporous sky into dim radiance without source.

He had not yet in his young life ever seen a city of man, except for the crude villages of his native Northlands; but he somehow knew no terrene metropolis could be like this. He became aware, just then, of yet another strangeness.

The air was cool and clear and scented faintly of blooming flowers. But the honey-hearted warmth of verdant summer lay beneath the dewy coolness of dawn. And that was—*madness*. For when he had been drawing ever nearer in his wandering to the great Jomsgard Pass that cleft in twain the Mountains of Mommur, it had been Phuol, the third month of winter. Yet no snow locked this land in its icy grip, and from the scented air and dewy lawns and flowering trees he had already seen, it seemed more like late spring—the month of Garang, say—or the month of Thyron in early summer. Which reminded him of another unanswerable mystery.

For it had been in the very hour of sunset he had lain down beside the weird jewel. But here it was dawn!

Thongor shook his head with an angry growl, as if to clear his mind of these mysteries. But already he suspected the truth: he was no longer in the world he knew, the world where he had been born, but in another. Or perhaps within the magic jewel the sequence of day and night was curiously reversed, and the seasons of the year as well. Mystery upon mystery —but their answers were of no importance. Whether or not he had been reduced in stature by some weird enchantment and now dwelt within the jewel, or whether the jewel was itself but the magical gateway which led to this strange new world, did not matter.

What mattered was that, wherever he was, he was prisoner of those that ruled this sorcerous world of timeless summer.

As he went on between his bird-masked captors, he stared about him with dawning wonder, forgetting his superstitious fears and the grim fact of his captivity. Everywhere he looked, vistas of radiant and enchanting loveliness opened before him: dim arcades of slender, twisting columns wherein small shops offered trays of fabulous gems, gorgeous embroideries, flagons of precious vintages.

Beautiful beyond belief, the city lay in the dim morning, and yet a shadow of unseen horror haunted it. For in the pale golden faces of the robed and bearded inhabitants, Thongor caught the look of fear.

Fear, too, lurked in their low, musical voices as they conversed, covertly eyeing the boy as his captors led him through the streets. Fear, and a glint of something else: perhaps—pity?

The boy stared about him, and he knew the city could not be real. Yes, it seemed solid enough, and doubtless was, but—unreal, for all its solidity.

He was led past a bell-shaped dome that glittered and flashed in the morning radiance. It was made of rock crystal, a cliff of pure crystal, a curving, unbroken dome, unlike anything Thongor could have imagined.

And the tower, the white minaret, built from one shaft of solid ivory. The seas and forests of the earth gave birth to no lumbering behemoth so vast as the unthinkable beast whose *single horn* supplied the snowy ivory for that solid tower!

Into a great, turreted citadel of sparkling jade and marble the warriors led him, and thence to an immense domed hall where his shackles were affixed to a ring in the floor. Food in a shallow bowl of some dark crimson wood, and a crystal flagon of water, were set at his feet. Then the soldiers left him.

Being Thongor, the first thing he did was to eat and to drink as much as his belly could hold. And, when at length his hunger and thirst were assuaged, he attempted to break either his shackles, his chains, or the ring in the floor. Tough young thews swelled along his strong arms; bands of iron muscle writhed and stood out in sharp relief across his deep chest and broad shoulders; his scowling face blackened with effort; but the sparkling metal, which looked like brass, was of an unbreakable hardness.

So, being Thongor, he lay down, resigned his problems to the turn of future events, and slept.

A gentle hand on his shoulder brought him to full instant wakefulness, like a startled jungle cat. The man who bent over him was old and lean and robed in white silken stuff. The cowl or hood of his gown was drawn, covering his features.

"Are you awake, boy? Do not fear me, I am a captive—a slave, like yourself," the aged one said in a quiet, cultured voice.

Thongor relaxed. "Why do you ask? Do I look asleep?" he growled curtly.

The old man shrugged, seating himself, tailor-fashion on the floor. "Alas, I cannot tell. I have no eyes with which to see whether you sleep or wake," he said.

Thongor bit his lip, angry at his own rudeness. "Your forgiveness, grandfather," he grunted. "I did not know you were blind."

"Not blind, my son—without eyes. There is, you will perceive— a difference."

Thongor shrugged. "I do not understand."

"I will show you, then, if you will promise not to be afraid of me. For, however dreadful my appearance, it is not of my doing, and I am no enemy of yours, however horrible to your sight my visage might be," the old man said.

And lifting one slender, wasted hand he drew aside his cowl and laid bare to the horrified gaze of the boy a sight of unthinkable terror. For he had no face, no face at all, merely a blank and featureless oval of pale, unwrinkled skin: no eyes or nose or mouth, or, if mouth there was, a veil of tight skin was stretched over the opening.

"Gorm…" Thongor said hoarsely; if it was a curse, it was also half a prayer.

"Our Lord Zazamanc is sometimes…capricious," the old man said gently.

8

Ithomaar the Eternal

"How did you come to be—like that?" Thongor asked in a low voice.

The old man veiled his horrible, blank visage behind that merciful mask of white silk and began to speak quietly. "Listen to me, my son, we have little time. I cannot answer your questions now, not all of them. In a very short while you will be taken from this place and brought before the Lord of this city, and it is my task to prepare you for that meeting. So do not interrupt, but let me speak swiftly of that which you must know in order to be spared such horror as I have endured.

"My name is Yllimdus, and I came to this place even as you did—through the crystal. My city is Kathool of the Purple Towers; in my youth I was a jewel merchant, and often led caravans into the Mountains of Mommur, seeking gem fields. On one such expedition, I achieved a rocky plateau and discovered, amidst the level tableland, a circle of standing stones and within that circle, a great gem: but I need not detail my discoveries and my experiences further, for you have known them, or you would not be here. Is it not so?"

"It is," said Thongor.

Yllimdus nodded. "Ages ago, when the world was young and the Seven Cities of the East flourished, there arose a powerful sorcerer, a strange man of deep wisdom and uncanny mastery of the occult sciences: Zazamanc the Veiled Enchanter. This strange being achieved heights of power unguessed at by mortal men; his lifespan he extended far beyond the endurance of human flesh; his searching gaze probed the hidden crannies of the Moon, the surface of distant worlds, the dark gulf between the stars. Yet for all his learning and magical arts, he was a thing of flesh and blood, and death comes to all that live, no matter how steeped in power. Zazamanc brooded long over his impending mortality, and at length perceived a method whereby he might cheat Death itself and outlive the eons.

"With his magical arts he constructed a crystal of durable substance; within that crystal he built a private universe where time could not come and Death did not exist nor could enter therein. A gorgeous city he constructed, raised by the hands of invisible and captive spirits, and therein a magic land was created, over which Zazamanc shall rule forever, an undying king, immortal and omnipotent as a god.

"This city he named Ithomaar the Eternal, for nothing within it can ever age or die. And the kingdom over which Zazamanc rules is the dwelling place of captive peoples such as you and I—unwary travelers, lured by the mystery of the crystal and its singing voice—who have entered into this magical land and cannot ever leave."

"These things are fantasies, grandfather!" Thongor growled.

"Alas, my son, they are utter truth," Yllimdus said gently. "Tell me: what year is it in the great beyond, the world from which you came?"

"Why, let me see; it is winter in the six thousand nine hundred and ninety-ninth year of the Kingdom of Man," Thongor said. There ensued a silence of some duration. Then—

"So long…so very long," whispered the old man with no face. "Ah, lad, it was spring in the Year of the Kingdom of Man four nine seven one when I came hither on that venture…*for two thousand years I have dwelt here in this accursed paradise beyond the reach of Time!*"

"Gods! Can this thing be true?" Thongor muttered.

Yllimdus sighed: "All too true, lad; here we can never die. Oh, I have prayed for death in my centuries…but we are beyond Death's hand, here, aye…and beyond the power of the Nineteen Gods themselves!"

"This sorcerer, this Zazamanc," the boy asked. "What will he do with me?"

A dim echo of horror entered the gentle tones of the ancient man.

"He will…play…"

9

The Veiled Enchanter

In this dim world where no sun shone to light the day nor moon to shed her pallid radiance by night, it was impossible to guess the passage of time. Thongor soon discovered this strange truth. Tall windows, narrowed, pointed, barred with thick grilles of that strange brass-like metal which Yllimdus had named *orichalc*, let in the dim, opal light. Thongor thought to observe the movement of time by the shifting across the floor of the patch of strangely colored radiance cast through that pointed, narrow window…but it did not move, nor did it wane.

At some unguessable time later, the warriors came to take him before the Enchanter for judgement. Yllimdus had warned him that to the proud, cold immortal who ruled this miniscule world, lesser men were slaves, toys, nothing but cattle. Here in this world his art had made him a very god, and he could play with his human toys as he wished. Men could not die in this dim, eternal world, but they could suffer. So, as the whim struck him, Zazamanc the Veiled Enchanter transformed them—mutilated them into weirdly horrible monsters. Some were quaint, droll hybrids: men with the heads of insects, women with flower petals instead of hair, dwarfed little beings, gaunt giants, men with neither arms nor legs who wriggled about like naked, pallid, fleshy serpents.

Yllimdus himself had been a courtier until his Lord wearied of his cautious advice and sage counsel. And thus, with a potent cantrip, the old man had been transformed into a faceless thing of horror. Thongor's eyes smoldered with rage and the nape-hair bristled on his neck like the hackles of some jungle beast. The wild boy was no stranger to cruelty. Nature herself was cruel, and men were her children and had inherited much of her ways. But the boy knew only the sudden, savage cruelty of swift death, or red roaring war, of man battling against man or against brute.

This sort of cruelty, casual, cold, cynical—this was new to him. And it chilled him with an unsettling mixture of horror and nausea and contempt. He wondered what sort of a man could so negligently and carelessly disfigure another man who had done him no greater ill than merely to bore him…if, indeed, Zazamanc was only a man.

For this was of the species of cruelty man usually suffered at the hands of playful and uncaring gods. Was, then, this Veiled En-chanter a god? True: he had created all of this miniature world within the jewel, and that was godlike.

And—a thrill of dread went through the boy at the thought—if he was a god, could gods be slain?

The warriors who escorted the savage boy through the mag-nificent palace of the Enchanter were curious beings themselves, and as he paced along in their midst, young Thongor stole many curious, covert glances at them in a covert fashion.

They were not bird-warriors like those who had arrested him beyond the city. These were cold-faced, pale, expressionless men. They were automaton-like, as the warriors in the fantastic avian costumes had been. But most of all they were like dead men some-how, in some grisly and necromantic fashion, imbued with the uncanny semblance of life, but devoid of life's animation.

Old Yllimdus had spoken of these, back in the prison hall. He had used a curious word to describe them—*avathquar*—"living dead." An odd, uneasy, disturbing word. Thongor's hide crawled at the touch of them, cold and flaccid, like the puffy flesh of corpses.

Yllimdus, who had been imprisoned for more than a year in the great hall, having incurred the dislike of his Lord, had warned him of these, and had said that not everyone came through the Jewel Amid the Seven Pillars alive. Some were drawn through, and were dead when they materialised within the miniature world. Perhaps it was these fresh cadavers, magically animated by some occult science that became the *avathquar*. It was a peculiarly unsettling thought, and he eyed them with guarded curiosity as they led him along.

They seemed completely drained and empty, with none of life's warmth and passion. He wondered if they truly lived, or if they were but automatons of dead flesh vitalized in some weird manner by the power of the Enchanter. They were splendid specimens of manhood, surely, tall, strongly built and handsome in a regular sort of way. But they strode along like puppets, looking neither to the right nor the left, their pale, stern faces hard and blank, no sign of alertness in their cold, empty eyes.

Bemused by such thoughts as these, Thongor saw little of the superb corridors and halls and chambers through which they led him: ever after he retained but a blurred impression of blazing tapestries seething with color and motion, or glowing figurines and statuettes of unearthly grace and lifelike detail, or of carved, marbled walls and fretted screens of ivory and soaring columns and arched and vaulted ceilings painted with weird and mythological frescoes.

At length they led him into a colossal hall floored with black marble like a gigantic mirror. Far above, lost in dim shadows, an enormous dome reared on thick columns of a sea-green stone unfamiliar to him. About the walls, more of the zombie-like warriors stood, motionless as graven images, immaculate in dazzling, sun-gold armor.

For these things he had no attention.

It was that which occupied the very center of the gloomy hall which seized and held his fascinated gaze. A tall chair of scarlet crystal, three times human height. And in the chair a man was seated.

10

Burning Eyes

Zazamanc bore the appearance of a slim, tall, youthful man with strong arms, long legs, and a coldly beautiful face, which bore no slightest sign of age. He was attired in complicated and fantastic garments of many colors: puce, canary, blood-scarlet, lavender, mauve, subtle gray, deep violet.

His raiment was unlike any costume that Thongor had ever seen or heard of. Tight hose clothed his long, slender legs; a tunic or jerkin, gathered and tucked and folded according to the dictates of some alien fashion, adorned his torso; sleeves of various lengths protruded one from the other. Long gloves were drawn over his lean, strong hands, and strange rings of metal and stone and crystal twinkled and flashed as he moved his fingers.

A cowl, trimmed with strange, purple fur, was drawn about his head but did not cover his face. This held and fascinated the boy. It was of a supernal, an unhuman, beauty. A high, broad white brow, arched and silken-black eyebrows, long imperial nose, firm, delicately modeled chin, thin-lipped but exquisitely carved mouth—these were his features.

They were flawless; without blemish. No wrinkle marred the purity of that godlike brow. No slightest shade of emotion lent warmth to the cold perfection of that face. It was like an idealized sculpture: cold, beautiful, pure, but inhuman.

The eyes alone held life and expression.

Strange eyes they were…black and cold as frozen ink…depthless as bottomless pits…cold and deep, but burning with a fierce, unholy flame of vitality. Behind their enigmatic gaze the boy somehow sensed a vast, cool, limitless intellect as far removed from the ordinary mind of mankind as man is from, say, the groveling insects or the squirming serpents.

They brought him before the tall scarlet throne and he stood erect and unbowing as that black, burning gaze swept him slowly from head to foot. With careful, judicious deliberation the Veiled Enchanter scanned him slowly.

When he spoke, and then only, did Thongor understand his cognomen. For, from brow to chin, his coldly perfect visage was delicately veiled behind a transparent membrane of some slight fabric, thin almost to the point of invisibility. Why a man should wear a veil which veiled nothing, and through which the eye could clearly see, was but the least of the mysteries Thongor had yet encountered in this tiny world of magic and beauty and depraved horror.

"It is a savage boy; doubtless from the Northlands; I believe I recall a race of strong Barbarians who dwelt of old on the wintry tundras of that portion of Lemuria," the Enchanter said idly. His voice was like his face: cold, perfect, clear, but devoid of warmth or animation.

"I recall the race; but that was…long ago."

For an instant it seemed to Thongor that the black flame of those eyes bore within their fierce depths a measureless weariness, an age-old boredom. Perhaps even something of—futility?

"He is young and strong, bred of brave warriors, I doubt me not. It might be amusing to see that strength…take him hence to the Arena Master. We shall see this youthful prowess on the Day of the Opal Vapors. Take him away now…"

The guards saluted with mechanical perfection, and led Thongor from the silent hall. Behind, sitting tall and straight and regal in the scarlet chair, the Veiled Enchanter continued staring straight ahead, into nothingness, with no expression on his cold and beautiful face.

11

In the Speculum

Zazamanc stood in his magical laboratorium. Corrosive vapours swirled about him, caught in twisted tubes of lucent glass. Fiery liquors seethed in crucibles of lead over weird fires of glowing minerals. Trapped forever between two panes of quartz, a mad phantasm screamed soundlessly, caught in a two-dimensional hell. Strange and terrible was this place of many magics: the air stank of dire wizardries; the brimstone odors of the Pit reeked therein.

The square stone chamber was oddly lit. Wandering, ghostly globules of insubstantial luminance drifted like bubbles of light, to and fro, ice-blue, scarlet, blinding white. Their shifting radiance cast eerie black shadows crawling over the uneven walls, clustering like frightened bats in the darkest corners.

A vast globe of silvery metal bore a strange image: a huge, insectoid thing, with a naked, exposed, and swollen brain, and black, glittering, compound eyes, squatting in green caverns of porous rock, where glassy stalactites and strange crystal outcroppings caught and flickered with vagrant wisps of light.

This was one of the Insect Philosophers who dwelt in the dead core of earth's moon, and with whom, by his art, Zazamanc sometimes conversed.

With a white crawling fungoid intelligence, on the twilight zone of the planet Mercury, he also communicated at times; and with a crystalloid but sentient mineral being on one of the moons of Saturn.

The insectoid thing with the monstrous brain faded slowly from the surface of the silver sphere. The image was replaced with a different scene. A sweltering area of burning sand where a half-naked boy struggled with a huge crimson beast. Zazamanc drew in his breath sharply, watching in suspense. The boy held, for weapon, a hooked sickle. His wild, black mane streamed about his yelling, contorted face; his strange gold eyes blazed lion-like through the tangle of his locks.

The crimson thing roared and foamed, and batting wildly at the nimble, leaping figure with heavy paws bladed with black claws like scythed razors. At length the boy darted within the reach of those grasping arms.

Zazamanc sucked in his breath and held it.

The sickle flashed, catching the light, as it swung in a wicked arc. It slashed through the distended throat of the roaring crimson brute and in an instant it lay gasping out bubbling gore on the wet sands, while Thongor stood panting, sweaty, streaming with blood, but triumphant.

Zazamanc uttered a curse and permitted the image to lapse into its component atoms of light. The surface of the silver sphere went black and dull.

Turning away from the speculum, the Veiled Enchanter crossed the cluttered, crowded chamber to a huge desk that was a cube of gray, cracked stone. On top of this a jumble of parchment scrolls lay sprawled in a litter of amulets, periapts, talismanic rings, and instruments peculiar to the magician's art.

Shoving aside two of these, an arthane and a bollime, the Enchanter uncovered a vast and ponderous book. This tome was of peculiar and alien workmanship: no terrene product of the bookwright's art, surely. The leaves were bound between two plates of perdurable metal, but a rare, unearthly metal, blue as sapphire stone, and filled with radiant flakes of gold light. The twin plates were deeply embossed with large glyphs of geometric complexity. And the leaves within were even more strange: of flexible, lucent stuff, glassy and crystalline and yet supple.

The pentacles, with which these leaves were inscribed, were of red-orange, green-black, silver, violet and a strange throbbing

color that seemed somehow to belong between the hues of helio-
trope and jasper, but which was a color not otherwise found on
earth and belonging to no spectrum of normal light. In some odd
fashion, these magical diagrams had been inked *within* the very
substance of the flexible crystal leaves.

Zazamanc opened the ponderous volume and began an intent
perusal of the sorcerous lore. The boy Thongor must die. And in a
grim and bloody manner.

And—soon!

But *how?*

12

Jothar Jorn

The arena stood on the further edge of the city of Ithomaar, a vast,
circular amphitheatre like an enormous crater. This bowl-shaped
depression had been scooped out of the ground by captive genii, its
sloping sides terraced into tiers and fitted out with curved marble
benches. The gladiators themselves, and the cages that held the
beasts they were to fight against, dwelt in subterranean crypts
below the arena floor. To these, the bird-masked and unspeaking
warriors conducted the youthful barbarian.

They brought him to a huge, fat, half-naked man who had been
working out with the swordsmen. He was crimson from his exertions, his massive torso glittering with sweat, and as Thongor came
up to him he was toweling himself dry and emptying an enormous
drinking horn filled with dark ale. One of the bird-guards proffered
a slim ivory tablet to him. It was inscribed with a brief directive,
written in emerald inks, in queer, hooked characters such as the
barbarian boy had never before seen. The man scruti nized them
quickly, then raised thoughtful, curious eyes to Thongor.

"A Northlanderman, eh? Tall for your age, and built like a
young lion. Well, cub, I doubt not those strong arms will provide
merry entertainment for our Lord, come the Day of Opal Vapors!"
His voice was hearty and genial, and his great, broken-nosed slab
of a face, beefy-red, glistening with perspiration, was cheerful and
honest. His little eyes were light blue and good-humored. Thongor

rather liked the look of him, and slightly relaxed his stiff, guarded stance. The gamesmaster noted this, and chuckled.

"My name is Jothar Jorn and I am our Lord's gamesmaster," he said. "You've naught to fear from me, lion cub, so long as you do as you are told, and quick about it, too."

"I am Thongor of Valkarth," the boy said.

The gamesmaster nodded, looking him over with quick, keen eyed. "Valkarth: I might have guessed, from the color of those eyes. Snow Bear tribe?"

Thongor bristled and a red glare came into his strange gold eyes. "My people were the Black Hawk clan, and the Snow Bear tribe were—are—their enemies," he said fiercely.

The big man eyes him with frank, friendly curiosity. "You're a bit mixed on your tenses, lad. 'Were—are'—which would you have?"

Thongor's head drooped slightly and his broad young shoulders slumped. In a flat, listless voice he said: "My people are dead, fallen in battle before the dogs of the Snow Bear; my father, my brothers…"

A sympathy rare in this primitive age shone in the small blue eyes of the big man. "*All*…of your people slain in war by the other tribe?" he asked in low, subdued tones.

Thongor's head came up proudly and his shoulders went back. "All are dead; I am the last Black Hawk," he said bleakly.

"Well…well…" Jothar Jorn cleared his throat loudly, and shook himself a little. "In that case, you will be hungry," he said in his hearty way. "Hungry enough to—eat a Snow Bear, shall we say?"

The boy grinned soberly, then laughed. And they went in to dinner.

Jothar Jorn bade an underling lead the barbarian to the common room where the gladiators ate at long benches, and set a repast before him such as the boy had not seen for as long as he could re-member. A succulent steak, rare and bloody, swimming in its own steaming juices, tough black bread and ripe fruit and a tankard full of heady ale. Thongor fell on the feast ravenously, reflecting that if *this* was captivity, then it might not be so bad, after all.

13

The Pits of Ithomaar

Ten days passed, and busy days they were. As a newcomer to the City in the Jewel, Thongor was curious about everything and kept his eyes and ears open. He soon learned that Jothar Jorn had entered the magic crystal only twenty years before: he had been gamesmaster of the arena of Tsargol, a seacoast city far to the south, head of an expedition into the mountainous country of Mommur, trapping beasts for use in the games then to be held in celebration of the coronation of Sanjar Thal, Sark of Tsargol. He, too, had glimpsed the jewel from afar, having left his trappers behind, hot in pursuit of a mountain dragon, and had been caught by the siren-like lure of the crystal even as had the Valkarthan boy.

As for the gladiators he trained, they were all Ithomaar-born and knew nothing of the outer world from which Thongor and Jothar Jorn had come. The boy soon found his place among them, but not without a few lumps and bruises. For the most part, the gladiators of Ithomaar the Eternal were full-grown men, and a mere stripling cast into their midst was fair game for a bit of good-natured hazing. But the young barbarian did not take very well to the playful roughhouse in the manner to which his fellow gladiators were by now accustomed.

The first man who tried to shove the boy around was a big, cold-eyed bully named Zed Zomis, the acknowledged leader of the gladiators. He ended up flat in the corner with his jaw broken in three places and a mouthful of shattered teeth, for all that he was ten years older than the boy Thongor, a head taller, and outweighed him by thirty pounds.

Three of Zed Zomis' comrades, who had gathered to watch their leader have a little fun with the surly outlander youth, promptly jumped on the wild boy from behind when they saw him dispose of their friend. Within the first few seconds of the tussle they discovered they had picked a fight with a lion cub in very truth. The *vandar*, as the jet-black lion of the Lemurian forest country was called, was twelve feet of steely, sinewy strength from fanged jaw to lashing tail tip, and a juggernaut of fighting fury: Jothar Jorn had nicknamed the young barbarian aptly.

To a boy from the savage Northlands, war was a way of life, and, for all his young years, the Valkarthan lad was no stranger to the red art, having been raised virtually from the cradle with a weapon in his fist. Northlandermen of Thongor's people dwelt in a bleak and hostile land of bitter wintry snows, and life was one savage and unending struggle against rapacious brutes, scarcely less rapacious human foes, and Nature herself, who was cruel and harsh toward weaklings north of the Mountains of Mommur.

Thus, to Thongor, fighting was no game, but deadly serious. And no one attacked a warrior of his kind in play, only in earnest. Thus, when Zed Zomis' bully boys sprang upon him from behind, it was no mere laughing tussle he gave them, but a grim, vicious battle to the death, from which they emerged with a number of broken bones; and one of them, at least, would limp forever.

Thus he made for himself a place in the pits of Ithomaar, and it was a place of considerable respect. The gladiators treated him with care thereafter, and not a few of them were quick to hail him as a friend. As for Thongor, he bore no ill will to the four men he had beaten and was as ready to be friends with them as with any man who treated him with dignity.

The boy thrived on the hearty meals the gladiators were served. These consisted of immense steaks swimming in hot gravy, raw vegetables, sweet pastries and a variety of good, strong wines. Of this menu, the last two items were new to his experience, and after a prolonged bout with the wine cups, from which he emerged a bit unsure of his footing and with a head, the next morning, that throbbed with queasy pain, he treated the fruit of the vine with much the same gingerly respect with which the older gladiators had learned to treat him.

From Jothar Jorn he learned something of the fighting skills as practiced by civilized men. The warriors of the Black Hawk clan had schooled him in the use of bow and arrow, spear and javelin, war-axe, and of course, in the art of using the great two-handed broadsword. He missed his own broadsword, Sarkozan, taken from him by the bird-masked guardsmen when they captured him. The sword was old, ancient, really, and it had passed down his line from father to eldest son from time immemorial. Some said the great sword Sarkozan had been wielded by none other than Valkh the Black Hawk himself, the famous hero who had been the founder of Thongor's nation—Valkh, Valkh of Nemedis, one of the immortal heroes who went up against the Dragon Kings at the close of the Thousand Year War—Valkh, who was of the blood of Phondath the Firstborn, in the twentieth generation of the direct male line.

That sword had, ages ago, drunk the blood of the Dragon Kings, reaping a red harvest there on the black beaches of Grimstrand Firth. Maybe the Nineteen Gods themselves had blessed it, when the heroes went up from Nemedis in the Last Battle, for it was written in *The Lemurian Chronicles* how of old They went among the men of the First Kingdoms.

Jothar Jorn trained the savage boy in such "civilized" weapons as dirk and dagger, rapier and hooksword, cutlass and scimitar. But the strong hands of the Valkarthan yearned for the loved, familiar heft of Sarkozan. And at last he revolted.

"But, cub! We don't fight with broadswords in Ithomaar—and, look, you can have your pick of weapons," the gamesmaster argued.

Thongor set his jaw grimly. "They have taken my sword from me. I want it back," he said stubbornly. Something in the set of that jaw and the glint in those blazing eyes told Jothar Jorn it did no good to argue, but argue he did, and plead, and even threaten. But to all his bellowings and coaxings, Thongor made but one reply:

"They have taken my sword from me. I want it back."

At length, Jothar Jorn talked himself hoarse and gave up. Who could say? Maybe a barbarian brandishing a broadsword would be a sensation in the Games. At least it would be—different.

"Get him his sword," he said, and shrugged, and left.

14

The Secret Gate

Now that Sarkozan was in his possession once again, Thongor began to plan his escape. He had no idea how he had come here, but he intended to return to the world he knew, one way or another. He was willing to die trying. For besides his appetite for red meat, his berserker courage, and his fighting ferocity, he shared another trait with the great cats of the jungle: he would not be shut in a cage. And Ithomaar was a cage—a very beautiful one, but a cage nonetheless. He had taken the measure of the folk of this fabulous realm, and he did not like what he saw, neither the dainty, gilded fops of the court who came to watch the gladiators at sword practice because it titillated them to see real men work up a sweat in brutal combat, nor the common folk of the city's shops and ways, with their listless faces, dead eyes, and hearts empty of hope.

The Pits were not guarded because there was no need to guard them. They were underground, hewn by invisible hands from solid bedrock, and there was no escape. Most gladiators never thought of trying to escape, because the life they had here was better than the one they had escaped from, with excitement and pride in their prowess, good meat and drink, and even women, occasionally brought in to serve their needs. But even at seventeen, Thongor knew he would rather die than live in a cage.

It was not long before he discovered the door in the wall. It was a slab of brassy orichalc and it bore, embossed upon its central panel, a hieroglyph whose meaning he did not know. What interested him was that the door was unlocked—had, in fact, no lock. In a roundabout way he questioned the other gladiators about it, eliciting little information. It was on the lowest level of the Pits and it was behind the beast-cages. Finally, drinking wine with Jothar Jorn, who had taken a liking to him, he mentioned the door. The brawny gamesmaster stiffened, his good-humored slab of a face paling.

"You don't want to find out what's behind that door, cub. Never go near it!" he grunted, eyes sober and almost fearful.

"I do not understand why it has no lock," Thongor said. "Where does it lead?"

"To the Tower of Skulls," said Jothar Jorn. And that was all he would say. His warning meant nothing to Thongor; the young barbarian knew only that it must lead down into the city itself, for there was no tower near the arena. Once in the city, he knew it should not be difficult for him to escape to the woodlands beyond, for Ithomaar the Eternal had no walls, which meant no gates, which meant no guards.

So that very night he made the attempt. He had eaten a good dinner at the long tables of scarlet *lotifer* wood with his comrades, but some of the meat and bread and fruit he had not eaten, but had hidden away in a sack he had fashioned from a scrap of cloth and kept hidden behind his cloak. As his comrades strolled into the common room, where lute players and dancing girls waited to entertain them at their wine, he sought out the jakes and, once alone in the winding corridors of stone, turned aside to the level of the beast-cages and the secret door of orichalc that went unguarded and unlocked.

He thrust the door open, finding a long, narrow corridor of damp stone. He went in, the door closing softly behind him. He went forward, the great Valkarthan broadsword naked in his hand.

15

The Thing in the Smoke

In a vast chamber beneath the Tower of Skulls, Zazamanc the Veiled Enchanter sat enthroned in Power. This throne stood on a dais composed of nine tiers of black marble, and it was carved from the ivory of mastodons. Set within the broad arms of this throne were the sigils whereby the Veiled Enchanter summoned the demons and genii and elementals that served his wishes in all things. At this hour he wore the Green Robe of Conjuration, and his left hand was set upon Ouphonx, the ninth sigil of the planet Saturn, which the Lemurians of this age knew by another name. Under his right hand lay Zoar, the third sigil of the Moon. Before him, on a tabouret of jet, lay the Crossed Swords and the wand called Imgoth.

Amulets were clasped about his wrists and throat. Pendent upon his brow hung the talisman the grimoires named Arazamyon, and upon it a certain Name was written in runes fashioned of small black pearls.

The face of Zazamanc went masked this day behind a single tissue of pale green gauze; through it the cold pallor of his handsome visage gleamed like an ivory mask, and his eyes glittered with frozen malice.

Sprawled upon the lower tiers of the dais lay the naked body of a sixteen-year-old slave girl, and beneath it a wet, scarlet pool spread slowly. Beside the corpse lay a razor-like dirk that had, only a few moments before, cut her heart from her naked breast. As for the heart itself, it had been hurled—a gory, dripping thing, still warm and throbbing with unquenched vitality—into an immense bowl of bronze, curiously engraved, wherein red flames slithered slowly.

Seated rigidly in his ivory throne, the Veiled Enchanter now called upon the Name Alzarpha. As the echoes of that Name died shuddering in the rafters of the high-roofed chamber, he began to enunciate in solemn, portentous tones the frightful names of the genii that ruled the Twenty-Eight Mansions of the Moon. Strange and uncouth were these names; many were never meant to be spoken aloud by the lips of men, and these were difficult to pronounce. However, as the green-robed figure spoke them one by one, the red flames that seemed to crawl and rustle within the brazen bowl turned first a sickly yellow and then a virulent green, the color of pus and corruption and decay.

From the ensorcelled flames there began to issue forth a thick, oily smoke. It coiled through the darkness of the mighty chamber, heavy and sooty, and within it was the stench of hell.

"...Zargiel!...Maldruim!...Phonthon!...Ziminar!" Name after name came rolling from the Enchanter's lips in slow thunder. As they rang through the somber silence of the subterranean vault, the nauseous vapor grew dense, coalesced, and began to assume shape and substance. Gradually there took form a weird, towering figure that loomed up against the gloomy rafters far above.

It was thrice the height of mortal man, and man-like in form, but only in that it stood erect upon two limbs and had a single head. For it was gaunt as a dead thing, covered with gray, greasy hide, wrinkled and warty like that of a toad. This demon was known to the grimoires as Xarxus of the Crawling Eye, and the Veiled Enchanter had long since bound it to his service by a terrible and unbreakable vow. Its long, lean arms ended in grisly pincers, like a gigantic crab's, and its head was unspeakably hideous. It had but one eye, and that was a hollow, fleshy pit from whose center slim tentacles sprouted: these flexed and slithered in a loathsome manner, and from this repellant and unnatural organ the demon's name was derived.

"I have the boy," Zazamanc said, when the demon had taken form. "But I cannot comprehend your warnings concerning him: he knows naught of me and is but a rough, untutored savage. I want you to read the future again, to discern if by his capture I have altered or averted the doom that you have foretold."

The demon stared down at him, tendrils crawling in the hideous, empty socket that was its only eye. When the tall thing spoke, it was in a voice deeper than ever came from human throat, but curiously flat and without resonance. It spoke even though it had nothing even remotely resembling a mouth, but this did not disturb Zazamanc, who knew that such as Xarxus did not require organs of speech but could resonate the very molecules of the air itself, or cause their thoughts to sound within the minds of those with whom they had uncanny converse.

I have warned you against having anything to do with this one, the demon said. *I have foretold that there approaches down the paths of future time one who is destined to be your bane and the cause of your death. You would be wise to send him hence from this universe you rule.*

Brooding upon his ivory throne, Zazamanc seemed not to have heard the words of the demon. "You can see further into future events than I can," he mused. "In my Speculum I have foreseen what will happen if he fights in the arena against my monstrous hybrids: his fighting prowess is such that he will escape victorious from every combat, if permitted an even chance and a good weapon. But it would be so easy to slay him…"

The demon shook its awful head, a familiar human gesture suddenly made horrible by his lack of human features. *There is little of the future that I may foretell with any degree of certitude, but this much I can say: the life of that one is linked with your own, and if you slay him, or order him slain, or set him in such danger that his death ensues, your own death will follow swiftly.*

Naked fear glittered in the cold, inscrutable eyes of the Veiled Enchanter. His death was the one thing in all the many worlds and universes that he feared, for he knew all too well what would befall him thereafter, and his soul shrank, shuddering, from the knowledge. His gloved hands clutched uneasily at the arms of his throne.

"Why do you refuse to read my future in any detail?" he queried in a thin, petulant voice. "You are bound to serve my will by the nature of the vow between us…"

It is not that I refuse, but that I am unable to comply, the demon said. *You are naught but a human, for all your control of magic, and the true nature of time remains hidden from your knowledge, a secret shared only between the Lords of Light and…mine own kind. Know, then, that time is like unto a maze of many thousand intersecting paths: at each single step you face a choice of paths to follow. Which path you may select in any given instance may be calculated, but to project the pattern of your choices further into the maze involves a geometric progression of possible choices, until the further ahead one seeks to predict, one is baffled before an infinite multiplicity of possible paths.*

"Read, then, what you can of my future," Zazamanc commanded.

Xarxus complied. *Every mortal has seven assassins, appointed by inscrutable Fate to be his doom. One or another or a third he may elude. Few men elude all seven. The youth you have so unwisely drawn into your realm beyond space will be the doom of Zazamanc.*

"Then I will slay him first! And thus avert the destiny you foretell for me."

The crawling eye of the demon stared at him sightlessly, tendrils writhing obscenely in the naked socket. *Death has never entered this universe of yours*, Xarxus said tonelessly. *Gladiators mangled in the arena regain their strength, their torn flesh knits: even this girl-child whose heart you fed into the flames will rise again. To strike down the savage boy with a bolt of force would be to let Death in…and once Death has entered here, he will not willingly leave. Beware, O Zazamanc, and guard thy portals well: for too long have you evaded the hand of the Destroyer of All, and he shall seek you out if once you let him in…*

With those words, the demon began to crumble and disperse, his pseudobody dissolving into the primal elements from which he had been formed. Zazamanc sat stiff and straight, his face an expressionless mask. But his eyes were shadowed with a terrible fear. He knew that a magician might defend his mortality with a thousand spells, but that the Powers that rule Creation have foreseen a loophole through even the most cunning defense. He knew, as well, that it is forbidden to assume the prerogatives of divinity, the first of which is life eternal. And however a wizard prolongs his life through arcane science, he never loses the dread of death; quite the contrary—the longer he lives, the more he savors life.

Zazamanc was afraid—for the first time in uncountable ages.

16

The Edge of the World

The secret passage was interminable. As Thongor prowled its length, Sarkozan naked in his hand, he expected to be attacked at any moment, but no such attack came. Doubtless the Veiled Enchanter used this tunnel to communicate with beast-cages, wherein many of his most extraordinary hybrid monsters awaited their turn on the sands of the arena. It was unlocked and unguarded for the simple reason that no one would dare disturb the privacy of Zazamanc and rouse his enmity by using it. But Thongor dared.

At last he came to its end and found a sliding panel that opened into an immense hall—the same hall in which he had first been imprisoned. This vast, shadowy place must, then, be within the Tower of Skulls.

The boy stood, glaring about him into shadows. If he could find his way out of here, he thought it likely he could escape from the city unseen and undetected, for Ithomaar had no gates or walls to detain him, and every boulevard led to the green fields and feathery forests beyond, and thence to the world's edge itself—the narrow, circular horizon of lambent vapor that marked the terminus of this microcosm.

And were he to reach the world's edge without being captured—what then? How to find his way back through the enchanted crystal to the land of Lemuria? The boy shrugged his shoulders, growling deep in his chest: it was not the way of the Black Hawk warriors to gnaw at more than one problem at a time. He would find or fight his way to the limits of this artificial world, and then worry about a way beyond it.

Suddenly he was not alone.

He knew it by the prickling of his nape-hairs, the way a jungle beast senses the presence of danger. The boy whirled in a fighting crouch, the broadsword flashing in his hand—to stare into the cold, inhumanly perfect visage of the Veiled Enchanter.

Zazamanc had melted from invisible air soundlessly, but the keen senses of the savage had detected his presence. In his right hand the magician bore an ominous baton of black wood, carven with twisting runes and capped at both ends with ferrous metal. Thongor would not have known it for a weapon, but such it was. It was the wand called Bazlimoth, the Blasting Rod. Within it, lightnings slumbered.

"You are strayed from the Pits, child," said the Enchanter in a cold, remote voice.

Thongor made no reply, but his strange gold eyes blazed lionlike through tangled locks and his weight was on the balls of his feet, ready for action.

The Enchanter slowly extended the black wand until its tip pointed at Thongor's breast. The cunning brain of the Enchanter seethed in a turmoil of unanswered queries—*had* the demon lied to him? How could the destruction of the wild boy bring about his own doom? True, Death had never entered here, but what of that? He could shrivel the boy to ash in an instant—and how could the act endanger him? Upon his cold lips a Word formed unspoken; suddenly the wand was vibrant with force. It throbbed in his hand like a live thing, eager to kill.

And in that instant a hand fell upon his arm and Zazamanc shrank with amazement and fury to find the faceless horror of old Yllimdus by his side. In his frenzy to blast down the barbarian, he had forgotten that his former councilor was imprisoned in this hall by his order. He shrugged off the hand of Yllimdus, his perfect visage a mask of fury. The old man fell back so that he stood between the rage of Zazamanc and the Valkarthan youth.

"Your end is near, Zazamanc," the old man said. "Your reign is over. Slay not this child, but permit him to return to the outer world from which you drew him: do this, and you may yet live."

"You dare lay hands upon your master?" Zazamanc cried, trembling with wrath. "Stand aside, fool, or die with him you would shield in your folly!"

"I do not fear death, for it is but an end to an existence of weary torment," the old man said quietly. "It is *you* who fear, for all too well you know what will follow in the instant of your demise."

Zazamanc flinched at these words, for he had never dreamt his councilors knew the nature of the vow between himself and Xarxus; for the demon was sworn to serve his will during his life, but upon the moment of his death, his spirit would enter the service of

Xarxus...and Zazamanc knew all too well the horrors that awaited him beyond the grave. He shuddered, his face livid and suddenly lined and weary with age, as if his supernaturally prolonged youthfulness was fading already.

"Die, then, worm!" he snarled, lifting the rod and loosing its dormant fires.

17

Letting Death In

The shadow-thronged hall lit suddenly with a flash of supernal brilliance that seared the eye. A thunderclap shook the domed roof and echoes bounced from wall to wall. Caught full in the fury of the bolt, the faceless man crumpled and fell, robe blackening, breast burnt away, a hideous charred pit.

Old Yllimdus spoke no further word, his head falling to one side as life left his shattered body. Nape-hairs rising with primal awe, Thongor blinked away the after-images of the flash and saw to his astonishment that in the moment of death the fleshmask crawled and shrunk and molded itself into the features of an old man. Noble of brow, weary and lined was that face, but, somehow, at peace.

Zazamanc shrank back at the sight. His enchantment was broken, but he did not understand it, for it should have persisted beyond death. A cold hand closed upon his heart, for at last the grim premonition of the doom he had for so long denied came home to him. He thrust his hands wide, face a writhing mask of naked fear.

"No—!" he shrieked, shrilly and weakly.

And in that instant, Thongor struck.

He sprang over the charred corpse of Yllimdus, booming his savage war cry. The great sword flashed as he swung it high above his head and brought it hissing down upon the shrinking, cringing form of the Enchanter.

Zazamanc staggered and fell to his knees, his face a crimson, torn thing. The black baton fell from nerveless fingers and rolled across the stony paving. On his knees he swayed, staring blindly up into the grim face of the half-naked boy who loomed over him like a vengeful specter. With quivering fingers he dabbed at his wound, peering in horror at his own blood. His dazed brain could scarcely comprehend what had happened: a thousand spells rendered him immune to death, invulnerable to assault. The sword blade should have glanced aside from his magically protected flesh, leaving him unharmed.

It was then that he saw the great glyphs acid-etched down the blade of the mighty sword, and knew their meaning—knew as well that no mortal hand had drawn those immortal and portentous sigils in the steel of Thongor's sword.

"*Aiii*," he moaned, rocking to and fro on his knees, while his l ife's blood leaked from him, drop by drop; "*Aiii*…it is Sarkozan… Sarkozan…*Sarkozan, my Bane*…"

Again Thongor lifted the broadsword above his head and brought it whistling down. Bone crunched, snapped: gore splattered. The severed head of the Enchanter flew from his shoulders to plop like a grisly fruit against the paving. The headless cadaver fell sideways to collapse in a spreading pool of scarlet.

Thongor's grim lips were taut. Beneath his bronze tan, his flesh whitened. His burning eyes widened in disbelief. For even as he watched, the bloody head…*shriveled*. The flesh tightened— dried—split, and peeled away from raw, naked bone that *browned* in moments. The fleshless skull grinned up at him from the gory floor. Before his unbelieving eyes, the gaunt bone grew pitted and sere; crumbled. The brain-pan fell in; the jaw detached to clatter on the stone. In mere moments there was nothing to be seen but a clutter of bony shards and dry dust…it was as if the centuries Zazamanc had denied had come rushing back upon him at the last.

It was even as the demon had warned. Zazamanc had let Death in and it had taken its toll, long overdue, at the end.

And Ithomaar was free.

* * * *

Thongor stood at the world's edge, where glittering mists roiled and crept endlessly, moving as if with a life of their own.

"Will you not come back to the real world with me, Jothar Jorn?" he asked.

At his side the burly gamesmaster rubbed his beefy jaw reflectively. "I don't know, lion cub," he grunted. "This world is a fair one, and snug enough, with *Him* gone from it. And no doubt all my old friends in Tsargol would be gone by now, or so changed with the years I'd not be more than a stranger to them. As for me, well, I'll stay here. Someone must take charge of things now; someone must keep order and rule here for those who will not go back to the world outside…it might as well be me, me and my stout lads."

"Will many stay, do you think?" the youth asked.

The big man shrugged, grinning. "Some of them, I expect. Many will leave, to find their places in the outer world; but many more will stay, for they were born here, and this is home to them, and a fair place it is, with an end to fear and evil magicking. But what of you, cub? Is it back to the frozen north?"

Thongor stared at the coiling mists, his grim bronze face unreadable.

"There is nothing for me there. Those I loved are dead, all, all of them. I will fare down the pass into the Southlands, to seek my fortune among the bright cities. Surely there will be a place for a man who can use a sword and can face Death unafraid…"

Jothar Jorn mused on the tall youth with thoughtful eyes. "Go, then, lion—cub no more, but a lion now, in truth! And—may you find what you're looking for, in the end!"

Thongor clapped his shoulder and turned away, striding into the seething mists and through the magic crystal into the great world that lay beyond, bound for the road that would eventually lead to the jungle-clad Southlands.

Thongor's path at last begins to bring him out of the vast tableland of the Northlands, until he reaches the very gateway to the southern kingdoms and the promise of the riches he has dreamed about for so long. Soon after leaving the magical realm of Ithomaar, he is again on a lonely, desolate road. But he is not to be alone for long.

DEMON OF THE SNOWS

1

Out of the Shadows

All day the lone traveler had trudged down the great Jomsgard Pass that cleft the mighty wall of mountains in two, and now, as the day died in crimson across the western horizon, he had come within sight of his goal.

From east to west across the world the wall of mountains strode like marching giants struck to stone by some dark enchantment. And, in very truth, they walled the world, dividing the wintry wastes of the bleak and barren Northlands from the golden cities of the jungle-girt Dakshina, as the Southlands were called. Tall they were and snowy-crested, these Mountains of Mommur, but the pass of Jomsgard broke their frowning battlements and gave an avenue to the weary traveler, such as this youth who stood with strong arms folded upon his breast as he viewed the awesome scene.

Here at this point the mountain pass narrowed until it was but little more than a footpath between towering walls of sheer, unbroken stone. They soared high aloft, those cliffs of granite, sloping to ice-clad peaks. Above the argent horns of the twin peaks the crimson of sunset faded to dim purple, whereupon the first sharp stars now ventured, one by one.

The taller of the twin mountains thrust forth a spur of rock above the pass, and upon that spur a high-walled keep was built. This was Jomsgard Keep, the hold of Barak Redwolf, the Lord of the Pass.

For a dozen generations of men the Northlander baron and his war-like ancestors had held the narrow way beneath the shadow of the sword, the spear and the arrow, exacting a toll of heavy gold from merchant caravan, homeless mercenary and wandering pedlar.

Unassailable by the skills of war were the high walls of Joms-gard Keep; commanding the head of the pass as it did, the old castle could not be taken by surprise, or storm, or even stealth. If ever there had been in all the annals of ancient Lemuria a castle unconquerable, it was the keep of Barak Redwolf.

And to his gates the lone traveler had come. The last of his savage tribe, in all the Northlands no hand was held out to him in comradeship, no kin had he in all the North, nor had he anywhere found a friend.

But the high walls of Jomsgard required many warriors to man them, and the tall towers needed sentinels to watch by day and by night. Here, from of old, flocked renegades and outlaws, men with blood on their hands and prices on their heads. Here, if any-where, the traveler thought to find a safe haven against the hostile clans and nations of the North. And if not, then southwards he would fare, down to the golden cities basking beside the sum-mery sea.

Cut from the hard stone of the granite wall, a wide stair rose from the level of the pass to the barbican-gate of Barak's keep. Guessing himself watched from aloft, the traveler mounted the stair and stood before the mighty portal—

And beheld a marvel!

For the great gate guarding Jomsgard castle was unbolted and—*ajar*!

Baffled, the youth—for he was scarce more than that—regarded the half-open gate with puzzlement.

Had some enemy crept into the citadel of Barak Redwolf? Had some force of warriors smote their way into the keep? Had some sly traitor, bribed with a satrap's ransom, left the door ajar?

Across his bronzed young shoulders, in a worn leather scabbard strapped to a baldric, the youth bore a great broadsword that his forebears had wielded in battle for many generations. Now, wary as some great cat, the youth slid the glittering blade from its leather sheath.

Bearing the great sword Sarkozan before him, the youth stepped within the portal.

And the blackness swallowed him up.

* * * *

The guardian of the gate had not, after all, deserted his post. For the youth found him just within the shadow of the barbican, face-down in a puddle of congealing gore.

The youth dropped to his knees, dabbling his fingers in the dead man's blood. Then he raised his wet fingers to his nostrils and sniffed keenly. At this height, and in this cold, dry air, fresh-shed blood cools swiftly and soon dries to brown scum. But the blood of the corpse was still damp. The man had been murdered, the boy guessed, a little more than two hours before.

On swift, silent feet the youth prowled the gloomy halls and chambers of the citadel, finding, here and there, more bodies, but nothing that lived. Neither did he find any evidence of battle—no signs which would have indicated that the castle of Barak Redwolf had been attacked by a force of warriors.

The men of Jomsgard Keep had been struck down one by one by something that had come upon them in silence and in stealth, out of the black shadows—

These thoughts were passing through the mind of the youth as he entered the inner hall of the keep.

He stepped through the gateposts and froze motionless, scarce daring to breathe.

For the blade of the knife which a small but firm hand held at his naked throat was sharp and cold as the kiss of death!

2

Terror in the Night

Flames still flickered upon the hearthstone of Barak Redwolf. They had not yet slumped to glowing coals.

By their orange light the youth was able to see the foeman who held him at bay.

Or—*foewoman.*

His eyes widened incredulously, and he uttered a short laugh. For a slim, long-legged girl held the knife at his throat—a girl younger, if anything, than himself.

Her skin was clear bronze, tanned by the sun and her cheeks were reddened by the icy winds. Her tresses, which lay in twin thick braids across her slender shoulders, were sun-golden. Her huge, long-lashed eyes were blue as sapphires. She wore rude garments of tanned leather, belted around her with chains of silver, and her feet were shod with buskins of supple hide. Clasped about her slim throat she wore gleaming amber beads, warm against her clear skin. She was very young—breathtakingly lovely—and very, very frightened.

The last was discernible from the way her firm young breasts rose and fell beneath her tunic, panting with quick, short, shallow breaths.

"Come, girl," the youth growled shortly, "take your sting away before you slice my gullet. I am no enemy to such as you. What in the name of all the gods has befallen here?"

The knife did not move from his throat; neither did the girl take her eyes from his face.

"Who are you, and why are you here?" she demanded, panting breathlessly. "Swift, now! And speak true, or my blade will drink your blood—"

"My name is Thongor, the son of Thumithar," the youth said.

"Where do you come from?" the girl demanded fiercely.

Thongor took a breath to steady himself. The girl's knife just touched his skin, and the blade lay along the great artery of the throat. One false word, one twitch of her hand, and his heart's blood would encrimson the rushes which lay strewn about the stone-paved floor beneath his feet.

"I am a Valkarthan, of the Black Hawk people," he said.

"How did you enter here?"

He arched his black brows. "The door was open; the captain of the gate lay dead in a pool of his own blood. I walked in to discover what thing had slain the man and left the gates ajar. Come: put away your knife; I am newly come to Jomsgard, and had nothing to do with whatever has struck here…"

The girl took her knife from his throat, although she did not put it away. Thongor rubbed his throat, wincing. Then he walked over to the fire and threw off his cloak of furs. The firelight gleamed on the thews of his bare, muscular torso. The girl followed him with her eyes.

"I am Ylala, the daughter of Thogar the Smith, of the White River people," she said at length, in a listless voice.

He said nothing, rubbing his palms together briskly before the burning logs. He was a lean, wolfish boy of perhaps seventeen with sturdy shoulders and strong arms: the corded muscles that rippled beneath his bronzed hide gave just a hint of the massive strength that would be his with manhood.

"My people pay tribute to Barak Redwolf, that our hides and furs and ivory may pass to the Southlander tradesmen," the girl said. "When times are hard, and there is no gold with which to pay, we pay in tribute of slaves. This year, the times were hard. I am the tribute," she said simply.

Thongor lifted his head and stared at her. His own people would have starved to the last babe rather than give a daughter of the tribe into slavery to such as the Baron of Jomsgard. Her limpid eyes fell before his stare, and her cheeks crimsoned. He said nothing, and after a moment he turned his scowling eyes from her.

By the glow shed by the leaping flames he could see the full length of the hall. Great benches of rough wood lined the walls; a rack near the door contained spears; bows and quivers full of arrows hung on iron hooks between brackets which held guttering torches.

There was only one dead body in the hall, and it lay at the foot of the low dais on which stood the chair of Barak Redwolf. It had been too dark in the antechamber beyond the half-open gate for Thongor to have made out the manner in which the gate captain had been murdered. Now, examining the figure which lay sprawled at the foot of the dais, he felt faintly sick.

He had seen men die in a variety of ways, but never a corpse like this.

The man had been *crushed* to death.

He nudged the corpse with his foot.

"Barak?"

The girl glanced over, then shuddered. "No; he was a bigger man, with a narrow head, amber eyes like a beast, and red hair. I think that man was Bothon, one of the chieftains."

"Where are all the rest of them?"

The girl shrugged.

"Where were you when these men died?"

The girl gestured to the back of the hall. "There is a room back there where they put me. I was brought here this day with dawn. Barak looked me over and liked what he saw. This…was to have been my…my bridal night…"

"Well, you were spared that, at least," the youth grunted. "But—you heard nothing, saw nothing?"

"The walls are thick, the doors were shut, and I was sick with dread," she whispered. "Sometime before sunfall I heard men yelling and the clump of their boots in the hall. I thought they were all drunk, or at some game or other. Then, when no one came for me, I ventured out. I found a man's body back there, behind the hall, and then this one here. I—I thought the keep had been attacked, and you, one of the attackers!"

The youth shook his head, long straight black hair brushing his square-jawed face.

"Not I," he said shortly. "Come—let us explore."

The girl cast a fearful glance into the deep shadows in the far corners of the hall. From such dark places, perhaps, nameless and unknown terror had struck through all this mighty keep, slaughtering men by dozens. And perhaps it lingered, even yet, in the gloom beyond the fire's glow. She felt the cold breath of that terror against her nape.

Then she looked up into the boy's clear, steady gaze. There was grim purpose in that gaze, and curiosity, too. But there was no fear. And suddenly she felt less fearful herself.

She rose to stand beside him. He took down one of the oil-soaked torches from a wall bracket.

Then he took her hand in his.

And they went forward into the darkness together.

3

Dead Man, Laughing

They came at length to a chamber decorated more sumptuously than the rest. The walls were hung with woven cloth in such colours and patterns as the weaver-women of Eobar prefer, and there were small tables of black wood here and there about, carved and set with ivory. There was carpet that had come from the looms of Cadornis, perhaps.

Ylala said that this was the room Barak Redwolf used for his—amusements.

One of the things he used to amuse himself still hung from the ceiling in iron chains.

It was, or had been, a man. An old man with a long thin beard and long thin arms and legs, and not much meat on the rest of him, either. He had been stripped naked and hung by his wrists while Barak did unpleasant things with heated irons to him. The irons still lay in a copper bowl brimful of hot coals, which still glowed amid pink ashes.

Ylala took one look at what the heated irons had done to the old man, then turned aside. Thongor put his arm around her until she stopped shuddering.

"Did you know him?"

She nodded.

"Was he of your tribe?"

"No. He was an old wizard, named Zoran Zar, who lived in a tower in the hills. They brought him in this morning. I heard Barak boasting that he would soon have the secret of his gold out of him. He thought the wizard had a hidden treasure trove. Is he—is he dead?"

"Quite dead," said Thongor somberly. "There is one thing about him that bothers me."

"What is that?"

"Look again at his face," the youth advised.

Steeling herself, the girl looked. Then she paled incredulously and looked away quickly.

Thongor nodded. "I agree," he grunted.

Instead of being drawn with pain, the wizard's face wore a most peculiar expression, considering how he had died.

He was *smiling*.

His lips were drawn back, exposing the rotted yellowish stumps of his teeth. His mouth grinned open. It was as if he had been just about to laugh when death took him.

Thongor said nothing. Men do not smile—much less break into laughter—under the caress of red-hot iron. Only the bravest of warriors, the noblest of heroes, can endure such torment with stoicism. And Zoran Zar, surely, had been neither.

It was strange, even uncanny. But there was much about this black castle that struck Thongor as uncanny, and he liked none of it. The gloomy castle, devoid of living inhabitants save for himself and the girl, its dark corridors weird with whispering echoes and crawling shadows, stank to him of magic.

He did not like magic, nor did he like magicians. Young as he was, he had encountered both during his wanderings, to his discomfort. Give him a foe of flesh and blood, and put naked steel in his hand, and he would do battle as bravely as might any full-grown man. But how can you fight ghosts or curses or enchantments with naked steel?

They went on, searching for some sign of life.

Behind them, dangling limply in the iron chains, the dead man hung, turning idly this way and that as a gust of wind moved down the draughty halls. The skull-like face of the old man still bore the rictus of silent laughter.

Thongor wished he knew what had made the old man smile.

* * * *

Within the span of an hour they had searched the keep from cellar to attic and found nothing that lived.

One more corpse, crushed to death as if in the embrace of a giant, they found at the head of the stairs leading up to the watchtower, but that was all they found, or almost all.

Nowhere was there the slightest sign of battle, nor any token that men had fought against men in the dark halls and empty rooms. No discarded weapons or smashed furniture or spilled blood. Nor had there been any looting, for casks of gems and gold lay in the cellars untouched.

It was inexplicable and frightening.

Returning to the main hall, they stirred up the fire again, piled on fresh logs. Then, while the flames roared up, and Thongor went to close and bar the great gate, Ylala made herself useful in the kitchens.

They ate before the flames, making a good meal from cold fruit, hot meat, fresh bread and rich, succulent gravy. They sampled, at first cautiously, then with enthusiasm, the thin gold wine of the Southlands, made from fermented fruit called *sarn*. Thongor had tasted wine but once before, while a prisoner in the enchanted city of Ithomaar; it had been too heady and exhilarating for one raised on the thin, sour ale of Valkarth. But this wine he liked, as did the girl.

They exchanged few words, feeling uncomfortable with each other. Girls and boys in their tribes were rigidly excluded from each other's company until of marriageable age. Only in the pits of Ithomaar had Thongor been alone with a girl before, and he did not quite know how to behave. As for Ylala, she kept a demure silence, her eyes downcast, except when he was not looking at her: then she lifted her eyes to his face, which she thought very handsome. To her, he seemed much more manly and serious and responsible than a boy his age should have been.

They slept for what remained of that night to either side of the fire pit, rolled in furs. But neither slept well or deeply; Thongor, because he was disturbed by the nearness of the girl, and by her loveliness; and Ylala, because she could not put out of her mind the thing they had found on the second floor of the castle.

It was a man's boot. With the foot still in it.

4

Barak Redwolf

When the great golden sun of old Lemuria lifted up over the edges of the world to flood the land with its light and drive away the darkness, the youth and the girl also rose.

They made their ablutions and breakfasted on a light meal, saving most of the meat against a future hour of need. Then they robed themselves in furs against the cold wind and the numbing snow of the heights, and fared forth into the mountain country.

Thongor had decided that there was nothing else for him to do but escort Ylala home to the caves where her tribe dwelt. He could not very well abandon her in the empty castle; neither did he deem it proper that she should accompany him down the great Jomsgard Pass into the southern country. So he must take her home.

They left at midmorning, and struck out for the plateau beside the White River glacier, where her people made their winter encampment. Besides a supply of food and drink, sleeping-furs and weapons, they bore with them a thick earthenware pot stuffed full of live coals, so that if need be on the way they could at least build a fire.

But they carried off from the castle of Barak Redwolf neither gold nor gems from the robber baron's treasure. Neither of them had any particular use for such loot, as there was nothing to buy in the waste; and Thongor, at least, had an uneasy suspicion that the wealth of Jomsgard Keep might somehow be tainted by the curse of invisible doom that had slain the baron's warriors to the last man.

Ylala, however, did not scruple to bear away with her a cruse of valuable lamp oil for her mother. Such civilized luxuries were hard to come by in the cave country.

They struck overland, Thongor going ahead to test the snow banks carefully with the long spear he had borne away from Barak's armory. It was well into Panchand, the second month of spring, and the thaws were eating into the thick-banked snow. Runnels of dirty water trickled down the cliff walls, and the footing underneath was loose and treacherous.

All that day they kept moving, pausing only occasionally to rest and refresh themselves. Toward late afternoon they surprised an *elphodon* drinking from a stream, which Thongor brought down with a single arrow. That night they sought refuge in an empty cave, built a fire, and roasted fresh meat from the carcass of Thongor's kill. They slept near together that night for warmth, achingly conscious of each other. With dawn they went forward.

They found Barak Redwolf near midday. Or what was left of him.

The baron must have left the castle at the height of the terror, creeping forth into the waste by a secret way. They had no way of telling where he might have been going, but he had not gotten far. Something had come upon him while he had rested, a little after dawn, by the ashes of a fire not long cold.

He had been crushed as if by some titan's hand. Only his lower parts were mangled; from the waist up he had not been touched.

The expression upon his face was one of sheer, unbelieving terror. Thongor regarded the dead man's face grimly. The baron had been a knave, a bully, and a tyrant. But he could not for long have held supremacy over his band of ruffians if he had not been a brave man, and a seasoned and veteran warrior. Hard-bitten men of such breeding do not die before the fangs of a beast or the spears of an enemy with such an expression of blood-curdling horror on their faces.

They went on, for there was nothing else to be done.

After a while Thongor cleared his throat and spoke.

"Was this Zoran Zar a powerful wizard?" he asked.

"So the old men of my tribe said," the girl replied. "They say he had tamed to his will, and pent up, the Demon of the Snows."

"What manner of creature is that?"

"I really do not know. The old men said it was a thing of utter cold that dwelt beneath the roots of the ice mountain," Ylala said.

Thongor grunted, and spat, but said nothing. He was not entirely sure that he believed in demons; on the other hand, he was not entirely sure that he didn't.

He wondered if Barak Redwolf had.

* * * *

They spent the second night under a low, shelf-like rock that afforded them some shelter from the wind and from whatever beasts might be roaming the snowy wilderness.

They slept in each other's arms.

Thongor had not intended this to happen, but it had. No sooner had he put the furs about them than the girl had come into his arms, pressing herself against him, burrowing her face into his shoulder. He was fumbling and inexpert at first, and they were clumsy in their eagerness. But the instincts lay deep in the blood of both, and soon they moved together, helping each other. When it was done, they lay gasping, and her face was wet with tears.

The second time it was easier, and much better. He was gentle when she needed him to be gentle, and fierce when she wanted his fierceness. This time there were sleepy, satiated smiles, and many warm kisses, but no tears.

They slept deeply and well that night, and woke with dawn, rested and fresh. And never again was there to be any strangeness or restraint between them, for as long as they were to be together.

Later that morning they came to the caves of Ylala's people. But there were none to greet them and the fires in the caves were dead and cold. Ylala had long born the cruse of precious oil to pleasure her mother. But nothing would ever pleasure her mother again, nor would anything ever again cause her pain. For she was beyond both pain and pleasure, when they found her remains on the outskirts of the caves, crushed as if by some immense hand.

5

That Which Kills in the Night

They found three other bodies besides that of Ylala's mother, and Thongor scratched holes in the snowy earth and buried them with their weapons and belongings beside them. Then he covered them over and piled high cairns of rocks atop the rude graves to keep the beasts away.

Then they rested beside a roaring fire, and took food, the girl dry-eyed, saying nothing, the boy grim and somber. There was nothing more to be done by them here.

The marks in the snow were clear and easy to follow, although they were unlike the tracks of any beast which Thongor had ever seen or heard of. It was more like the path made by a crawling worm or a serpent than anything else, he thought to himself, that shallow, wriggling, smooth depression in the snow. But if worm indeed it were, then the thing was twice as long as a tree is tall.

They followed it up into the hills, reaching the crest by afternoon. Here they found the tower of the dead wizard, Zoran Zar; it was more of a house than a tower, a four-sided stone building only a little taller than it was long.

Inside, they found nothing. Barak Redwolf's men had been thorough, if not neat. Old books written in languages Thongor could not understand lay cast about, scattering the stone-paved floor with paper. Crockery was smashed in the fireplace, which stank of queer chemicals for which Thongor had no name. Curious small idols of lead and clay and brown stone lay toppled over or smashed. The furniture, what there had been of it, was broken or overturned.

Here and there, Barak's men had pried up stone slabs from the flooring, hoping to find gold buried beneath them, somewhere. There was no sign that they had found any.

Outside the stone house, holes had been dug in the earth. Neither was there here any sign that treasure had been found, such as empty sacks or broken chests.

Here on the heights the wind had blown away most of the snow and the earth was raw and muddy. It was easier to track the devil-thing.

The tracks led to a hole in the earth, like a covered well. The cover, a rounded slab of mountain granite, had been manhandled away and there were signs in the mud that men had knelt here as if to probe the depths of the pit with long poles or spears.

Thongor examined the stone lid curiously. It had carefully and painstakingly been carved with cryptic symbols in a language he could neither speak nor read, but which he had seen before, once or twice, in his travels. They were the characters used in the secret language of magicians. The weird runes were potent and powerful, he knew; it stung the eyes until they watered just to look upon them.

Bidding the girl stand back, he unwrapped their store of fresh meat, tied a thong about it, and dangled it over the lip of the well. The odor of meat was rich and tantalizing on the fresh air.

They heard, both of them, a slithering in the depths of the earth, as of some ponderous and mighty thing—*stirring.*

Then a blast of frigid air smote them. So unearthly was the cold that breathed up suddenly from the pit that ice crystals formed in their hair and upon exposed portions of their bodies.

At the sight of that which came pouring forth out of the pit the girl screamed—horribly. Even Thongor felt his skin crawl and his nape-hairs stir.

It was like a worm grown unthinkably immense—mountainous in its hugeness—soft and pulpy and obscenely naked.

White it was, with the unhealthy pallid whiteness of a thing that has never, or seldom, been exposed to the glare of the golden sun.

It had no eyes, no nostrils, no features of any kind. Except for a wet, squirming, repulsive, toothless orifice that should have been a mouth. This obscenely working hole closed over the dangling meat. Oozing a fetid slime, the orifice gaped open again, hungry for more flesh.

Thongor flung his spear into the white thing, but it did no harm, merely slicing a path through stinking, colorless pulp. Then he put an arrow or two into it, which it did not seem even to feel.

The gaping maw of the thing, dripping slime, veered suddenly toward Ylala, where she stood frozen with horror as if rooted to the spot. The blast of arctic cold that breathed from the wriggling length of the worm-thing chilled her flesh, made her blood flow sluggishly. In a sudden spasm of revulsion, the girl flung that which she held, for some reason, in her hand.

It was the cruse of oil.

The stopper came loose when the container thudded against the monstrous worm. In seconds, pale yellowish oil ran all over the head and upper portion of the thing, dripping into the gaping, wetly-working maw.

Thongor whirled, caught up the pot of coals and flung it.

Hot coals spilled out and splattered the worm from its blind head to the upper portion, which extended out of the mouth of the well. Mindlessly, the worm chomped down on the live coals.

Then it recoiled suddenly, uttering a shrill, ear-splitting hiss of pain. Steam swirled up, obscuring the thing as it whipped its pulpy head to and fro.

Flame shot up as the coals caught fire in the spilled lamp oil. Writhing tendrils of flame meshed the white worm, bit in cruelly. For perhaps the first time in the measureless eons of its monstrous life, the Demon of the Snows felt the unendurable searing touch of pure flame upon its soft, cold flesh.

Wriggling in spasms of agony, the worm-thing oozed back into its pit.

It vanished from view, but they could hear its shrill, squealing cry; and the earth shook to the fury of its torment.

Oily black smoke, mingled with live steam, seeped from the yawning mouth of the pit.

Thongor rolled the stone lid back into place until it once again covered the well. Sunlight gleamed on the deep runes cut in the smooth stone. They blazed with wrathful warning, strong with power.

"Is it—dead?" Ylala panted, shivering in his arms.

"Gorm knows," he grunted. "But, dead or alive, it cannot pry the lidstone away of its own strength. Those signs were cut there to keep it imprisoned safely far below. Let us hope that never again men come this way, hungry enough for gold to lift the stone and set loose that which was never meant to be seen by the light of day."

* * * *

All day the travelers had trudged down the great Jomsgard Pass that chopped the mighty wall of mountains in two, and now, as the day died in crimson over the western horizon, they had come within sight of their goal.

The Mountains of Mommur bestrode the horizon like a great wall of stone, shutting away behind them the icy kingdoms of the bleak Northlands—Eobar and Valkarth, and the many tribes and clans that wrung a meager sustenance from the wintry wild.

Below them the pass sloped down into the warm and summery lands of the Dakshina. There a curtain of morning mist lay over the grassy meadows and the dense jungles. Far to the south, and farther still, morning smote to gold the towers of Kathool and Pa-tanga, and the seacoast cities. Sunlight glittered in the waters of the great gulf, and gleamed on the curving ribbons that were the jungle rivers feeding into that gulf.

For Thongor of Valkarth it had been a long and wearisome road, down from the cold vales of the ultimate north, down across the snowy valleys, across the great plateau, and the mighty glaciers, and the sky-tall mountains. But he had reached the edge of the golden Southlands at last; surely there, among the wharves and shipping, in the barracks of the soldiers or the palaces of the kings, among the green farmlands or in the noisy marketplaces, he could find employment with his keen eye and steady hand, strong arm and brave heart. For a man who was not afraid to face death at sword's point, the Southland with its wars and golden cities was the place to seek his fortune.

For the girl at his side, he felt willing to try. Together they would face whatever might come. Thongor was no longer alone, and his heart swelled within him at the realization. The girl, perhaps sensing his thought, smiled up at him, and her hand crept into his. Hand in hand, side by side, they began the last trek down into the Southland together.

Thongor's relationship with Ylala is not destined to last. Perhaps she realizes that he is shaped for a life of turbulence and conflict in which she could only ever play a minor role, or perhaps he knows he is marked by powerful forces for a life without ties at such an early age. For whatever reasons, they do part, somewhere in the uplands of the northern Dakshina.

Thongor does not have long to mull over any regrets. The world here seethes with dangers, his life threatened at every step.

THE CREATURE IN THE CRYPT

1

The Hounds of Hell

O mighty Lord who sits upon the Throne
     Of Lotus leaves dyed full with blood!
Thy rolling eyes like suns and moons above—
Cause them to glance on us alone
     When, from amid the woes which towards us flood,
We plead of thee a boon of father's love.

O thou who once contested Valka's crown
     With mighty arm and well-timed blows
And whelmed the demons with resistless power,
Who crushed the skulls of foes with great renown,
     Who reigns concealed from whence no mortal knows
By Vandoth's Bolt until this present hour!

Grant us again thy valor to behold
     And free thy lands from those who would despoil,
Divide, destroy, and crush our pride.
And send to us a king of courage bold
     And let his foemen's blood enrich our soil!
Cause him to wield thy blade, thy chariot ride!

> —The *Crimson Veda*, Book 68, hymn 8
> To Vandoth of the Blood Lotus

The day had been long already, and full of toil, when a young, heavily muscled form, journeying southward from under the shadows of the towering Mountains of Mommur, had noticed the first signs of pursuit. Picking up speed, he did not waste backward looks to confirm what his keen ears told him, that he had become the intended prey of a pack of Talondos Hounds. These were beasts of which no fossil evidence survives today, combining features of our crocodile and wolf. They moved with surprising stealth and speed, given their heavy armor and size, their sense of smell hardly needed now that their victim's form was so clearly etched in the light of the great golden Moon of elder Lemuria.

There were several of them, and once they caught up to the single human form, he sold his blood dearly, exchanging it for two of their lives before escaping in a burst of speed, his arrows spent and his sword reluctantly abandoned, jammed in one of their armoured carcasses. His great strength necessarily waned as he still managed to put some distance between him and his pursuers, now perhaps a bit less eager to run him to ground, especially since the evening temperature was rapidly falling.

The man, running now on sheer endurance, was Thongor of Valkarth. His continent is now long vanished, even from the theories of ethnographers and students of mythic lore: Lemuria, the great incubator of primal life forms, some of which survived the eons, others not. Man was one such successful experiment, though today's specimens seem degenerate and colorless by comparison. Thongor's species developed here earlier than anywhere else on the globe, sharing the continent with jealous competitors including the great saurians and a few other mammalian species fit to battle them or escape them. Jealous, too, was the great Indian Ocean, as it is called today. Its eager waves lapped at Lemuria's shores, awaiting the day they should be able to swallow it whole, save for a sprinkling of surviving islands.

The climate of the lost continent was a paradoxical combination, cold at both extremities, warm in its central regions. The north was given over entirely to towering mountain cliffs whose heights were ever shrouded in snow drifts; while, a day's flight south, the jungle-clad plains were exposed to the fury of the equatorial heat, which declined further south toward primal Antarctica, where legends, ancient even then, whispered of the lurking presence of strange pre-human intelligences.

Having descended the mountain regions of his birth, Thongor had been tracing a horizontal course along their base, seeking occasional refuge in hillside caves or higher eyries when his encounters with the plainsmen grew too dangerous. Now it was the pursuit of the Talondos Hounds that made his golden eyes, miniature twins of the moon above, seek some sign of a mountain-face cave. And he found one. Far enough above the level terrain to discourage the Hounds, it would yet demand of him all his remaining strength.

The bargain mentally made, Thongor began the ascent, finding the tiniest of jagged hand and footholds. The snapping and hissing of the pack below grew fainter as he finally heaved himself over the lip of the ledge and into the cave. The sleep of exhaustion overtook him at once, and he slumped against the cool rock, heedless of any new danger the cave itself might present.

2

The Cave of Wonders

When he next awoke, a full day had come and gone, and with it, his pursuers. The golden moon once again eerily illuminated the landscape, as well as a bit of the interior of the cave in which Thongor found himself. By its filtering rays he could see that what he had taken for a small hole in the rock face was the merest antechamber of some larger, hidden labyrinth. A sharp turn revealed the presence of a complex, if crudely delineated bas-relief mural. The subject matter was nothing strange to the barbarian's golden eyes, for it depicted scenes of embattled figures, possibly representing any of the bloody sagas of his, or of any, people.

His native curiosity urged him to explore, especially as the recesses might offer a more than adequate refuge from any returning Talondos Hounds. But to see better, he would need more light. And unless the cave had been carved for the benefit of the blind, it seemed likely that the means for making light ought to lie near at hand. A moment's tentative searching confirmed his expectation. His questing hand met a rusting iron bracket set shakily into the stone wall, while his booted foot encountered a clay jar. He judged that it ought to be a jar of fuel oil.

A quick whiff of the gummy deposit at the bottom told him he was right. Several brackets further on he found a dried-up reed torch, almost a brush. He scrubbed this into the congealed bottom of one of the jars until he had enough to light and ignited it using the flints he kept in his pouch.

In the first moment the torch flared too brightly, then settled down. But in the initial flare Thongor could make out the full panorama, a cave stretching some twenty yards, its uneven floor and stalagmite-fanged interior covered with heaps and bins of treasure and other ancient objects. As his eyes began to adjust to the gloom, his memory filling in the gaps of what he could no longer so clearly see, he went deeper into the shaft, examining what he could. An occasional oath escaped his lips.

It was a surprise, then a wonder, then something suspicious: all manner of objects were heaped before him in disarray, implying they had been pilfered many times, yet finally left unmolested. Here and there stood statues, apparently of various gods and totems, some of them irreverently tilted against the walls, others carefully set in carved niches.

A few were vaguely familiar, while others seemed like more primitive versions of conventional deities. There, for instance, was elephant-headed Chaugganath, but his countenance was wooly and shaggy. Another was nobly human in form, his great mane of hair seeming to merge with a storm cloud, his beard with the cataract of rain, and he held in his mighty fist a levin-bolt. Surely this was Father Gorm. Others had multiple arms and faces. Thongor had heard there were nineteen gods, though he did not know why there should be so many, but there were not nearly that number here.

Leather bags, clay pots, and metal tubs overflowed with polished sea-shells, which might have been used by some tribe as currency, though the very concept was relatively new to Thongor whose people had used only barter to meet their simple needs. Scattered feathers in profusion suggested the long-ago decay of a supply of arrows left by the guardians of this storage place. Occasional metal boxes which did not seem to be mere containers sported what looked like dull gems and pointless studs, some of them round and grooved at tiny intervals. What use these might serve, the barbarian knew not and so passed them without further glance. His eye fell next on the clay likeness of a fat sun-lizard. He knew what a succulent treat its living counterpart made and wished urgently that he had one to satisfy the hunger he suddenly felt so keenly!

He cursed in amazement as a nearby noise of disturbance betrayed the skittering presence of the clay reptile's living twin! Swiftly disemboweling it with a rusty knife, he cooked it impatiently in the tarry smoke of the torch and devoured the morsel in an instant. The taste was not bad, but the meal seemed to lack any substance. He put it down to voracious hunger no one tidbit could satisfy. That his wish was so quickly met he did not pause to consider.

Thongor increasingly felt a desire to leave the peculiar haven. There was an uncanniness to the place that made him feel he was taking some great risk simply by being there. But the night outside was cold, and he knew predators could not be far off. It seemed more prudent to stay and brave whatever might challenge him here, which was probably no more than his own superstitious imagination.

He continued to examine the amassed loot, laying his hand next to a chest of gemstones of various hues, though all strangely dull even in this torchlight. He knew enough of the ways of civilized men to know that trinkets like these would be deemed valuable, and he at once resolved to take with him a goodly supply when he left. But then he wondered again why the treasure was still here undisturbed. Surely he could hardly be the first to stumble upon the place.

A hoard of a very different nature next met his eyes: a great stone bin filled to the brim with skulls! Thongor gasped, and his small nape-hairs began to stir. Were these the remains of previous intruders? On the other hand, he had noticed no recent disturbance of the dusty floor, much less any signs of struggle. He had once heard that some of the ancient kings and priests amassed their own bones with those of their predecessors in this fashion. Was it then a crypt?

Further scrutiny revealed a jar of leather and palm-papyrus scrolls. The latter fell to fragments at his touch, though he had instinctively been gentle. The leather scrolls proved more durable, though no more helpful to the illiterate young man. He lifted his eyes from the puzzle-like glyphs lining the red-dyed page, only to drop the scroll in surprise as a figure appeared beside him, seemingly out of nowhere! He relaxed somewhat as he beheld, not the form of a fighting man, but rather that of a wizened old man, not unlike the painted shamans of his own people.

The ancient spoke not a word but stooped to retrieve the leather scroll. As Thongor looked on in wonder, a whispering voice broke the long silence of the chamber, intoning some chant in a tongue Thongor knew not, though he fancied he recognized one or two divine names. Interrupting the stream of what seemed to him gibberish, Thongor made to speak to the man in his own rude language. His words had an effect, if not the intended one, for at the first of them, the old man fell silent and disappeared! And the scroll had vanished with him. Again, a wish had been fulfilled for a moment, only to tease him!

Now determined to flee this cursed place, whatever dangers might await him without, Thongor made one last sweep with his fading torch, seeking perhaps some cloak against the cold, some weapon to make his way safer. Surely no ghostly guardian could begrudge him these?

But, a few yards away, barely visible in the gloom, yet hitherto-unseen, was a great throne, and seated upon it a skeleton, which examination revealed to be clad in the rags of once-fantastic vestments, as well as an antique crown. This last had once adorned the broad forehead but now formed a great collar around the bone-bare neck. Every instinct bade him flee, but Thongor lingered to gaze upon the figure and at the weapon it held in its rotting claws, across the arms of the throne.

A great, unsheathed length of steel, it seemed to have played the role of royal sceptre as well as of savage cleaver. It was festooned with jewels, but these blazed with the glory that had been absent from the massed rubies and sapphires he had seen piled in bins and baskets. Stranger still, they seemed to glow with an inner radiance, as Thongor's torch had now died out. The blade was brilliant silver without a trace of rust.

Thongor of Valkarth knew he must have it. Not so much greed as a sense of destiny impelled him, for, in truth, he feared it as much as he lusted for it.

Reluctantly, the youth who blanched at nothing began with disgust to peel away the flaking fingers of the thing in the crypt. As he freed the last on the left hand, he felt...*resistance*. Wondering and aghast at what this might mean, the young giant stepped involuntarily back.

"Gorm's blood!" he blasphemed unconsciously. What his transfixed golden eyes beheld was the sudden bulking and rejuvenating of the desiccated form on the throne. He watched in detached fascination as if what transpired there had nothing to do with him, as indeed perhaps it might not. The head became a blur as its skeletal dome began to rise from its age-long slump forward.

And when Thongor could see it again, the head was massive and proud, blue-skinned like that of the fabled Rmoahal nomads of the cast, skull as bare as before save for a single oily black braid. The ears were pointed and bore silver hoop-rings. The nostrils flared. The eyes bulged slightly, and there were *three* of them, one perched above the others, moving concurrently with them in his direction. The powerful form began to rise, one arm hefting the huge sword, a second reaching out for Thongor, and an additional pair emerging from concealment as a great cloak swept back from them. The crown again rode his brow.

3

The King from the Past

The Valkarthan reached instinctively for his scabbard, his hand closing on empty air. The fact registered but dimly as his hair stood on end and his breath grew short. He decided to take the first blow, if only to gauge the giant's strength. He allowed himself to be grasped by the shoulder and thrown to the wall, where, as anticipated, the piles of various objects broke the force of his impact. He rose bruised, casting about for some weapon.

Initially he took refuge in evasive maneuvers and striking inconsequential blows, which seemed to register as he dealt them but which failed to slow down his strange opponent an iota.

Thongor began to throw some of the larger objects at his enemy. None harmed the giant, but when one or another of the divine images found its mark, Thongor noticed how the stone or metal seemed to cause the monster's bluish flesh to spark and smolder in a peculiar way. He had thought the nature of his adversary a mystery to be pondered later, at his leisure, should he escape with his life. Now he began to realize that the solution of the mystery would be his only effective weapon.

With a terrible reverberation, the giant figure began to speak, though in a tongue Thongor knew not. Yet nonetheless he began to experience a sense of *recognition*. Had he seen something like this creature's form depicted in the wall mural? Yes, he had. More than once. Haloed deities had bowed before this blue-skinned monster, presumably a king or a god himself. If the barbarian's own experience was any clue, the giant must have defeated them all in battle, proven his worthiness to be their king. And would he prove now to be Thongor's master, even in death? Not if the Valkarthan could help it!

He gathered his strength and leaped at his foe. His boots were apt weapons: the giant fell backwards, though at once he rose up, none the worse for the bruising assault. Frustration lent new fury and power to the few blows Thongor managed to launch while not avoiding the arcs of the great silver sword. He fought with renewed energy, if no more effect. He judged that the creature before him was truly flesh, had become flesh, but was somehow more. Alien flesh absorbed the impact of the youth's blows, but the thing was no ghost, else Thongor's flailing fists had met no resistance.

As the two circled, Thongor's eye caught something he had not noticed before: a shield. A shining relic, of little use for offence by itself, and perhaps the twin of the sword the blue giant held fast. The giant saw it, too, and both dove for it. Thongor came up with it. He knew the blue-skinned behemoth scarcely needed it to fend off his blows, so there must be some other advantage to his possession of it—or perhaps an advantage to him in Thongor's *not* having it.

Stepping away from the creature, Thongor hefted the shining disk so that he might behold the approaching form of his foeman over his shoulder. It seemed insanely foolish, but in that moment, he had found the crucial weapon that had thus far eluded him: *knowledge*. For now he understood the true nature of his enemy.

In the reflective silver, that metal celebrated for cancelling every spell, Thongor saw but an animated lattice of ancient bones, some of them trailing cobwebs and bits of desiccated gristle. Alien, antehuman, preternatural it was, but it was finally a rotten tree of bones, and, laughing, Thongor swept them aside with the shield. They sprayed across the chamber, many of them collapsing into the omnipresent dust. Struggling against his own fears, he had at last prevailed with the aid of a moment's thought.

The great sword fell with an almost musical ringing clang. Holding the shield fast, Thongor bent down to retrieve its partner. He made to leave the treasure shaft forever. But on second thought, he stooped and stared about again, looking for the fallen crown of the phantom god-king.

He found it, twirled it around an index finger, and toyed with the momentary temptation to place it on his own brow in a pantomime inauguration. The empty throne was just behind him, as if he had freshly risen from it.

As he stood there, the awful fatigue of the last two days' exertions fell upon his shoulders. How good it would feel to take a rest upon the dusty throne! Perhaps a healing nap of an hour or so before going on his way. Unconsciously he sat upon the throne.

Without his noticing any passage across the threshold of sleep, dreams nonetheless began to fill his head, and he saw himself reigning from that throne as Sark of all Lemuria! Just as this vanquished being had once reigned in his heyday of the remote past?

And of a sudden Thongor beheld his likeness displayed in the mirror face of the shield: it had become one with the blue-skinned, three-eyed visage of his fallen opponent! Horrified, casting both sword and shield from him like a pair of hungry vipers, Thongor, destined perhaps one day to be king, but not this day, sprang from the throne as from a well-laid trap and made his way down along the shaft to the welcome freshness of the night air.

* * * *

Down on the lower slopes below the caves once more, Thongor was alert for the sound of the dread Hounds of Talondos. There was neither sight nor scent of his recent pursuers. Pausing a moment, he took the risk of retracing his running steps till he came upon the bleeding heap from which he had earlier dared not stop to retrieve his sword. Now he braced one foot on the stoney ribcage and yanked the Valkarthan broadsword free, wiping the blade clean of the creature's foul blood with a handful of leaves.

Resuming his southward course, Thongor's steady stride devoured the miles. At length he stood still, and in the light of the golden moon he gazed again at his reflection, this time in the mirror-face of his own familiar sword. Thankfully, it was his natural face.

He knew not what destiny awaited him: surely it had been foolish to entertain the thought of his one day sitting a throne. He laughed aloud now. But he knew his path lay south, and it was time to be on his way.

Reaching the southern jungle lands at last, Thongor encounters a new world, where quick wits and an even quicker sword keep him precariously alive. He soon establishes himself as a useful fighting man and signs up for military service in the legions of Arzang Pome, the ambitious Sark of Shembis, one of the largest of the city-states.

MIND LORDS OF LEMURIA

1

Jungle Silver

The handful of *kroter*-mounted soldiers thundered into the glade, the intense sunlight of old Lemuria mottling their harsh features through the overhanging foliage. Only half their original number, these survivors were, on the whole, neither stronger nor cannier than their late companions, just luckier—with perhaps one exception. Command of the unit had fallen to a young barbarian from the frozen peaks of Valkarth, a complete stranger to these climes, but seemingly indifferent to the stings of clinging vine and bird-sized mosquito alike. His name was Thongor, and some months earlier he had entered the service of the fat Sark of Shembis, the tyrant Arzang Pome.

The ways of civilized men seemed no less than madness to the strapping Valkarthan, accustomed as he was to the barest code of survival in a hostile world. But the decadent Pome's madness was real, even by civilization's standards. His madness was a greed for silver. Hushed rumor had it that the Sark required the precious metal for some unspeakable alchemical rites aimed at securing eternal youth. And, while believable, these whispers might be a simple cloak for insatiable greed where the metal was concerned. Perhaps the be-jowled monarch just had a liking for it.

But for whatever reason, it was his silver lust that had sent this mixed band of palace guards and mercenaries on what thus far had been a futile chase into unmapped jungle. Some wandering mage had sold the Sark a wives' tale of a lost city buried in the depths of the *lotifer* forest, a rich and proud city whelmed in ancient days for its overweening pride by the Nineteen Gods. Surely a city so proud must have shared the oblivious ruler's imprudent lust for precious metal, and so he sought to emulate their crime, risking their doom. If there had ever been such a place, a half-fabulous city with no name that even the itinerant storyteller could remember.

But greed let no chance go unopened, and here they were, most of the men sick and disgusted. Their original commander, a high-ranking member of the elite guard, had already perished from snakebite, several others from deadly fruit. Wild beasts had thus far remained at a distance, but as the men's numbers shrank, this would almost certainly change.

Thongor had assumed command, and no one with an objection had any longer the strength to challenge him. He would do his best to watch out for the men. He liked not the bargain the Sark had struck: how many men might be spent in search of superfluous loot that probably didn't even exist? He decided he would press on but a little further into the rank growth, far enough to justify the report that a search had turned up nothing. Then he would turn back and take his chances as the bearer of bad tidings. He explained his scheme to the men, and none gainsaid him, all eager to be back in the Shembis wine shops and brothels if they should live so long.

Such thoughts occupied him as Thongor guided the foremost of the mounts carefully through the strange terrain. It suddenly grew thicker again, slowing them down to a maddening crawl. He congratulated himself on having avoided a path grown dense at the far end with spiky vines, but as he turned left, the company raggedly following along…

Disaster closed like a vise! At once there was nothing underfoot. A hunter's trap, he thought momentarily as his stomach lurched with the unexpected descent. But the fall continued too long, and it was only before he crashed to solid floor beneath that he realized he had found what he sought. The vines and bushes of a thousand years had silently covered the tunnel mouth leading to a great underground complex.

2

Caverns of Madness

It was not long before consciousness returned, and thanks to his wilderness-bred instincts, it returned like a pouncing *snow*-vandar. His head ached, but Thongor's full black mane, square-cut across his forehead, had cushioned the blow. His silver-plated helmet was nowhere to be seen. He rose up on one elbow, turning in every direction, trying to pierce the shadows with his curious golden eyes, to see how his men fared, men who had made a mistake in following him.

Thongor cursed himself as he paced across what seemed an extensive chamber, stooping over body after body, finding a broken neck here, a fatal concussion there. All he could find were dead, but not all were yet accounted for. Of a sudden he saw a trace of lambency, a strangely colored light shining round a corner of the cavern wall. Had the other survivors, and there could be no more than four, he estimated, had they awakened before him and gone on without him, deeper into the shaft? It seemed unlikely.

Tightening his sword belt and choosing a dagger from one of the sprawled forms, Thongor made for the light. But before he could round the corner, crouched in a stance anticipating attack, he was surprised by an advancing form that seemed to throw itself upon him like a vast blanket. Dry like a snake, yet viscously unstable like some jellyfish, the thing sought to smother him, but he whipped his broadsword from its sheath like lightning and hacked desperately at that which held him. It neither bled nor made any sound.

But a faint buzzing, of which the barbarian had been but subliminally aware up to now, began to heighten in pitch and urgency. Thongor ripped and sliced, tearing with one hand as he cut with the other, but the living wave of alien flesh began to get the better of him, attaching itself to his face, cutting off his breath. For the second time in under an hour, he lost consciousness.

This time he awoke to the buzzing, become so loud that he could not ignore it. He tried to move. Frustrated in this, he next tried at least to gain his bearings, focusing his eyes. This was difficult. He seemed to see but a pinkish blur, though there was a hint of motion somewhere within the roseate haze. It registered that the hue was nothing natural, but the same as he had seen reflected earlier on the cavern wall. It emanated from no single source, yet it filled the very air around him, and its strength extended no farther than mere inches beyond a great circular tube that held his immobile form.

As his eyes became accustomed to the weird haze, his peripheral vision revealed the arrangement of four other containers, presumably like his own, in a rough semicircle against the irregular cavern wall. At some point in the distant past, some one or some thing had troubled to smooth the rocky surface, yet without bothering to straighten the natural walls. Thongor's world knew a crude version of glass, though mirrors were usually constructed of polished silver. He had never seen the like of what held him captive now, a perfectly smooth, seemingly thick cylinder of transparent shielding.

And it was the same with the others. The tale of the wandering mage had been no idle one, then, though whatever treasure might lurk here would seem to be far too costly to recover. Thongor thought with grim irony that he would be a rich man to escape this place with the treasure of his life.

He thought he could make out the blurred lines of the remaining companions within the other tubes. Three he had not known well, but the fourth and the easiest to recognize because of his short stature, was one Tam Tavis, a boy too young for the dangers of this ill-fated mission, but headstrong enough that he would not be left behind. Thongor had seen in the strapping youth a reflection of himself in earlier years, a boy budding into manhood quickly, with instincts and reflexes, not to mention precocious strength, that would one day serve him well on the battlefield. There was no school for adventure better than adventure itself, as he had learned amply, so he had put up no real opposition when the lad had pleaded to be taken along. Now Thongor rued his decision. He had long ago lost count of the number of foemen's lives he had taken. But it was a new and distasteful thing for him to count the squandered lives of friends.

The Valkarthan's golden eyes turned to the sudden appearance of that alien entity he had fought and failed to defeat. His brow flared into a fever of rage as he traced the heavy, shifting motions of the shapeless silhouette before him, his anger rising even faster with the chagrin of defeat. And for all this, his spine began at once to tingle as he felt the creeping tendrils of a foreign consciousness entering and mingling with his own. The rising panic abruptly ceased, however, as his mind's eye began to feed on vast scenes crystallizing from a mist of seeming forgetfulness, as if he were awakening from a long sleep and coming to himself, a self he had forgotten he knew.

He was unaware that his square jaw fell slack and drooling as his vacant eyes gazed down the centuries, through the memories of his inhuman host. Together the unlikely pair beheld a great vista of which discredited legends spoke: the infinitely ancient migration through the cosmic aethyr of a legion of sentient comets. From a neighboring sphere they came, the immemorial Children of the Fire Mist, so designated in the forbidden *Testament of Xanthu*, ostensibly salvaged from the collapsing fanes of elder Mu.

They had arrived on the new-made earth, seeking among the myriad forms of burgeoning life some spark of intelligence that they might fan into flame, perhaps out of sheer benevolence, perhaps for recondite reasons of their own. The Lords of the Fire Mist had the uncanny ability to transfer their own intellects, incorporeal as they were, into whatever physical forms they chose, so long as these possessed at least some malleable mindstuff. They sought by this means to heighten the faculties of these crude beings, to hasten their evolution to full awareness.

The first objects of their attentions were the scarcely sentient pseudopodic creatures whose likeness Thongor had lately battled. With these beings they eventually won great success, their mottled blue-green rubbery forms at length evolving into the mighty blue-skinned Rmoahal warriors of the southern plains. But these proved too mighty for the Mind Lords to dominate. They had done their work too well. After long years they ventured another experiment in what Thongor would have deemed blackest sorcery.

The Sons of the Fire Mist chose a species of small, tailed mammals, bulge-eyed and bulb-fingered, tree-swingers, bug-eaters. Thongor's vision, which falsely seemed a memory, traced the progress of these creatures up the ladder of apedom to nobler form and feature, and he knew he had witnessed the very origin of his own tribe: Man.

Thongor now knew, and indeed took for granted, that the loath-some form of the thing he had fought and which now shared his very soul was a specimen of that earlier, long-ago age of experi-ment, before the furry branch-swingers took their first involuntary steps to humanity. Here was one of the first intelligent beings from earth's dawn age. How long had it bided the ages? He sensed a great anger and a greater…covetousness. This one of the archaic Mind Lords of Lemuria wanted what he, unlike his ancient col-leagues, had been denied: a fully human form to inhabit.

Their ancient mission had succeeded. Wisdom had been ignited in the breasts of earthly creatures. Had the rest of the Children of the Fire Mist abandoned the planet again, returned to their adjacent sphere? If so, then why had they left this one behind? Thongor found he could share none of the creature's memory at this point. Here the lone Mind Lord became guarded; was this, perhaps, from ancient habit, when he needed to shield certain heretical or trea-sonous thoughts from his more enlightened fellows?

3

Alien Flesh

The Valkarthan lost consciousness again, instantly, as if it had been snuffed out like a temple candle. When he again awakened, no sense of the passage of dreamtime betrayed how long he had been out. He knew at once that the paralysis had left him, and he made to flex his limbs. His initial thought was surprise that there was no ache—until he beheld in horror members which answered to his commands, albeit clumsily, but were not his own!

Worse yet, they were not even remotely human. Of course he knew himself the prisoner of his rugose and monstrous host, more truly and damnably a prisoner than he had been when paralyzed. He was back in the clear tube, and his ungainly tentacles thrashed helplessly against the smooth, concave surface. He found he was able to see what transpired without, but his sight was somehow *different*. Nothing seemed to point in any one particular direction. Relative height and width fluctuated. Colors shimmered into and out of the familiar spectrum range.

His human form was free—and occupied! He saw the image of Thongor of Valkarth admiring himself in a mirror, as if a man should consider a new robe or suit of armor! Gradually, his living image drew forth its scabbarded longsword, again belted to the hip, and made clumsy swipes with it through the stagnant air of the cavern. But the thing that held his body hostage was rapidly accustoming itself to the reflexes and instincts of its new home. Thongor's body as well as his mind had learned his martial skills, and that made them available to the usurper.

But it also appeared to work in reverse! Thongor at once felt more in control of the repulsive alien form he had inherited. He was for the moment no less a captive, but he knew that things needed to change but slightly before new possibilities could begin to form. Nor was this the only change.

The Mind Lord in Thongor's body now held the blade in one hand and manipulated some glowing studs on a chest-high metal surface. The mist filling one of his men's cylinders began to dissipate, drawn back through tiny holes in the base. The man within began to shake himself awake, lacking the paralysis Thongor had experienced. Then the cylinder retreated into a recess in the cavern shadows above, leaving the man free and gasping a lung full of the stale but welcome air.

His eyes visibly brightened as he recognized him whom he took for his brave commander. Inside Thongor's prison tube, the Valkarthan could hear no sounds, but he saw that the soldier spoke pleasantly to his commander's image, awaited a reply, looked puzzled—then crumpled with his life's blood jetting in a geyser from the severed stump of his head.

The helpless mind of the captive Valkarthan raged in impotent fury as he saw the same performance repeated by the incarnated Mind Lord, who seemed to imagine he honed his battle skills by similarly butchering the rest of the Sark's dazed troops. No doubt one and all perished thinking Thongor had betrayed and murdered them! He vowed his foe should pay dearly for this outrage!

But now the false Thongor made to open the prison-tube of the last of the men, young Tam Tavis! The blue-green sheath that was the Valkarthan's body shook with unaccustomed—human—fury; Thongor knew he must somehow find a way to prevent this final atrocity.

4

Thongor against Thongor!

He saw a single, dim chance and acted more by instinct than by design. Thongor's mind had begun to feel, as if by the acquisition of a new sense, that it could mimic some of the mental feats of the thing whose alien form he now wore. He focused his oddly distorted vision upon his own stolen form, but it remained obtuse to his probing. The entity must have taken precautions against the trick Thongor now tried. But the barbarian would not be daunted, not with his young friend's life at stake. He focused next upon the awakening form of Tam Tavis. Thongor had a dreamlike apprehension of running, exerting himself in a race to reach some far point as soon as he might, straining every nerve. And then he was beyond the physical form he had occupied—and into that of Tam Tavis!

Thongor knew he was taking several risks at once, not the least of which was that the boy, awakening inside the terrible, utterly non-human form of the Mind Lord, would instantly go quite mad. Already in his brief career of adventuring, Thongor had beheld a number of sights to shake the soul, though mind-transference with this awful being might have unhinged him without the shared memory-vision of the Mind Lord to make sense of the events for him. And he knew Tam Tavis had no such advantage. Gorm grant the boy would awaken with the creature's brain-instincts as a safety net.

For his own part, Thongor could not help rejoicing in wearing a more accustomed form, blood pumping through muscled arms and legs from a central heart (for the adepts of ancient Lemuria knew already this much of the body's systems). He was shorter now, but his perspective was much more familiar than the strangely filtered perceptions of the thing from the planet Venus had been. There was but little sluggishness in the lad's limbs as the adrenaline drove out the last vestiges of the alien sleep gas.

The black-maned, golden-eyed giant facing him appeared to freeze for a moment, surprised, but quickly making sense of what had happened. It was plain he had not deemed the barbarian or his race so capable. In that moment of his foe's hesitation, Thongor darted forward to grasp the hilt of the dagger he had earlier picked up from the fallen body of a soldier. His mighty opponent had not expected the move, just looked at the blade in Tam Tavis' hand and smiled, raising his own great-bladed sword.

The two men paced and circled, the younger crouching like a hunting *vandar*, the jungle lion of Lemuria. Both had blades extended, but the disparity between the two weapons daunted Thongor not. Indeed, he feared his own prowess with the blade, not daring to contrive to kill his opponent—himself! Which would prevail: his strength, or his skill?

The first blow was that of the Mind Lord, a clumsy but powerful thrust, which Tam Tavis' body, agile as a cricket, easily sidestepped. "Go ahead! Flee me, human! I have waited all these *kalpas*, and I can spare a few minutes more!" The intonation was not quite right, as if the thing inside were only beginning to get used to the human vocal apparatus.

"Fool!" the Lemurian youth gasped with the exertion, "You have waited so long only for death!" He knew how laughable that sentiment must seem. Even if he were able to overcome the massive form whose death-dealing capacities he knew better than anyone else, it were mere foolishness to seek to kill his own body! Better to find some way to get it back—if he could evade its increasingly skilful blows!

As he considered his next move, Thongor noticed that the amorphous body of the Mind Lord was now flailing with agitation. Plainly, the mind of Tam Tavis had awakened in its new abode and liked it not! But was the young mind also going mad? Was it as Thongor had feared? If so, here would be another innocent death charged to his account. But he dared not entertain such thoughts at the moment if he hoped at least to save the body of his young friend, to say naught of his own soul.

He saw now that the boy's agility exceeded his own, just as his weight was much less than Thongor's. New stratagems suggested themselves like recruits on a parade ground. Thongor took advantage of his borrowed skills to leap upward and grasp hold of a fang-like stalactite. He hoped to gain a moment's breathing space this way, but he had not counted on the slippery nitre and began at once to slip. So be it; he would come down on his opponent's head. His own form stood uncertainly below, trying to spot his vanished quarry amid the dense shadows, seeing his sudden descent too late. If only the younger man might knock the older unconscious without further damage!

But the mighty frame of Thongor of Valkarth shrugged off the blow and assumed a fighting stance once more. Thongor's mind felt keenly the lack of his great barrel chest and ample lungs, for he could not now replenish his wind so quickly. He noticed from the corner of his eye one of his men's shields that had been sent bouncing and rolling by the initial impact of his fall and made its way into the present chamber.

He evaded the lunge of the larger form, which still had not grasped how to check and channel its own inertia, and he ran for the shield, grabbing it. His foeman stood foursquare once more and brought down the sword like a headsman's axe. The uplifted shield saved him but sacrificed itself, shattering against the superior blade; nor could it prevent the raised arm beneath it from taking the edge of the sword.

Thongor knew his time must be near. He shook his head to scatter some of the blood that had splattered into his eyes and looked toward the cylinder where the now calm form of the Mind Lord reposed. Had the mind of Tam Tavis collapsed as his body was about to? Or dared Thongor hope that he had made the adjustment, that perhaps he was discovering, as Thongor himself had, what new abilities were available to him?

"I salute you, human! You have afforded me valuable exercise! For I must go in your form and in your name back into the world of men. With my knowledge of the science of the Children of the Fire Mist and the combined labors of your fellow humans to aid me like worker ants, I shall soon master this world and devise a means to return to my own, where I will at last gain revenge upon those who abandoned me on your primitive globe for my imagined crimes. You are indeed honored to have played a role in such a grand scheme, and I shall remember the sacrifice you are about to make." Withal he lifted his sword for the final blow.

And delivered it. Blood and consciousness alike began to flee the young body, and Thongor's lone thought was that he should thus perish in the body of his friend, both murderer and victim.

5

Thongor Berserk!

But in a moment he was aware again, as if someone had nudged him out of a fresh nap. He saw the same scene from a different angle, and from several feet away. The colors were distorted and the angles somehow skewed. He was back in the shroud-like form of the alien! That must mean that Tam Tavis had managed to return his mind to his own body—just in time to meet his death in Thongor's place! Thongor had been unable to supplant the Mind Lord, but he had sensed the other had his guard up to prevent it. Tam Tavis had met no such opposition.

Neither was the doomed lad's heroism quite at an end, for Thongor watched in astonishment as the failing young warrior managed to grasp one of the shield fragments and throw it unerringly at the head of his towering opponent, still bent over him, gloating in his cheap triumph. Surprised fully as much as Thongor himself, the Mind Lord in his stolen body reeled with the impact of the blow, staggered, and fell oblivious.

Thongor knew from experience that such mazing could not last long. If he were to make one last attempt it must be now. He concentrated till sweat would have poured from his brow, save that he had none. He felt again the sensation of running a desperate race, and all at once he awoke in his proper vessel, shaking off the momentary blackout.

Meanwhile the cylinder, under the mental control of the shapeless thing within, receded into the stalactite roof and the Mind Lord began to ooze toward freedom and renewed attack. Thongor felt again an eerie suction at his very soul. But he had learned enough from his enemy to know implicitly how to cast up a barrier against such invasion. Then, exulting to dwell once again where he belonged, he fell to the combat he had so long been denied.

He knew where to strike a human to kill him instantly. This was different, more like cutting and hacking at whipping sailcloth. But berserker rage kept him at his task till eventually only quivering fragments of the once-threatening mass remained scattered about the uneven floor. The warrior allowed himself a deep breath and noticed that he was not, as expected, covered with splashes of blood and ichor. He could not guess how the creature had lived nor yet precisely why his blows had been able to kill it. But Thongor did know well the entity's capacity to reintegrate itself. He used his dagger and the sharp-edged shards of the destroyed shield to tack the sundered pieces of the thing into the cavern floor and walls where thick growths of lichen and moss provided sufficient purchase.

Finally, having contrived a rudimentary harness, he hoisted the lifeless body of the young hero Tam Tavis back to the surface and began pushing the covering of jungle foliage down into the pit it had first concealed. When this was done, he cut more from the brush and dumped it down the hole. Lighting a dead tree branch he had discovered, he cast it down into the abyss and made away as quickly as he might, carrying the body of his friend, fleeing the ascending stench of alien flesh.

As the sun broke the horizon again, Thongor gained his bearings. It was back to Shembis, where plenty of enemies awaited him, but where none of them bore his own face.

Thongor quickly tires of the constraints of military service and for two years he lives as a thief and a swashbuckling adventurer, roving the jungles and wild lands of the Dakshina. His reputation grows, as does his prowess as a fighter and he wins the chieftainship of an outlaw band. Now, at the age of nineteen, he is a formidable opponent, his name known and reviled by the same nobles of Shembis that he once served.

SILVER SHADOWS

1

A Merry Company

The golden Moon of lost Lemuria filled the skies, providing little cover for those who plied certain trades as far away as they might from the scrutiny of the law. But Zakeela the courtesan showed no particular preference for her customary shadows as she strode brazenly down the Street of Taverns in the most dubious section of the city-state of Shembis.

Many eyes, filled with both surprise and desire, followed her as she pursued her purposeful way. She had a goal but no fixed destination, for it was a particular man she sought, without knowing where exactly, which drinking house, to find him. So her heavily shaded, smoldering eyes sought for any clue before she would give in to the inevitable and try each tap room one by one. But fortune favored her, and it was her gem-ringed ears that found what she was looking for.

Toward the end of the street, where it ended abruptly at the city wall, one of the smoke-hung, glowing doorways gave forth a sudden clatter, as if a whirlwind had entered the place and set about its work with terrific force. One would normally avoid the source of such ominous sounds but these were not normal circumstances, and so Zakeela made for the tavern as swiftly as she could, retaining her professional composure, and grateful that the ruckus had subsided by the time she got there.

The eyes of the men within, quickly tired of one spectacle and already seeking another, turned on rank to observe her coming, though many as quickly turned away again, realizing no doubt that they had already drunk up their funds for the night. The barkeep's sons were busy sweeping away the debris of a struggle, shattered chairs and the like, but otherwise the scene was surprisingly placid, calm following the storm. So Zakeela's eyes resumed their keen scouting. Almost at once she spied the man she had sought.

He sat in the corner, one guessed for tactical reasons, and wiped his lips as he set down a foaming tankard, not likely his first. She slunk to the other side of the taproom and tried to blend in so as to observe him for a moment unseen. The young giant towered over three drinking companions who, from the looks of it, held their liquor less well than he, since all three without exception were now face down on the table. The other shook back his shoulder-length mane and wiped the sweat from his brow, his chopped bangs falling back into place.

The face, mainly unscarred, appealed to the harlot, who saw many male faces but appreciated few of them. His eyes were clear and quick and unusual for some reason which, at this distance, she could not quite identify. His cheekbones were high and prominent, his nose slightly aquiline, his jaw strong. He had all his teeth, if her glimpse spoke truly. The burly youth wore a scarlet tunic emblazoned in black with the device of a swooping *graak*, the prehistoric pterodactyl which yet lingered in the skies of Lemuria. From a wall hook depended a great black cloak. Wristbands hugged his forearms, looking as if they might once have served as manacles. And now Zakeela saw that he was looking at her.

As she crossed the crowded, reeking room she kept her eyes on his, thinking in this way to form some estimate of him before they exchanged words. He remained an enigma, and not least because of those eyes, which she could now see were miniature replicas of the great Lemurian moon above, for they were gold in color. This lent the warrior's rugged face an incongruous hint of the ethereal. But that was scarcely the only surprise in the scene, for she could now see that the three men with him at the table were all dead, their ruined faces soaking up a pool of their own oozing blood.

"You need more lively dining companions, young sir, if you don't mind my saying so."

A quiver of a smile crossed his face. "They are just tired out, poor things. A few moments ago they were quite frisky, I assure you. The fools sought to test their mettle against me, a stranger, and their junior. I sat them here to warn others. I prefer being alone." These last words seemed, on second thought, intended for her.

She decided to come to the point. "You are the Black Hawk of Valkarth?"

His brow furrowed; it usually meant trouble when he was recognized. "Who seeks me? And why?" He sat up straighter, the ale forgotten.

She looked around, aware of many eyes upon them. Seeing her discomfort, Thongor of Valkarth reached over and pushed the nearest corpse from its perch, kicked it away, and motioned for his visitor to join him. "Mind the blood. You'll not want to stain that pretty outfit. Now, what have you to say?"

"I serve those in high places in this kingdom. My master seeks one such as you to secure him some…lost goods. There are dangers involved, but the pay will make the risks worthwhile, I assure you."

"I would hear more. What is it that he seeks? His own goods, stolen from him? Or does he covet the treasure of another? And of what sort are these dangers?"

"Are you afraid, then?"

Thongor laughed. "Fear is a vice I gave up long ago, girl. But a man likes to know what he's up against."

"Well spoken," she said, feeling sure that her master's choice was a sound one.

"And who is your master? From the looks of you I can see he must pay splendidly indeed for services well rendered."

Her cheeks crimsoned, for the first time since she could remember, and her voice dropped. "I am sent by the Sark, Arzang Pome himself."

Thongor's golden eyes widened slightly. "I can imagine my name is well enough known to him. I can imagine as well that he might want to lead me into a trap."

"I think you misjudge my master. He is not one to lose sleep over assassinations and thievery such as follow your name. In one such as you he sees only the commodity of a talent he may use to his advantage."

By this time, the young giant had arisen and secured his cloak to his shoulders, from whence it belled out like a sail as the pair quit the stale air of the drinking house and proceeded down the street, retracing the courtesan's journey of but half an hour before. "This is not the place to bargain over the Sark's business. Lead on."

His suspicions still sounded like an alarm gong, but Thongor knew that danger always presented opportunity, provided a man were quick enough. So he kept his eyes and ears open for treachery, as well as for the chance to render some of his own if needed. He had been in the world of civilized men but a short time, but his wild senses were keen to the serpentine wiles of city folk.

"Where are you taking me, Zakeela? The palace of Arzang Pome is to the South."

"We are not going there. Another will explain your mission. The Sark likes not to deal directly with…"

"With my kind!" Thongor laughed in derision. "Well, that makes the two of us even, I guess!"

2

Whispered Mysteries

"I like not the look of this place. It stinks of black sorcery!" The Valkarthan instinctively loosened his great broadsword in its scabbard, for all the good it might do him against intangible perils such as he half-anticipated.

"Aye, that it would, young sir, for we have entered the magicians' quarter, and this is the dwelling of Belshathla the magus," said Zakeela, afraid now that the barbarian's superstitious dread might be getting the better of him. "But all's well. I swear, there is no trap." She was about to rap upon the ponderous wooden slab. But as her small knuckles fell, they met no resistance, the door already sinking inward of its own accord.

A cracked voice from within sounded frail greetings. "Zakeela? Is that the Black Hawk with you? Why, of course it is! Who else would it be?" A comical figure threaded his maddeningly slow way through twisted piles of strange contrivances and devices. The doors of half a dozen scroll cabinets lay open, some cock-eyed on bent hinges. Inscribed papyrus scraps and *phondath*-parchment leaves were universally scattered, and cabalistic charts festooned the low walls. Heaps of the debris seemed occasionally to shift as if living creatures, whether the sorcerer's pets or experimental subjects, were given free run of the place. A couple of bracketed torches gave wan light, supplemented by the strange glow of various crystal globes in which scenes of far-away sights seemed to flicker. There was a near-inaudible hum pervading the place, as of occult energies at whose nature the uncouth barbarian could not guess. But for all that he saw, the greatest danger in the place appeared to be the low beams with which his raven-locked head nearly collided more than once.

The old mage Belshathla was a bearded, swag-bellied gnome, tenuously borne aloft on precarious spindle-shanked legs. There was little of menace, much of the burlesque about him. And yet his eyes did seem to sparkle with a peculiar vitality. A stained apron gave him more the appearance of an apothecary than that of a mighty sorcerer. Thongor held his peace, somewhat at ease now, but waiting for more evidence upon which to base a judgement on the old man.

The courtesan Zakeela embraced the squat figure as if he had been some long-lost uncle. Thongor felt more relaxed still, enough to venture a remark. "Are these the accommodations of a court magus? Forgive me, my lord, but…"

The wrinkled face split in a grin. "It is true I serve the Sark of Shembis. But I am not one of his court, nor do I seek any wealth save the riches of learning that surround me. And besides, the more tokens of favor one receives from the powerful, the more tightly their talons fasten upon one." At this, a shadow passed over Zakeela's pretty countenance.

"So, my dear, you have not yet told our young friend the nature of his task? Very well; allow me. Young sir, I can tell you only so much, because a crucial element of the challenge that faces us remains a mystery, even to one such as I. Still, I will tell you all I know."

"First," the impatient Valkarthan demanded, "what is it I am to seek?"

"A hoard of silver, that much I know, if legends tell truly. A hoard surpassing the dreams of men, a fortune amassed before the dawn of men by the very Dragon Kings themselves! You will know that our sovereign Arzang Pome, a greedy man all round, has an especial fetish for silver, prizing it even above gold and electrum."

"Aye, his standards, banners, pennants, even the chasing of his *kroters'* bridles gleam of silver, much to the despair of the many poor lining the streets of his city." At these words, Zakeela's own numerous argent trinkets, presents of her royal master, began to hang heavily upon her.

"That is indeed so, Thongor of Valkarth. And you will ask why we are concerned to aid him in gaining even more. As it stands, nothing will stop him in pursuing his obsession. But a man obsessed is a dangerous man. And we but seek to minimise the danger to which he may expose us all. For if the silver treasure truly exists, there is said to be a potent curse upon it."

Thongor growled deep down. "I knew it had to come to that sooner or later! Of what sort is this curse? That which seeks out the despoiler after the fact and strikes him down? Or perhaps a guardian set to forestall attempts to steal the treasure?"

The wizard's rheumy eye sparkled to observe the curt and business-like manner of the young mercenary, a good omen. "The latter, so far as I can determine, for my manuscripts tell of many over the ages who have sought the treasure and perished miserably in the attempt. Of no man is it written that he made away with riches only to be tracked down by some nemesis. But of what nature that guardian spirit may be, I know not. Only two words are told of it: 'Silver Shadows,' and beyond this nothing is known."

"And the location of this great treasure? Is a long journey involved? I will need provisions…"

"Few, I should think," mused Belshathla. "For the treasure lies buried in a cavern deep beneath the Sark's own castle. Indeed, the old legend was the reason he chose the site."

3

Paths of Peril

Shortly after dawn, a rested and well-fed Thongor, accoutred now in black link-mail supplied by the Sark's largesse, embarked upon his task. He had not seen the voluptuous Zakeela since the previous night, but he hoped to see more of her whenever the present business might be over. For now, he made his way swiftly and silently down the surprisingly smooth path of a tunnel, far below the surface, below even the sewers, of ancient Shembis. Many men had passed this way, perhaps those treasure-seekers of whom legend told dolefully, perhaps simply workmen of the Sark who had done preliminary spadework to make his access easier. Here and there were signs of recent workmanship, not least the infrequent torches bracketed to the damp walls. Their wan light seemed more to smolder than to glow, dampened in some strange manner by a hidden foulness in the very air.

The Valkarthan's equipment, by choice, was meager, for he trusted in his good right arm and in his great broadsword Sarkozan, with its strange elder-world sigils. The weapon never left his side, this mighty blade, which he had taken from the fallen corpse of his father, Thumithar, and which was said to have come down his ancestral line from Valkh, the Black Hawk, founder of the clan. Thongor held the blade firmly in his clenched fist, and it almost seemed that the engravings along its surface shone against the all-pervasive miasma of the place. But now was not the time for such musings.

As the old savant had told him, there was no lengthy journey involved, so of victuals he carried none. Slung over his shoulders were a pair of large sacks in which he might bring back specimens of the forbidden silver should he succeed in vanquishing whatever guardian might seek to prevent its theft. But the fabled loot must far exceed the capacity of a single delver; hence Thongor's task was but to clear the way for the Sark's more timid servants to come and bear away the rest.

Just ahead, around a bend in the tunnel, traces of voices—Thongor judged two—carried to his ears. Had other fortune-hunters, not in the Sark's employ, sought to forestall his mission? Or was there treachery in store after all? Ready for anything, Thongor sprang into the midst of whatever scene might await him, seeking the advantage of surprise.

But it was he who was surprised, and very much so. For what filled his eyes was the familiar yet completely unexpected form of Zakeela the courtesan—spread-eagled on a set of wooden crossbeams, her sweating, naked flesh gleaming in the torchlight.

Stunned only for a moment, Thongor turned, sword already raised, to face the girl's captors.

"What in the Eleven Scarlet Hells is this?" he barked, eyes narrowing. He stayed his hand, for it was plain the two dull oafs, though well armed, intended him no harm.

One, considerably alarmed, managed to sputter, "Hold there, Black Hawk! We were sent to aid you! For a second there, I thought you the guardian of the treasure!"

"The Sark sent such as you to join the fray? And what of Zakeela? What mischief is this?" Thongor stepped to her side and undid the silken scarf that had been used to gag her.

Her eyes frantic, Zakeela gasped, "Thongor! Praise the Nineteen Gods! The Sark thought it might go better with you if he placated the guardian of the treasure with a human sacrifice. These ruffians abducted me in the middle of the night and bound me here. Arzang Pome reasoned that you might come upon the monster, whatever it may be, already busy or perhaps sated. I have passed many hours here with no sign of the guardian, but only the lewd mutterings of these base fools."

Thongor began to unfasten her bonds. One of the Sark's men protested, "Here, now! It's Sark's orders—she's to be fed to the thing from the tunnel! You can't..."

Thongor's swordpoint was at his throat in an instant. "And why not offer him a pair of sacrifices, fatter ones and far more tasty? I care not for the mad reasoning of the Sark! The task is mine, and I'll not be party to the slaying of the innocent."

The other man, older and craftier than his partner, now spoke up. "There's no need for bloodshed, young sir. I quite agree. But orders is orders. Still, there's no one to know better if we three reached a bargain, eh? We take turns with her, see, and when we've all had our fill, we leave her to the Sark's pet beastie!"

He looked genuinely surprised when the young outlander's gaze only grew more fierce. The Black Hawk lifted his sword, signalling that the others should do the same, as he had evidently done with words. He would settle the issue in a more definitive way. But it was not to be.

"Thongor! He comes! The guardian!" Zakeela cried.

The others took to their heels, back the way they had come. Zakeela stared in disbelief as Thongor dropped into his combat stance. Strange sounds, as of a great weight dragging on the ground, crushing the gravel beneath it, warned of the imminent advent of some unthinkable monstrosity, but Thongor busied himself with cutting through the ropes that chafed the tender flesh of the desperate maid.

"If I am defeated, I will not have you left captive to the thing's depredations!" So saying, he freed her, then wheeled just in time. Like a swarm of deadly jungle flies a massive form swept into view with speed seemingly impossible for such great bulk. It thrust a great limb at the raven-maned head. Thongor dropped, grazed by the blow, which he could not entirely avoid. He sought to gather his fleeing wits and to bring his sword arm into play, knowing his foe would allow him no quarter, no margin for error. Before he could strike, however, he heard an unearthly shriek from the monster. Zakeela had somehow managed, with arms still stiff from captivity, to grab one of the torches and cast it into the thing's face.

Thongor rolled aside and regained his feet in a bound. "You're a wonder, girl! I owe you both our lives—but begone now! I'll fight my own battle!"

Knowing she could not hope to strike so fortuitous a blow a second time, and equally aware that the barbarian sought only to mask his concern for her under his protest of manly pride, Zakeela did as she was ordered. Thongor was alone with the guardian of the treasure.

For a moment, he and the creature stood poised facing one another, and he got his first clear glimpse of it. Filling most of the enclosure, the towering ape-like form was a living fortress of iron muscle barely contained beneath a scaly reptilian hide. The thing might well be a survivor of the vanished age of the fabled Dragon Kings whose own sorcery had ended in their doom, though shuddered rumors hinted that here and there some of their species might survive, planning the renewal of their ophidian empire.

It was a large measure of Thongor's fighting skill that he approached each contest as a gambler approaches the table, quickly assessing and calculating the situation and its opportunities. Fear he knew to be a fatal luxury and so did not allow himself to be whelmed by its onrush. Danger and death he took for granted. They were but his opponents in the game, and he began to calculate how to beat them. He knew that the size of the creature, for all its power to intimidate, must be a tactical disadvantage in these close quarters. Whoever had conjured it here must have overlooked that, trusting to its frightful ferocity as a sufficient weapon.

He had to stay clear of the vicious talons of the thing, scythes mounted on living tree limbs, striking with the force of a battering ram. Each blow, already falling like a rain, dislodged fragments of stone from the narrow walls, with no apparent discomfort to the monster. Agility must tell the tale. Thongor dodged, feinted, dived. He swiftly realized that he could trick the guardian into sparring with his shadow in a repeated pattern, a dance, if he could pick a path between the scaly limbs, evading the mighty but clumsy blows, and then repeat it. For its part, the lumbering behemoth seemed to trust in no more than persistence and, if it could manage it, speeding up its pursuit, like a dog chasing its tail.

At first Thongor made no effort to strike with the sword, hoping to lull the dull-witted guardian into believing it was no more than a game of chase. As he circled the saurian figure, he noted with dismay that his foe bore the scars of many previous battles, many previous victories, for he could see the fragments of several sword and knife blades protruding from various spots on its broad back and tree-trunk legs. It appeared the weapons of previous opponents had simply broken off and given the monster no pause. How could he avail against such a foe?

One of the lumbering monster's blows found its mark and hurled the young warrior through the air. His link-mail did a little to cushion the impact, but Thongor nonetheless had the wind driven from him. By willpower more than anything else, he rolled aside and narrowly avoided the brunt of the oncoming attack. He had been hurled further up the length of the subterranean hall and now found himself in position to behold at least a bit of the legendary silver hoard itself. What he actually saw, having but a moment to spare for it, was the seemingly self-generated bluish glow of the silver treasure. In this depth there could be no daylight for it to reflect, and the color was wrong for reflected lamplight. But here came the dragon-thing again.

Thongor remembered how the mage Belshathla had spent an hour or so the previous night engaged in some mummery over his young guest's broadsword, as if he had recognized something in the faded engravings along its ancient blade. Perhaps there might be something to the old man's superstitions. At any rate, Thongor now found that he had enough space to swing the sword without encumbrance, and with a gasp of a prayer to father Gorm, the uncouth deity of his people, he let loose a blow at the thing's slavering head.

It met no resistance! And yet, his senses amply honed by many combats, Thongor knew he could not have missed his target. He guessed that he owed to the old savant's spells and blessings that his sword did not shatter on impact as many others had before. His blade was useless as a weapon: he accepted that and looked for another. And surprise was always a handy weapon, so he turned on his heel and ran for the heaped treasure, a seemingly foolish gesture as it could only bring his opponent after him with increased fury. What Thongor hoped to gain by this desperate stratagem not even he knew. But every other path was closed to him. If any open door remained, it must lie in this direction.

4

Voices from the Past

Zakeela fled down the tunnel path until she tripped over something that lay in the shadows at her feet. It was her clothes, heaped in a pile where the Sark's men had left them after stripping her. No doubt they had planned to sell the rich brocades and silks and convert the profits into heady *sarn*-wine. She reached mechanically for her garments and hastily donned them, as if some instinctive female modesty overruled even the panic she felt. Arzang Pome, he who had betrayed her, had in the days of his favor bedecked her with various pendants and broaches of his favorite precious metal, and she made to pocket these rather than take the time now to arrange them. But one of them, a large silver disk polished to mirror-like clarity, caught her eye as a glimmer of torch light seemed to kindle it into unnatural illumination. The strange light made her feel sleepy for a split second, then she saw, or imagined she saw, in it the wizened face of her mentor Belshathla. There was no sound, but she felt sure she could read the old man's lips as he spoke to her. Was it a dream? Had she fainted in her terror?

"…long last discovered the riddle of the Silver Shadows! It was in the *Scarlet Edda* all along, if one but had eyes to see it! I found the clue in a glyph on the Black Hawk's sword! Then, just now, it all made sense! My dear, here is what you must do. Otherwise your champion stands no chance…"

Moments later, Zakeela gathered her wits and plunged down the tunnel, back in the direction of the growing sounds of struggle. She passed the broken crossbeams upon which her former master had intended she be sacrificed as a titbit to sate the monster. She noticed the stone debris fallen from the walls and marveled at the power of the demon that had dislodged them, fearing for the safety of the young Valkarthan. Then she came into view of the pair of combatants. Thongor's situation, she saw, was desperate. He picked up and threw at the creature what stones lay to hand, but none had any effect. It was all he could do to side-step the deadly lunges of the thing. She was sure he might have evaded it long enough to regain the safety of the tunnel and flee as she had done, but he had not. Apparently flight was not in his makeup.

Hoping not to distract him for a fatal instant, she nonetheless called out for his attention. "Thongor! Here! Strike him with this, if you can!" And she threw something as far as she could in his direction, hoping Thongor would manage to reach it before his untiring foe did. He succeeded, owing to the fact that his enemy, little more than an animated engine of destruction, possessed not the curiosity to note the object she had thrown, like the apple of discord, into the fray.

Stooping down to grasp the shiny object, then side-stepping another attack, Thongor saw that Zakeela had thrown him a mere trinket and, if he were not mistaken, one he had earlier seen her wearing. It was some manner of broach wrought cunningly from silver in the shape of a scimitar. He was to smite the giant reptile with a toy like this? He smiled briefly at the devotion that must have moved her to this gesture of desperation. But as swift as thought, here came the lunge of the titan, and he instinctively made to deflect it. He thrust forth the fist which still grasped the sword-ornament, and to his amazement he saw it rake the reticulated hide of the beast. Where it touched the creature, it sparked and smoked, and the thing recoiled. There was a queer kind of flash of negative light, if such were possible, and then he again faced the giant figure, little having visibly changed.

He cast the toy aside and drew his sword once more. Futile gesture as it might be, he resolved to go down fighting. Heedless of the probable outcome, Thongor swung the mighty broadsword like an ax directly into the monster's heaving chest—and a great bloody swath appeared! He brought the sword down again and cleft deep into one of the pillar-like forearms. He had passed at last from mere defence to attack, his more accustomed role, and it felt good!

The scaly fiend now stood bewildered by pain and surprise, if Thongor read its inhuman countenance correctly. It screamed in agony as the Valkarthan chopped again and again at its staggering form, letting loose geysers of steaming gore and stinking reptilian blood. In mere moments, Thongor was soaked in the noisome stuff, but in the berserk rage that possessed him, he scarcely marked it. Long after the guardian of the treasure had ceased to be any threat, Thongor kept at it, like a grim and remorseless butcher, till the tunnel floor was littered with the sundered parts of the lifeless carcass.

5

The Riddle Solved

Zakeela looked at her champion, as he turned from his bloody work, with a mixture of horror, relief, and desire. Some of this she thought she saw mirrored in the barbarian's strange golden eyes, the only part of him not drenched with gore.

Thongor looked at himself and laughed. "I'm not a pretty sight, I fear. But if it's a pretty sight you want to see, my princess, look yonder." He pointed with his dripping sword to the gleaming silver hoard. There were heaps upon heaps of goblets, crowns, shields, breastplates, statues, as well as a number of utensils harder to place, things that might easily have been designed for the use of non-human anatomy, as that of the Dragon Kings.

"We'll be rich on this stuff." Thongor the professional thief spoke now, all thought of the preternatural horrors of the past hour clean forgotten. "I swear that fat bastard Arzang Pome will lay nary a bejewelled finger upon it. Somehow we'll get it out of here ourselves, and…" With that, the Valkarthan stooped down and sought to gather into his arms a sample of the hard-won booty.

Zakeela murmured, "My lord, I fear…"

At once Thongor found his arms empty of treasure, and the whole subterranean hall likewise! He looked around him with outrage and bafflement. "By the Flame Lord! What witchery is this?"

She could not suppress a laugh, hoping not to enrage him further. "It is witchery indeed! As was that whereby you were able to slay the guardian! As I fled, the spirit of the mage Belshathla came to me and bade me cast you the broach. A thing of silver, it proved fatal to a creature of black magic. It dispelled the sorcery that shielded the monster from all harm, so that you might engage it in fair combat."

Still confused, Thongor asked, "But how can that be? After all, it was the guardian of a hoard of silver such as no man ever saw!"

"That was the riddle which the mage at last deciphered. There was never any treasure—only silver shadows, an enchantment placed there by the Dragon Kings, or by some sorcerers at any rate, to lure greedy mortals to their doom."

"Then I have very nearly paid with my life for the greed of another!"

She came to him and embraced him, heedless now of the foulness with which he was soaked, kissed him, and said, "My warrior, let us make haste to depart the city, for Arzang Pome will soon enough learn that no treasure is forthcoming, and he will surely believe you have made away with it."

"As I would, if only I could, by Gorm!" Thongor laughed, then swept up Zakeela in a great embrace. "Come, my would-be princess, let us back to the house of Belshathla. I suspect he has resources to aid two fugitives. We'll settle up with Arzang Pome another time."

Thongor's buccaneers continue to cause havoc among the rich merchants of Shembis, until Arzang Pome, the infuriated Sark, begins a determined campaign to bring the troublesome pirate to heel.

KEEPER OF THE EMERALD FLAME

1

The Sign of the Skull

The Daotar Dorgand Tul shifted gingerly in the hard saddle, scratched irritably at the bite of a stinging insect, and wished for the thousandth time that he had entered the priesthood rather than obeying his father's desire by purchasing a commission in the legions of Arzang Pome, the Lord of Shembis.

He was a fat, soft-faced little man, with quick, clever eyes, a petulant mouth and a waspish temper. For all his silver-gilded cuirass, jeweled honors and the martial-looking longsword that hung at one plump thigh, he seemed distinctly out of place at the head of a punitive company of warriors. And, indeed, with every league his troop penetrated into the dense jungles his dissatisfaction with the military life grew more profound.

The bad-tempered little Daotar was hot and weary, and his buttocks and thighs ached from long hours on *kroter*-back. He sat slouched in the saddle, dreaming of a soft couch, cooling breezes from the gulf, nubile slave girls at his beck and call and tall, frosted goblets of spiced wine. He wondered if he would ever feel comfortable again.

For seven days and nights now he and his troop of warriors had plunged ever deeper into the jungles of southern Kovia, until by now he was heartily sick of the whole business. The massive crimson boles of soaring *lotifer* trees rose all about him; snaky vines dangling from low branches overhead caught the plumes of his helm; stinging gnats whirled in buzzing clouds about him as he guided his plodding *kroter* through thick bushes of *tiralons*, the strange green roses of ancient Lemuria. Behind him, half a hundred footsore warriors toiled along, their mail smeared with sap and black with mud, and they longed for the comforts of civilization no less than he.

For the ten-thousandth time he cursed this Northlander savage and his gang of bandits, whose elusive track they followed. The bold young Valkarthan raider had been harrying the caravan routes for the past six months, and his depredations cut deeply into the revenues of Arzang Pome, who delighted more in the clink of fat gold coins than in the caresses of all his women and his perfumed boys. At length, stung beyond endurance by the daring of the bold young bandit chieftain, the Sark of Shembis had sent a troop of warriors on his trail…and it was the sad fate of Dorgand Tul to be the commander of that troop.

The day was wearing on apace. Ere long the gold disc of Aedir the Sun god would expire in crimson splendor on the western horizon and the thick jungle night would cloak all of Kovia in darkness. It was the night that Dorgand Tul feared most, for then the monstrous predators were a-prowl—the slinking *vandars*, the great black lions of the Lemurian jungles, the savage Beastmen, and—most dread of all—the colossal jungle dragons whose enormous size and ferocity rendered them virtually impossible to kill.

Dorgand Tul shivered at the thought. The days were exhausting and muddy and vile with the steaming jungle reek—but the nights were made hideous by the coughing roar of hunting reptiles and the glare of hungry eyes through the blackness, mirroring the flicker of the watch fires. Already he had lost two spearmen of his troop to the jungle brutes, and, were it not for the fact that his own tent was set each night in the very centre of the camp, the plump little Daotar would have trembled to the depths of his soul for his own precious hide.

Just then his *kroter* shied, almost toppling him from the saddle. He seized the saddle horn in one fat fist, straightening the plumed helm, which had slipped down over his eyes, with the other hand and snarling a blasphemous curse as he saw the cause of the disturbance.

The bushes ahead parted and the muddy, haggard figure of one of his advance scouts appeared, making a sketchy salute.

"Well, what is it, Yazlar? Don't tell me you have lost their trail again?" he demanded shrilly.

The old scout shook his head. "No, Daotar. It continues straight ahead. I estimate they are now only four hours ahead of us."

"Well, what then?"

The scout turned, gesturing for Dorgand Tul to follow, and vanished in the underbrush. The fat little officer thumped the *kroter*'s ribs with his booted heel and guided the weary beast through the bushes, whimpering a curse as thorn-edged leaves stung his hand. The *kroter* shouldered through the glossy-leafed bushes, and Dorgand Tul found himself in a little clearing.

The glade was small, hedged about with densely packed trees. Reining the beast to a standstill, the officer glanced about, and then his eyes caught an ominous and grisly emblem and he froze, while a small thrill of apprehension ran over him.

A tall pole of gaunt black wood thrust up from the muddy earth at the edge of the clearing. Atop the pole was affixed a grinning, naked human skull. A cryptic hieroglyph was etched in crimson paint on the brow of the death's-head. The eyes of Dorgand Tul were caught and held by that coiling, crimson symbol.

"The sign of Omm," whispered the old scout.

The fat little Daotar paled, swallowed, but could not tear his eyes from the blot of bloody color blazoned on the grinning skull. It held his gaze with a horrid fascination, like the cold enigma in the eyes of a snake.

"Did the bandits…pass it?" he asked at last, in a weak voice.

The old scout nodded, his lank, gray locks swinging. "They did," he said somberly.

A flame of malignant delight blazed up in the eyes of Dorgand Tul. New energy surged within his weary, flaccid form. He snatched up the reins and wheeled the *kroter* about and plunged through the bushes by which he had entered the clearing. The first bedraggled warriors of his troop were just catching up to him as he retraced his path. A scarred, hard-faced sergeant came forward to receive orders at the Daotar's impatient gesture.

"Turn the men about, my man. We shall camp for the night in that large clearing we passed through an hour or so ago. And then back to the city!" the Daotar crowed delightedly. Then, at the look of blank incomprehension in the sergeant's eyes, he laughed with vicious humor. "The barbarian in his flight has led his bandits past the Sign of the Skull…and ere night falls across the world, he will be in the power of Shan Chan Thuu!" he smirked.

The sergeant's eyes widened in black, horrified amazement. His lips parted and he whispered to himself a dread phrase at which his men shuddered…and which even cooled the malignant joy in the heart of Dorgand Tul, and made the fat officer fumble at his throat, where a protective amulet of blue paste dangled on a silver chain.

"The Keeper of the Emerald Flame…"

"…Only the Nineteen Gods can save Thongor of Valkarth now," the grizzled scout said under his breath.

2

Something in the Dark

Thongor of Valkarth was baffled.

He crouched in the crotch of a great tree, his keen gaze studying the jungle behind his track, and deep in his heart he felt a nameless qualm…a distinct yet shadowy unease. Something was wrong, yet he did not know what.

Lithely he swung down from his perch, dropped to a lower branch and clambered down a dangling vine, to drop lightly to the thick grasses of the clearing as might a jungle cat. His warriors, who had been resting while he sought the upper levels, rose now to their feet, turning questioning eyes upon their young chieftain as he appeared.

For a moment he stood silent, brows knotted in puzzlement. As the men of his band watched him, waiting for his words, there was not one among them who did not gaze at him with admiration. He was superb, the half-naked young barbarian, his bronze body with the thews of some savage god. Black and heavy as a *vandar*'s mane, his unshorn hair fell across his broad, naked shoulders, framing a stern, impassive face, strong-jawed and manly for all his youth.

Beneath scowling, black brows, his strange gold eyes blazed with sullen, wrathful, lion-like fires. Few men could meet the gaze of those somber, burning eyes, for behind them smoldered the fighting fury of a barbarian, whose savage heart had never learned the cooler temper of civilized men.

His powerful torso was clad in the plain black leather of a Lemurian warrior. A great cloak was flung back over his shoulders and a massive girdle bound his taut, rock-hard mid-section. The leather strap of a baldric was slung across his chest from shoulder to hip, and from it hung in its scabbard a mighty Valkarthan broadsword. A crimson loincloth and black leather boots completed his war-harness.

"What is it, Thongor?" one of his lieutenants demanded, as the long silence of their young leader began to puzzle the men.

The barbarian shook his head. "Strange, Chelim! The Shembian troops are—*going back*!"

Chelim, a tall, massive Zangabali with shaven pate and gold hoops in his ears, scratched his heavy, stubbled jaw thoughtfully. "Maybe it's a trick?" he suggested. "Maybe they split up, one group returning, the other sneaking around, hoping to catch us off guard, once we were convinced they were all turning back."

Thongor grunted. "Not a chance. I counted heads as they went through that big clearing near the lightning-blasted tree. Every man-jack of the troop is bound in full retreat."

A scrawny, rat-like little man with one eye sniggered. "Chief? Maybe seven days o' jungle muck and *vandars* in the night convinced them this is no place for Arzang Pome's warriors, eh? A lot of craven-hearted dogs, those Shembians, anyway!"

Thongor grinned. "Well, maybe you're right, Fulvio. At any rate, we'll take no chances on being surprised. We'll push on—even past nightfall—until we find a place that can be stoutly defended. On your feet, men. Mount up, and let's get out of here."

* * * *

Night fell, shadow-winged, across the edges of the world. Stars glittered like jewels in the dark sky, and soon the great golden Moon of elder Lemuria emerged from her palace of clouds to bathe the black jungles of Kovia in her silken, shimmering light.

Thongor and his bandits made camp in the hills, where sheer walls of rugged stone enclosed their position on three sides. The hill slopes were covered with loose, fragmented shale. Thongor believed that it would be impossible for any force to creep up on their position without dislodging underfoot a rattling miniature avalanche of broken rock, whose noise would give warning of the advance of the foe.

They watered their *kroters* in the small stream that trickled by the foot of the hills, built a fire to keep the beasts away and made a rude supper, gnawing on cold joints of meat and dry cheese, washed down with thin, sour ale in waxed skin bags.

Then, setting his sentries, Thongor curled up on a bed of dry leaves under the shelter of an overhang of rock, wrapped his great cloak around him against the night chills, set Sarkozan, his great Northlander broadsword, near to his hand and fell asleep almost instantly. Even his giant frame was weary from the long trek through the jungles, and from boyhood he had learned the knack of falling asleep at will. His boyhood, spent on the wintry plains of the wild north beyond the Mountains of Mommur, had taught him the survival skills known only to a barbaric people such as his own Black Hawk tribe. To survive in a rugged, frozen land, where the forces of hostile nature were leagued with savage enemies and monstrous predators against human life, one learned early—or one did not live long. Thongor learned—and lived.

It was four years since all of his tribe had fallen in battle against an enemy tribe. Since that savage day, he had left the north. Down across the wintry steppes he had come, through the rugged mountains. He was a hardy, bronzed youth of seventeen when he reached at last the lush jungle lands and splendid, glittering cities of the Dakshina, as the Southlands of Lemuria were known. And for the two years since that time, he had eked out a precarious living as thief and wandering adventurer, and now, most recently, as a bandit chieftain in the wilderness of Chush and Kovia. He had joined the caravan raiders eight months ago, and fought his way up the ranks to the leadership of the band, slaying the former chief, Red Jorn, in a barehanded battle to the death.

Some might think it odd that a youth of nineteen, scarce more than a boy, should lead a band of experienced warriors, most of whom were half again, or twice, his age. Odd, perhaps, but not illogical. For Thongor, from the first hour he had entered the ranks of Jorn's raiders, had proved himself bold, fearless and indomitable. As for his men, seasoned veterans all, their very lives depended on the quality of the leadership of the band, and if the young barbarian, not yet twenty, could prove his superior gifts, they were willing to swallow the fact that he was younger than the least of them.

The secret of his swift domination of the bandit company may have been summed up in a single phrase: at nineteen, Thongor had faced more perils, fought more foes, seen more of death, war and adventure, than any man of them.

It was his savage intuition that roused him now—

The scrape of leather sandals on rough stone. The click and rattle of a dislodged pebble.

The boy snapped in an instant to full, tingling alertness. Yet, in the transition from sleep to wakefulness, not a muscle moved in all his mighty frame. To the eye of any watcher, he was still slumbering in heavy sleep.

Again, the faint sound. And now his keen senses told him it came from directly above his rude couch. *Someone was descending the face of the steep hill. Someone was crouched just above the rock under which he lay.*

He rose lithely to his feet, drawing a long dagger from his girdle. The broadsword he let lay—it would make too much sound to draw the blade, and he would need his hands free. As silent as a jungle cat, the barbarian padded to the brink of the overhanging ledge. Emerging from under the low rock, Thongor rose slowly to his full height, flattening himself against the side of the wall of stone.

Dimly in the moon-silvered gloom, he could make out a crouching figure, black against the sky. It seemed to be surveying the bandit camp. One hand clutched a long spear, and it was the heft of this spear that had dislodged the pebble.

Like a striking snake, Thongor seized the unknown watcher.

3

Jungle Girl

He dragged the fiercely struggling figure down to the ground and sought to pinion its lithe arms. But it was as if he had seized a spitting, wriggling armful of clawed fury. It writhed and snarled in his grip like a maddened wildcat. Sharp nails drew lines of scarlet across his bronze hide and drew stinging furrows in his chest, cheek and shoulder.

Suddenly Thongor gasped with astonishment, released his captive and sprang back. For in their struggle, his arms had gone around the chest of his opponent from behind, and his hands had touched—not the flat, muscular hide of a male warrior—but the warm, pointed breasts of a young girl!

Illana the Moon Lady had receded behind a cloud moments before; now she displayed the glory of her unveiled visage, and by the sudden wash of silver light, Thongor could clearly see his foe.

It was a half-naked young girl, of his own age or a year or two younger, who crouched, stone-bladed dagger clenched in one small, capable fist, challenging him to continue the combat. Her slender body was bare save for a strip of fur worn low about her hips, and twisted about her slim loins. This and leather sandals and a bauble worn about her throat on a thong constituted her only garments.

Very lovely she was in the silver moonlight, her hair long, black, a shining cascade that poured over sleek shoulders and down her slender back to the firm rondure of her little rear. Her legs were long, adolescent, graceful. Her breasts were shallow but firmly rounded, warm, pointed. They rose and fell as she panted, and their surging rhythm drove his hot young blood to interesting speculations.

"Come, girl," he growled. "Forgive my rough handling—I did not know what you were in the darkness. Come, let us be friends— I make no war on women."

She crouched, wordless, moonsilver glinting on the flinty blade in her fist.

He straightened, laughed and tossed away his dagger, showing her his empty hands. She stood up reluctantly, fingering her stone knife, and finally thrust it into a *phondle*-skin sheath tied by thongs to her loincloth.

When she smiled, the pale round oval of her face, framed by shining black hair, was inexpressibly lovely. He felt a small pulse thud hotly at the base of his throat as he watched her bare body move in the moonlight.

"I am Thongor of Valkarth, the chieftain of this band," he growled. "And I thought you were the vanguard of a troop of Shembian soldiers!"

She voiced a husky laugh. "I am Zoroma of the Pjanthan," she said, "and I feared you were a troop of," her voice dropped, "*ghosts!*"

He gave a grunt of laughter. "We are flesh and blood. But, tell me, girl, what are the Pjanthan? Never have I heard of them till now."

"Jungle hunters," she answered. "There are many tribes like ours in Kovia—how can you not know this?"

He rubbed his jaw ruefully. "Frankly, I know nothing of Kovia, save for the jungles around Shembis, the Dolphin City. We are bandits who raid the Shembian caravans, but now we have been chased deep into this jungle country, unknown to us, by the Sark's soldiers. I fear we raided one caravan too many!"

"It is as I thought," she said enigmatically. "You are strangers. Few dare come into these regions of the jungle—even the legions of Shembis never enter here."

Thongor wondered why—wondered if the answer to that question might not also explain the curious retreat of the warriors of Dorgand Tul—but before he could ask, his sentinels, attracted by the sounds of their struggle, and the conversation, came over to where he and the girl stood, to see if everything was well with their chieftain. And by the time he had reassured them and, learning that the girl, Zoroma, hungered, saw to it that the remnants of their meal were put at her disposal, the girl's curious remark had slipped his mind for the moment.

She slept for the remainder of the night in his bed of leaves, under his cloak, while he stood guard to make certain that none of his men, who had not seen a woman in weeks, did not abuse the hospitality he had offered her.

Many times her eyes stole to his stalwart figure as it stood before the overhanging rock, black and silvered bronze in the moonlight. But, at length, she fell into a fitful slumber, from which she did not awaken until dawn.

* * * *

They breakfasted on cold water from the stream and the small scraps of meat and cheese that remained uneaten. Then they pressed forward. Thongor was still uncertain as to whether the pursuing troops had retreated completely or were circling around, so he moved his men out early with all possible speed.

Zoroma rode his *kroter* and he walked alongside the beast. The trail through the hills was rough and rocky, but they made better speed over clear, dry ground than they had the previous days, hacking a path through dense jungles and the muck of rotting leaves.

The sun burned high above like molten gold in a cauldron of searing brass. They were hot and dusty, but he urged them on, with brief and infrequent rest stops.

"Do your people, the Pjanthan, dwell nearby?" he asked her.

"No. Many leagues to the west."

"How is it, then, that you are roaming these hills alone, so far from your tribe?" he asked.

"I am searching for a youth who is…lost," she said.

"A brother?"

She shook her head. "My lover. Him who…was to have been my mate." There was a note of somber sorrow that haunted her low, hesitant voice.

"And your people would not assist in your search? They would permit a mere lass to stray so far, in so hostile a land, all by herself?" He grunted and spat. "Mine are a savage people, too, and no soft-gutted city-dwellers. But rather than permit a maiden to venture alone into peril we would sacrifice half the fighting strength of the clan!"

She moistened her lips hesitantly.

"They…they fear to penetrate the borders of this region," she said in low tones. And she explained that it was under a bad omen; she used a term which Thongor understood as—*taboo*.

He said nothing. His people, too, knew the terrors of the darkness and the curse of all omens. The Black Hawk people of Valkarth were not immune to the strength of the taboo…but never would the stalwart heroes of the North have permitted shadowy terrors to come between them and the protection of their womenfolk. Privately, he decided that these Pjanthan were either weaklings, or fools—or both.

But he did not want to offend her.

Frequently that morning as he strode along beside her *kroter* his lambent gaze strayed to her bare brown thighs, rounded calves and slender, tapering ankles...to the proud lift of her naked young breasts, her sleek, flat abdomen, the rondure of her little rump. And, whenever she thought he was not looking, the girl's huge, dark eyes took in the swelling arch of the boy's deep chest, his flat belly. His long, powerful arms.

It was nearly noon when they came upon the white, grinning skull mounted on a black pole, set up like a silent warning directly in their path.

4

The Shadow of Shan Chan Thuu

Zoroma shrieked as the naked white skull loomed up in their path. The *kroter* shied nervously and Thongor growled an oath and sprang to catch the bridle before the beast could panic into flight. The girl sat shuddering, her terrified eyes fixed on the grisly emblem of warning that grinned at them from atop the black pole.

Thongor examined it narrowly.

"We passed such a thing in a jungle clearing last evening," he said. "I thought it a warning sign reared by the Beastmen, but the hairy folk of the jungles would not be here in these harsh hills. Do you know what this thing means, girl?"

"It bears the sign of Omm," she said weakly. "The emblem of Shan Chan Thuu!"

"And what might Omm and Shan Chan Thuu be?" he growled.

Her face pale, her dark eyes haunted by fear, she shuddered, for all the baking heat of the dusty hills. It was as if a clammy, crawling wind blew against her naked spine.

"Have you never heard of Omm?" she asked faintly. "Indeed, you are strangers to the jungles of Kovia..."

"I told you our accustomed territory lay to the north, in the wilderness of Chush," he said impatiently. "Come—out with it, girl!"

"Omm is a legend in this land...an age-old city that dates back to the dark days of Time's Dawn...when the children of Nemedis first came into this realm out of the Ultimate East, to lay the foundations of the Nine Cities." Her voice fell to a whisper, and there was something in her tone, a crawling note of cold menace and elder evil, that lifted his nape hairs and roughed the skin of his forearms with the thrill of premonition.

"No one knows where the Lost City of Omm lifts its eon-crumbled towers, but legend whispers that it is the cradle of an evil deviltry…a lore of science-magic foul with the slime of chaos, and black with the horror of man's cruelty," she whispered. "Such is the unholy legend of Omm."

"And what of Shan Chan Thuu?" he pressed. "Is it some black god of the Pit?"

She shuddered. "Perhaps that is what he is, after all…but he was mortal once, an ancient devil-wizard out of Omm who came into this land and raised his own black citadel among these very hills, wherein to pursue unmolested by his sorcerous brethren his strange worship and his stranger arts. That was two hundred years ago, men say…"

"And he lives yet?" Thongor demanded, incredulously, though a brief memory of Zazamanc in the ancient city of Ithomaar stirred in his mind.

The girl shrugged slim, bare shoulders, tawny, pink-tipped breasts lifting. "They say he prolonged his life beyond the limitations of mortal flesh…that he bartered his soul to chaos for some vast magical price—"

"—*The Emerald Flame!*" a voice gasped behind them.

Thongor turned to see that his lieutenant, Chelim, had heard the girl's fable.

"Have you never heard of it, lad?" Chelim grunted, his shaven pate gleaming with perspiration, his powerful muscled arms gray with rock dust. "A fabulous jewelled treasure—I've heard the same tale as the wench relates—the old Omnian sold his immortal part to possess it! They say 'tis a wealth of gems of a kind unknown to men—the ransom of a dozen emperors! And the old wizard long since dead!"

A speculative gleam shone in the fierce eyes of the young barbarian. "Gems, eh? And this death's head means we are approaching his fortress, or whatever it is? It is supposed to warn men away from his treasure house?"

The girl nodded. Thongor and the burly Chelim exchanged glances.

"What do you think, Chelim?" the youth growled. "Will the men let old fables fright them from a treasure like this?"

White teeth flashed in the bald giant's tanned face. "Not Jorn's Raiders, lad! They'd dare the horrors of the Pit itself for a handful of gold!"

The girl watched them but said nothing.

"Where is this place?" Thongor asked.

She pointed. "Directly in our path, but—"

He waited. "But—what?"

She bit her lip. "Nothing…"

* * * *

After a brief consultation with his warriors, Thongor led the march forward. Some of the men had demurred: that scrawny little thief, Fulvio, whined that it was not wise to disturb the bones of dead wizards, for life clings long about the dust of those sorcerers who have sworn the awful Vow to Chaos. But Thongor laughed and mocked their fears.

"I have faced and fought gods, ghosts and devils—men, magicians and monsters, before now," he grunted. "And never yet have I found a thing that cannot be killed!"

And so the bandits rode on, ignoring the grisly warning that grinned down at them from the black stake, the ominous crimson symbol coiled between its bony brows.

And Zoroma rode with them. But now she was silent, and her face was tense and haunted. For all the hot moonlight, it seemed to her that they rode through gathering shades of darkness, as if a dread shadow lay over all this dead, dry land.

The shadow of Shan Chan Thuu.

5

Black Citadel

As the long shadows of late afternoon stretched across the rocky hills of Kovia, they came within sight of the ruined tower. It had been built atop a round knoll and it thrust high up above the surrounding barrens. Gaunt and stark and ominous was that dead citadel, the only sign of man in all this waste.

Thongor studied it with narrowed eyes, thoughtfully. It was odd, he thought, that the transition from lush, steaming jungles to this harsh and barren land should be so abrupt. One moment they were cutting a path through sweltering underbrush—the next their boot heels crunched in dry soil where not a single blade of grass grew. He had not even glimpsed a mold or lichen, such as one might find underneath boulders or on the shadowed base of rocky cliffs, even in the most desert-like of wildernesses.

It was more than odd—it was uncanny.

It was as if that black citadel that thrust its broken walls up into the dim gloaming were the centre of some cosmic contagion that had cast its evil blight over all this land about, draining the life and the vigor from every living thing. Not one single sign of life had they seen since leaving camp the night before. Not so much as a crawling scorpion, carrier hawk or a venomous serpent.

All of this land was a land of death…

From this distance, the citadel was a black, featureless mass—a clotted cluster of shadows, of which no details could be discerned. But it was evident that the structure was of far greater antiquity than the legends hinted, for the extent of decay was extraordinary: Thongor could see fallen columns, shattered architraves and entire sections of wall that had collapsed into moldering ruin. Surely, the passage of a mere century or two could not account for so extensive a degree of ruin. It would take millennia—perhaps even eons—for a stone structure to crumble like this, particularly in a desert wilderness, whose aridity should preserve worked stone, not hasten its decay.

The rocky eminence whereupon the black citadel stood was in the exact centre of a vast bowl-like depression, a disc-shaped valley, like some enormous crater. The floor of this crater was a stretch of desiccated sand—dead as the surface of the moon.

They rode across the breadth of this huge depression, the hooves of their *kroters* crunching and squeaking in the crystalline sand. Thongor stooped and picked up a handful of the strange stuff. It was not sand at all, but rock—stone that had been subjected to some weird force that had sapped the hardness of the mineral until at length it crumbled into this coarse substance.

Under the pressure of his fingers, the sand crystals crushed to fine powder, like dry wood ash. *What uncanny force had leached the solid strength from living stone?*

They rode on.

As they drew nearer, it became easier to make out the details of the structure. And they became aware of its true size—distance, a trick of perspective, or perhaps the absence of any nearby object large enough to measure it against, had somehow concealed the truth of its proportions.

It was the largest stone edifice that Thongor or his warriors had ever seen. It may well have been the most enormous man-made structure on Earth at that time. Indeed, it would have dwarfed even the pyramids of Egypt, or the mighty Sphinx itself, had those relics of ancient Atlantis been built in the age of Thongor, the dim Pleistocene.

* * * *

The colossal stone wreck was one of incredibly detailed and curiously unfamiliar architecture. The eye became lost in a maze of balconies, towers, colonnades and buttresses. The mind was baffled and confused among the mad profusion of wall and arch and wing and extension. It was not so much one building as a cluster of buildings, all built together in a man-made mountain of stonework. The nature—the origin—the uses—of the citadel were impossible to make out.

It was like nothing else on Earth.

The extent of the decay was incredible. The outer walls, which were as much as twenty paces thick, and built of solid stone, had crumbled and lay fallen, scattering the slopes of the high place with enormous cubes of broken stone, each weighing several tons. Minarets were toppled and square turrets leaned crazily or strewed the earth with rubble. The whole outer surface of the enigmatic ruin was worn and pitted, as if bathed for countless centuries in the glare of some intolerable radiation. From the rough, porous condition of the outer walls, Thongor got the feeling that solid *inches* of stone had melted into powder, sifting down from the face of the structure.

As they approached nearer, they became aware of yet a further element of mystery. They felt an uncanny sensation of being close to some enormous and living—*thing*.

It was hard to say precisely what there was about the shadowy citadel that gave them the feeling that it was, somehow, alive. Like a titanic idol, hewn from a solid mountain of dead black stone, carved by the denizens of some unthinkably remote eon, it squatted, brooding, amid all that dreary waste of death and desolation.

There exuded from the dark structure an aura of cold menace. The black openings of windows gaped like the eye-sockets of a skull. The cold wind of fear blew from the towering colossus, like a chill and fetid breath from the mouth of the Pit itself.

The men muttered among themselves, signing their breasts with the names of half a hundred gods and totems and protective spirits. Thongor alone remained impassive. He had looked death and horror in the face often enough—and he had laughed!

* * * *

When all the west was a welter of crimson vapor where Aedir the Sun lord lay expiring in scarlet and gold, they reached the summit, and colossal portals loomed before them like the yawning jaws of a dead behemoth.

Within they found a vast, echoing hall whose roof, supported by stone columns like marble sequoia, was lost in clotted shadow far above. Galleries and antechambers in incredible number branched away from this central hall. All was a murmuring emptiness of dim shadows and whispering echoes.

For a very long time, it was evident, the hall had lain untenanted.

Moldering rubbish littered the stone paving of this gloom-drenched hall in which one hundred men could have marched abreast without brushing the walls to either side. Thongor poked among the rubbish of dry leaves, rotten bits of cloth and nameless scraps of ancient leather—and the toe of his boot dislodged a human skull.

Zoroma stifled a cry.

He knew she was thinking of her lover. But this could not be him. The bone of the skull was brown and scabrous with antiquity.

Thongor dispatched some of his troop to explore the nearest galleries, while assigning to a limping rogue named Randar the task of stabling the *kroters* in an antechamber close by the front gate. Then, while a few men under the command of a grizzled old swordsman from Thurdis marched off to take a look at the far end of the colossal hall, he drew his lieutenant, Chelim, to one side.

Zoroma stood, staring blankly about her with wide, apprehensive eyes, absently fingering a protective amulet of white crystal that hung between her breasts. She did not notice as the men stepped apart for a consultation.

"Well, what do you think?" Thongor inquired.

Chelim rubbed his nose, which had been broken once or twice and clumsily reset, and sniffed.

"I don't like it, lad," he muttered. "I get the feeling this place is somehow *alive*—watching me—waiting for me to take a false step, before it pounces; or does something even worse."

Thongor grunted: he had the same feeling, and he liked it little. "This can't be the citadel of Shan Chan Thuu. Not if the old Omnian sorcerer only lived two hundred years ago! This place has been abandoned for thousands of years—and its true age must be measured in millions of years. Look at that area of wall: the facing stones have decayed away, littering the floor with dust. Why, it would take ages to do that."

"Aye, lad—and those columns, see how they're cracked and split and pitted? I've seen the sides of *mountains* that looked younger…well, the old legend must be wrong; the sorcerer must have found this place as it is, and made it his dwelling, rather than building it himself."

"I think you're right," the youth grunted. "No one man—wizard or no—could build anything this big. It is a task that would require a nation." He paused, fingering the hilt of his sword. "I have heard that in the ages before the Father of the Gods created the first men, this world was ruled by wily and malignant creatures known as the Dragon Kings of Hyperborea…and that they entered in the land of Lemuria when all their land was lost beneath the eternal snows of the boreal pole."

"Yes, I've heard the same tale…You think this is some ungodly palace or temple or shrine left over from the fall of the Hyperboreans?"

Thongor nodded. "I do. For I have seen many of the kingdoms of man, and looked upon his cities, yet never till this hour have

I seen this fashion of building…not in my homeland, or among the shadowy foothills of Mommur, or in Kathool or Thurdis or Zangabal, or even old Tarakus, the Pirate City or any of the cities of the Dakshina. This is, must be, a survival of some forgotten age before the coming of man."

Chelim's face was stolid. "Gorm alone knows what pre-human deviltry these ancient walls have looked upon…or what shadowy forces may linger within, waiting for the chance to spring to life again."

Thongor uttered a rude expletive. "Keep this in mind, friend. I've seen much that the world affords in the way of dangers—ghosts and monsters and dark gods—but never have I encountered anything that could do me physical harm and which could not itself be destroyed!"

Chelim grinned. "Aye, there is that! Sharp steel is a mighty remedy against things in the night."

The leader of the men Thongor had dispatched to explore the farthest reaches of the hall came up to them then, and their conversation ended.

"Well, Thad Novis, what's it like at the other end?" Thongor asked.

The grizzled old Thurdan paused to catch his breath from the long hike. "Just more of the same, Thongor: galleries leading off in every direction, chambers opening into halls and corridors—this temple, or whatever it may be, is like a city, a whole city under one roof!"

They ate what few scraps were left, finished the ale, and bedded down for the night in the echoing vastness of the central hall, save for those whom Thongor designated as sentries of the first watch.

That night the first of them died.

6

The Thing that Walks in the Night

Deafening, filled with unendurable agony and horror, the scream rang out through the gloomy castle.

Wakened suddenly from fitful, uneasy slumbers, the bandits sprang up, cursing, snatching up their weapons, staring about for the enemy that had struck abruptly and without warning—but there was nothing to be seen.

Thongor, who had taken a small antechamber off the central hall for his bedchamber, appeared naked in the doorway, Sarkozan, his broadsword, glittering in his hand. Sentries peered about with wide eyes and white faces, but nothing untoward was to be seen. Yet *something* had happened—they could not all have dreamed that horrible shriek.

At Thongor's command, a head count was taken, and one man was found to be missing. It was a fat, red-faced rogue called Kovor. He had bedded down with the main body of the men, who lay in a ragged circle around the huge bonfire they had built against the night chills. Now his pallet was empty.

One of the bandits suggested Kovor might have stepped outside to answer a call of nature. Thongor dispatched searchers to investigate, but they found nothing.

Urging the sentries to be wary, Thongor bade his men to return to their interrupted slumbers, and withdrew into his little room again. But hardly a single warrior of the band so much as closed his eyes through all the rest of that fear-haunted night.

At dawn, the men refreshed themselves with water from the small quantity they had dipped out of the running stream the night before, when they had camped in the hills. Then the young barbarian organized them into search parties and carefully directed the exploration of the central portion of the monstrous edifice.

In case anyone became lost in the maze of suites and corridors and chambers, he commanded them to scratch the symbol of an arrow on the sill of every portal through which they passed, pointing back the way they had come, so that in any eventuality they should be able to find their way back to the central hall. They trooped out, under search leaders designated by Chelim.

They found what was left of fat Kovor an hour later. A runner was sent back to fetch Thongor and the girl.

"We could *smell* it before there was anything to see," panted the wild-eyed bandit as he guided the chieftain through the maze of dusty chambers. "Then we found—*this!*"

Zoroma moaned, covered her eyes and turned away.

Even Thongor, toughened as he was, felt his belly writhe and heart sicken within him as he peered beyond the portals of the room of horror. It was a huge, square room, unadorned, its floor one solid piece of unbroken stone. The only element of decoration was a square design cut in the exact center of the floor.

Floor, walls and ceiling were splattered with gouts of blood and gobbets of raw flesh. The stone chamber stank like a slaughterhouse. Kovor had, literally, been torn apart. No fragment could be found that was any larger than a man's thumbnail. His sword, dented and broken, lay in one corner. His reeking gore flecked and dribbled the interior of the hollow stone cube like a ghastly scarlet dew.

Chelim, who had also been summoned, came up and stood at Thongor's shoulder, a grim, sickly look on his ugly face. "What kind of thing could have done anything like…this?" he muttered. "There isn't even enough of him left to bury and say a couple of words over…"

"Fat, puffing, complaining old Kovor…" Thongor said slowly.

There was not much else that a man could say.

* * * *

All that day they searched the endless rooms of the vast citadel, but nowhere did they find any sign of recent habitation. If the ancient Omnian sorcerer had, in truth, made the unearthly castle his habitation, they had yet to come upon the place wherein he had dwelt. There would be books, bits of furniture, athanors and crucibles and aludels and the other apparatus of the magical sciences.

That night, ferociously hungry, they again settled down to sleep, but terror haunted the dreams of every man, and they started awake at the slightest sound.

Toward morning, the second man died.

Thongor staggered to his feet, kicking aside his cloak, cursing vilely, knuckling the sleep from his bleared eyes, grabbing up his naked broadsword. From her pallet across the chamber, Zoroma stared, white-faced.

"Not—another one," she whimpered.

But it was so. The echoes of the mad scream still sounded through the vastness of the gloomy structure.

The second victim was discovered to be one Orovar, a stolid, close-mouthed Pelormian who had few friends among Thongor's troop. They did not find his bloody remnants, although they searched all the next day. But he was missing, that was certain.

Thongor questioned his sentries closely. He had put the fear of death into them the evening before, threatening to disembowel any man who slept on sentry duty. But he knew the men were so frightened they would not have dared to fall asleep, not if they had gone a week without rest. Only one of the sentries had heard or seen anything in the least suspicious. None of them had noticed Orovar creep stealthily from his pallet, but one hesitantly said he thought he had seen something—something tall and black and thin—walking silently in the night. He had thought it was a trick of the eyes, of his overstrained nerves, or just a curious shadow cast by the flickering of the flames. But now he was no longer so certain.

Something that walked in the night. Something tall and black and thin. Something that—*killed.*

That next morning, Chelim drew Thongor aside, leaving the old Thurdan veteran, Thad Novis, to organize the search parties.

"What do you say, lad—shall we leave this place before it takes us one by one?" he asked.

Thongor's strange gold eyes were inscrutable. "Is that what you advise, Chelim?"

The huge Zangabali shrugged, the golden hoops in his ears glinting in the morning light. "You are the chieftain," he grunted. "But we have no food or water left, and are not likely to find any in this accursed ruin. And the men are very frightened and are beginning to whisper among themselves. All the jewelled treasure in the world will not tempt them to stay much longer in this devil-haunted mausoleum. Thus far you have held them here because they admire and trust you; but before too much longer their fears will get the better of them and they will begin slipping away, by ones and twos, into the hills."

Thongor folded his arms upon his chest, and bent his head, brooding on the stone paving. At length he lifted his black mane and looked at Chelim.

"You can leave if you like. But if I go from this place now, without finding the solution to this mystery, it will haunt me for all the rest of my days," he said.

7

Zoroma Vanishes

Thongor came awake suddenly. He could not tell precisely what had awakened him, but something was wrong. Those ultra-keen senses of the barbarian, which are dulled and vestigial in softer, city-bred men, triggered him to alertness. He lay motionless, pulses drumming, searching the gloom with keen eyes and listening ears. He had found it difficult enough to get to sleep, his belly growling with hunger and thirst raging in his throat like a small red demon, but eventually he had drifted off into a fitful, uneasy slumber. Now some faint signal, some vague premonition of danger, drove sleep from him.

Lifting himself on one elbow, he searched the darkness of the far corner of the room where Zoroma slept.

He had not touched her, although he wanted to, and although he sensed her own response to his manhood. Not since he had learned she mourned her lost lover. Although a barbarian, the boy was not without a certain rude chivalry in such matters. But he could not trust the more ruffian-like of his bandits to leave her unmolested—hence he had offered her the protection of his presence. Now his eyes searched the corner where her pallet lay.

And saw that it was—empty!

A tingling shock drove the last vestiges of sleep from him. He sprang to his feet, buckling his warrior's harness about him, dragging on his boots loosely, not bothering to buckle them securely. His face was grim and impassive, and his eyes burned like fiery coals. If anything had happened to the girl—?

Out in the vastness and echoing silence of the central hall he found the sentries awake and alert, and he questioned them urgently. None had seen or heard anything unusual, and not one of them had noticed the girl as she had crept from the small side chamber she shared with the barbarian youth.

"Shall we rouse the men?" asked one of the guards.

Thongor considered briefly, then shook his head, tousling his coarse black mane. "Let them sleep if they can. The wench cannot have left more than a moment or two ago, and she cannot possibly have gone far. I shall search for her myself," he growled.

Snatching up a burning brand from the fire, he strode off into the darkness. Some indefinable impulse led him in the direction of that dread room in which fat Kovor had met a terrible fate. He could not have explained his reasons for selecting this goal, but he had long since learned to trust his hunches, for the barbarian had a wilderness trained intuition, better developed than most.

The gigantic pile of masonry echoed about him, ringing with his rapid strides. He strode along, searching every shadow with alert eyes, scrutinizing the dusty paving for some trace of Zoroma's small, bare feet. His cloak rustled behind him and his loose boots flopped. He bore the torch in one hand; the other held the hilt of his naked broadsword.

She had either taken another direction, or she had moved more rapidly than he had guessed likely, for it took him some ten minutes to reach the distant chamber wherein Kovor had so horribly died at the hands of the unseen opponent.

The enigmatic structure was as dark and silent as a tomb. And tomb-like was the noisome stench that hovered in the cold, dusty air. Thongor uttered a low growl, as might some prowling predator who detected the scrutiny of invisible eyes.

At length he came to the portal of the cube-shaped chamber and peered within. There was no sign of the vanished girl. The crusted flakes of Kovor's gore, dried now to brown scabs, still clung to walls and ceiling and floor. But although Thongor searched every corner of the stone chamber, he found no token to suggest that Zoroma had come this way.

His brows knotted in bafflement. Every presentiment in his savage breast urged him that she had stood in this room but moments before, yet she was not here. His jungle-trained nostrils almost caught the warm, sweet odor of her tender flesh hovering on the stale fetor of the air. But his eyes found no evidence that she had come this way.

Baffled, he prowled on. But the endless rooms beyond were deep in the dust of millennia. No one had entered them in countless ages, that was obvious.

He doubled back and entered the room again. He stood motionless, searching with every sense for the slightest sign of some thing wrong. There was—*something*—about this room that obscurely bothered him, but he could not give a name to the vague unease that stirred his primitive soul.

It was an odd room, the walls totally devoid of any ornament, unlike most of the others, whose surfaces were sculpted with weird and alien geometrical designs in low relief. The only attempt at any sort of design was the shallow square cut in the exact centre of the floor.

On sudden impulse, he squatted down and peered closely at the crack in the stone floor, holding the crackling torch closer.

A muffled exclamation escaped his lips.

Earlier, when he had scrutinized the room following the strange doom of Kovor, the cracks that formed a perfect square in the floor of the chamber had been thickly packed with dust. Now that dust was gone.

His strange gold eyes narrowing in thoughtful surmise, the young barbarian studied the square design cut in the solid stone of the floor. Could it be a trapdoor, leading to unknown regions below?

They had not, in days of searching, found that portion of the black citadel wherein Shan Chan Thuu had made his magical laboratory. Could it not lie in unexplored crypts hollowed out of the heart of the hill?

He inserted the tip of Sarkozan in the crack and probed and pried. Was it only his imagination—or had the stone block shifted ever so slightly?

Now he wedged the blade of his small dagger in the other side of the crack, and played both steel blades against each other for leverage. The stone slab creaked—groaned. Working with infinite care, wary of snapping either of the steel blades, he slowly wedged the sword and dagger deeper into the knife-thin crevice, and began to work the slab loose.

When he had pried the stone slab up at one end so that he could get a grip with his fingers, he released the broadsword and closed his hands over the lip of the slab—and threw all the steely strength of his mighty thews into one tremendous effort.

With a harsh rasp of stone against stone, the slab lifted slowly. And Thongor stared down into a weird and wonderful world.

8

The Crypt of the Sorcerer

From the mouth of the black opening a green glare flickered. It bathed his impassive features in a lambent jade luminance. By that elusive radiance the youth perceived a flight of worn and ancient stone steps that descended from the level of the secret door.

Sheathing his dagger but keeping the great Valkarthan broadsword bare in his hand, the young barbarian stepped through the trapdoor and lowered himself until his booted feet touched the topmost step of the ancient stone stair. He descended cautiously, eyes roving from side to side, alert for the slightest sign of danger.

Beneath the floor of the citadel he found an immense cavity hollowed from the stone of the hill whereon the edifice was reared. At the foot of the stair he found the stone floor bed splattered with a ghastly crimson. His jaws tightened grimly. The gore must be the remnants of Orovar of Pelorm, who had vanished on the night following the disappearance of Kovor. But what, then, of Zoroma? Did the tattered remains of her young body bedew some far corner of the crypt? Perhaps—and perhaps not.

He recalled that, as yet, the ghastly scream that had twice rung out to signal the demise of two of his band had not yet sounded the death knell of the jungle girl.

He prowled through the crypt without finding anything of further note. Here and there portions of the stone floor were encrusted with a noisome, scaly residue that suggested the dried blood of earlier victims. He searched on, seeking the source of the curious flickering green light that dimly illuminated the recesses of the enormous vault.

In the far wall he found a dark opening and strode in warily, finding a gloomy passage of ancient stone. Cautious as a jungle cat, he padded through the dark passage, which soon widened into a vaulted chamber even more enormous than the one he had quit.

Huddled in one corner, Zoroma lifted dulled eyes and tear-wet cheeks to him.

"*Gorm!* Are you unharmed, girl?" he burst out, surprise and relief mingled in his tones. Woefully, she nodded.

He strode over to the corner where she sat huddled. "How did you come to this dismal place?" he asked.

She shook her head mutely. "I…I know not. It was like a dream. I seemed to hear a voice that called my name…a voice that seemed to come from a great distance. And I followed it, like one entranced…followed it to the room where your man, Kovor, died."

"And found the trapdoor in the floor?"

She nodded listlessly. "It stood open, and a dim green light beat up from the opening in the floor…still the far, faint voice called, and it seemed in my dream that I could not resist the urgency in that voice…it drew me on…down the stone stair…to this place, where I found…I found…" Her words died in a choked sob. Bare shoulders shook as thick waves of her shining black hair fell across her tear-stained face. And it was then that, peering about, he saw that this corner too was scaled with the dry crust of long-shed gore.

"Alatur!" she sobbed, holding out one hand.

"Your lover?"

She nodded mutely. Clenched in her fingers a bronze talisman flecked with dried blood could be seen. She wept, and he let her weep, knowing it the best remedy for woman's sorrow. He raised his head and peered about alertly.

"A voice that calls one, as in a dream, to the hidden place of death," he mused. "There must be more to these crypts than this—come, lass. Let us explore further."

Fear leapt suddenly into her great dark eyes. "Should we not be gone from this place before…before…*it*…comes?"

He revealed white teeth in a swift, wolfish grin. "Probably you are right," he growled. "But it goes against my ways to retreat from danger—and never yet have I faced a foe that cold steel could not kill!"

He helped her to her feet and they went forward through the green-lit gloom. As his eyes roamed about restlessly, ears straining to catch the slightest sound, he felt the pressure of unseen eyes, but could see nothing but bare, worn stone about him. The walls of these crypts radiated an almost tangible aura of cold menace, but still he went forward, searching for something to kill.

Why had not the unknown, murderous thing torn apart Zoroma? Was it perhaps because it sensed his own presence, and the swiftness of his approach? Perhaps…he would find the answer to that mystery soon enough, he somehow guessed. He would find the answer to many mysteries here, he knew.

* * * *

They came at length into anther chamber, larger than all the others. And on the threshold, Thongor halted abruptly, amazement written upon his features, and an oath of astonishment on his lips.

The floor was heaped and littered with treasure!

The far walls bore chests and shelves of ancient wood, whereon moldering objects lay scattered. Huge old books of thick-leafed parchment, bound between boards of carved wood, or plates of ivory, or bound in the scaly hides of dragons.

A long bench of black marble bore instruments of the sorcerous arts—a brazen astrolabe, a huge hourglass filled with dark crimson powder, mortar and pestle, and a great deal of broken crockery— the remnants, he doubted not, of crucibles and vats and cucurbits and other devices of the alchemist's art. There was even a gigantic instrument of verdigris-eaten bronze, a weird conglomeration of rings and hoops, with an engraved bronze spear at the center. Thongor dimly recognized it as an armillary sphere, whereby a necromancer may follow the movements of the stars and planets through the celestial circle of the zodiac.

Over everything lay a thick, gray blanket of dust, and the heavy webs of dead spiders festooned the walls. The floor was heaped with a splendor of treasure and trash. Bits of old, worm-eaten wood, dried bones, the withered remnants of ancient mummies, globes of dusty glass, the wink and flash of gems, thick gold coins, bright goblets of precious metals, crumpled scrolls and scraps of antique parchment, rust-gnawed blades of dagger, axe, sword and spear, dented helms, casks of gems, all manner of bottles and vases and phials, filled with colored powders or nameless oils—all lay jumbled together in a trash heap of decay and neglect.

With a muttered oath, Thongor strode over to examine the drifts of wreckage that bestrewed the floor. Gems crunched under his boots and ancient coins spilled, clattering, down the sides of the heap as he disturbed their ancient rest.

It was from this moldering pile that the lambent green light shone.

He dislodged a clattering avalanche of broken bottles and spilled jewelry as he dug down through the heap. Suddenly green flame bathed his bronze torso in flickering light. A muffled exclamation burst from his lips as he gazed down at the incredible thing his searching fingers had discovered.

"Thongor! What is it?" Zoroma cried.

He turned, grinning exultantly in her direction, holding up the flashing object he had found. *"The Emerald Flame*—by all the gods!"

9

Secret of the Emerald Flame

It was an incredible thing—and its value must have been fabulous. It was like a great collar and heavy pectoral, but it was fashioned entirely from strange gems whose like the barbarian youth had never before encountered. The gems varied in size from that of a kernel of corn to great lumps as large as hawks' eggs. They were uncut but polished smooth, and they were the pale, lucent green of clear water or the fresh bright jade of young leaves.

In the heart of the jewels an elusive wisp of flame danced and flickered. This wavering flake of fire was the fierce yellow-green we call chartreuse. Not all of the gems contained this wisp of flame at their hearts—there must have been a couple of hundred gems in the heavy collar, which, when worn about a man's throat would lap over his shoulders, chest and back, covering them with a mantle of flickering jade fire. Some of the jewels were dead and dull and lusterless, but most were alive with inner flames that danced with an ever-moving semblance of life.

Thongor stared at the treasure in his hands, for incredible it was in very truth. There was the ransom of a hundred captive kings in his heavy handful of living green fire. With the wealth this collar represented a man could purchase an empire—nay, a dozen!

He laughed delightedly, drunk with the exultation of his discovery, and lifted the collar to set it about his throat—

And then a bony, claw-like hand clutched his ankle in a vise-like grip of steel.

He stared down, his face contorted with astonishment.

The hand was as scrawny as an eagle's talons: scarce more than bare bone sheathed in scaly, desiccated, parchment-like skin, woven together with dry sinews like cords of cat gut. It was the hand of a thing long dead and withered…but it clung to his ankle with incredible living strength and tenacity.

He stepped back, dragging his captured foot. A thin, gaunt arm appeared, coins and parchment tatters spilling away. Dried flesh hung in ropes and tatters to the brown old bone. But the thing, somehow, *lived.*

Now the rest of the mummy came into view, a hideous thing with a bony mahogany face that was as fleshless as a skull and to whose bald brow a few shreds of desiccated skin yet clung. The eye sockets were deep and hollow, mere black pits of shadow, but within them eyes blazed with cold, awful fires of malignant hatred. The eyeballs themselves, Thongor could see, had dried to beads of yellowing gum, but still they burned with cold, inhuman vigor and intelligence.

His skin crawled with a thrill of horror as he saw that the dust of centuries filmed those naked, burning eyes!

Behind him somewhere the girl screamed with sheer terror as the living dead thing arose into view, clutching his leg in an unbreakable grip. And Thongor somehow knew that even after centuries of death, Shan Chan Thuu was still the Keeper of the Emerald Flame, and by whatever nameless sorcery animation lurked yet within its withered flesh, the mummy of the old Omnian magician still guarded its ancient trust.

Thongor swept his sword up and chopped an awkward blow at the scrawny arm. But it was tough as sun-dried leather and although the keen edge of Sarkozan cut through a shred of dried flesh and snapped a thread of gristle, naught else was accomplished. The vise-like grip on his boot tightened inexorably. Already his ankle was numb from the paralyzing pressure of those withered talons.

On sudden inspiration, he recalled that in his haste in dressing he had not bothered to buckle the boots securely. Thus, with a twist of his leg, he tore his foot out of the boot, leaving it in the grip of the mummy's hand, together with a few square inches of his hide. He sprang backward, clumsily, thrusting the collar of glittering green flame into his girdle so as to free his hands.

The grinning jaws of the long-dead sorcerer gaped in a sound-less howl of rage. Convulsively, the bony claws closed on the empty boot like a steel trap. And then Thongor saw the ferocity and demoniac strength that had torn his men asunder into bloody gobbets—for in a mindless fury the claws of the mummy ripped and tore the tough leather of his boot into rags.

His jaw tightened grimly. If once those bony claws closed on his flesh, he would be maimed for life. Whatever the nature of the force that animated the wizard's mummy, it lent unbelievable strength to the withered lich of Shan Chan Thuu. Now the thing came lurching down the mounded treasure toward him, bony arms reaching for him, eyes aflame with a reptilian ferocity.

Behind him the girl watched, her face milk-white, hands to her cold cheeks, eyes wide and filled with horror.

10

When Dead Men Walk

Thongor circled the stone chamber slowly, fending off the mummy of the ancient wizard with the gleaming steel of the broadsword. With jerky, ungainly strides, the thin brown thing stalked after him, its burning gaze fixed on the mass of gem-fuelled flame that flashed and scintillated at his girdle. It closed with him suddenly, and the youth took his stand and swung the mighty broadsword in a whistling blow that caught the mummy full in the side.

The impact of that slashing steel would have slain a living man. Gaunt ribs, over which leathery hide was stretched drum-taut, crunched and splintered. The mummy staggered, but did not seem to feel the blow in the slightest. Another stroke caught the mummy's forearm, splintering the bone and shattering the wrist joint. The blow, which would have put any mortal warrior out of action, did not in the slightest impede the skeletal lich. The young barbarian felt his skin crawl with horror.

How do you kill a thing that is already dead? he wondered.

Again he circled the chamber, followed by the staggering mum-my that stalked tirelessly after him, bony arms outstretched to rend and tear his flesh.

Fumio and Orovar had, doubtless, stood still, mesmerized by the uncanny powers of the dead sorcerer—helpless to move as the grasping claws ripped their bodies asunder. But Thongor was free of the spell—which indicated that a man who was awake was immune to the magic of Shan Chan Thuu, who gained his powers over the minds of sleeping men by whispering to them in their dreams his eerie, siren song.

It occurred to Thongor to wonder for what reason the mummy had lured the two men and the girl, Zoroma, into his grasp. Merely to protect his treasure of ensorcelled gems? He frowned thoughtfully: it was not likely, for until he had penetrated to the secret crypt, they had not known of it, and thus posed no threat to the mummy's treasures.

Why, then, this bestial fury—this necromantic urge to kill?

Suddenly, it came to Thongor, as if by sheer intuition. That collar of green gems, some of which were inwardly lit by eerie, writhing emerald flames, and some of which were dead and dark, unlit and lusterless.

Something the boy knew of the dark, perverted cult of chaos, for his adventures had brought him into proximity with their grisly worship and unholy rites ere now. He knew that the gifts of chaos were never bestowed freely…that always the seeker after wisdom and power had a grim and terrible price to pay.

What price had Shan Chan Thuu paid for his magisterium?

Thongor had a horrible suspicion that he already knew. For each weird gem in that mighty collar, the old Omnian wizard had taken a human life…and the flickering, restless flames that beat within those green crystals, as prisoners might beat against the bars of their cells…*each flame was a captive soul.*

And there were still a score or more of dark, lusterless gems at whose cold heart no captive flame danced.

"Great Gorm!" he breathed hoarsely…and the curse was more than half a prayer. No reason, now, to wonder that life clung with unnatural tenacity to the dried, dead mummy of Shan Chan Thuu. For his spirit would not be free of its ancient curse until every crystal which composed the Emerald Flame was horribly in-lit!

* * * *

Zoroma watched as the young warrior circled the stone-walled chamber again and again, followed by the shuffling steps of the untiring mummy. The horror of their predicament gradually dawned upon her frozen mind, which was gripped in the icy clutch of supernatural terrors. Why had she violated the precepts of the tribal elders and sought out this haunted castle? She had known that her lover, Alatur, was lost…for no man who entered the realm of Shan Chan Thuu ever left it alive.

Her vain and foolish quest had accomplished utterly nothing. And it would soon bring a ghastly doom down on herself and on the stalwart barbarian boy who now battled on heroically—but so hopelessly—against the animated mummy of the ancient wizard.

Thongor, too, knew that it was only a matter of time before he would fail to elude the grasping claws of the mummy. And once that bony grip closed on his arm, he would be helpless to oppose its unnatural strength. His strength was failing even now. Days of toil and tension, sleepless horror-haunted nights and the lack of food and water—all these had taken their toll even of his magnificent young physique. In a moment—or an hour—his weary legs would falter or stumble, and the claws of the mummy would seize him in their unbreakable grip…and those mad eyes burning from black pits sunken in that gaunt, grinning skull would be the last sight he would see in this life.

Fiercely, he redoubled the fury of his attacks against the stalking dead man. Sarkozan whistled through the fetid dead air, smashing a thigh bone here, slicing through a taut ligament there—terrible crippling blows that seemed to cause the walking dead thing no discomfort.

One shattering blow stove in the side of the bald, bony brow, extinguishing the mad glitter of one scummy, dusty eye in a shower of splintering bone. Yet on it came, grinning with a rigor of hellish mirth!

Another terrific blow cracked the bony pelvis. A web of black lines ran jaggedly through the dry brown bone, but did not slow its tireless advance. The weary boy was panting with effort now, his face black and congested, his naked breast rising and falling. The broadsword in his hands seemed to weigh like a ton of lead and the taut sinews of his arms trembled with the effort of wielding it. It was only a matter of time before—

Zoroma screamed!

His booted leg stumbled against the ruin of a broken chair and suddenly he felt himself falling. The broadsword spun away from him and rang like a struck gong against the stone flags of the paving. Then he lay sprawled, his feet entangled in the broken rungs of the chair, the air knocked out of him by the impact of his fall—and before he could clamber to his feet again, the mummy lunged like a striking serpent and he felt the dry, bony claws clutching at his throat and stared up through rising red mists into the single glaring eye of Shan Chan Thuu.

11

Flaming Death

The clutch of the bony claws was crushing his throat. A numbness went tingling through his body and his skin crawled with loathing at the touch of the dead sorcerer. Dimly, through the rising haze that obscured his vision, the young barbarian stared up into the ghastly, grinning visage of the mummy as it loomed above him. Its bony jaws worked soundlessly, and he could smell the dust-dry odor of the breath that blew from between the brown fangs, sour as sweat.

He fumbled desperately, seizing the gaunt wrists in his numb and suddenly powerless hands, and strove to tear the vise-like grip loose. But all his young strength was helpless to dislodge the clutch of the mummy. The muffled thunder of his pulse was loud in his ears. Faintly, as if from a vast distance, he could hear Zoroma screaming his name.

Then blackness rose about him and it seemed to Thongor that he fell with weird slowness through veils of dim vapor, ever darkening around him…and he knew that soon his mighty spirit would be but one more captive flame flickering within an eternal prison of cold crystal.

* * * *

Terror broke the cold paralysis that had seized the girl. She sprang forward, crying Thongor's name, casting about her frantically for some weapon to use against the murderous mummy. On a long, low table of acid-stained black wood she spied a heavy carboy of clouded glass, and snatched it up.

Sustaining its massive weight with numb, trembling hands, she staggered to the struggling pair—raised the heavy container above her head—and brought it down with a shattering blow upon the naked skull of Shan Chan Thuu. Bone crunched, glass cracked, and a noisome chemical stench permeated the air suddenly. The whole back of the mummy's skull was crushed inward by the force of her blow, and from the broken carboy rivulets of a heavy fluid seeped, crawling over the bony back and shoulders of the sorcerer.

Suddenly it staggered erect, releasing the half-conscious barbarian youth. It peered about at her with one mad, blazing eye. She stood frozen, watching a strange and miraculous transformation take place. The heavy fluid, which had soaked into the desiccated flesh of the mummy—*smoked.*

Burst into flame!

An oily, metallic vapor went whirling up from the mummy's wriggling, jerking torso. Now its entire upper thorax was one seething mass of crackling flames. Whatever virulent fluid the carboy had held—some powerful acid, no doubt—the centuries had not lessened its fierce potency.

As the mummy, wrapped in crackling flame, went staggering away, Zoroma dropped to her knees beside the half-conscious youth and cradled his head on her bare thighs. Was he dead? Had the crushing claws quenched his young vigor? No—he lived—for now his perspiration-smeared chest rose and fell, drinking the fetid air deep into his oxygen-starved lungs. Even as she watched, the blackness drained from his congested features and his eyelids flickered. The youth voiced a hoarse, inarticulate growl and forced himself up on one elbow, staring with amazement at the wizard's mad contortions.

As if it was capable of feeling pain, the burning mummy staggered and cavorted about the stone-walled chamber, writhing and flapping its flaming arms, in a macabre dance of death. The ghastly scene was made all the more gruesome by the utter silence of its struggles. For although the bare fanged jaws moved and mouthed horribly, as in mute agony, no sound escaped it.

Frozen with horror, they watched the dance of the flaming death. The leathery flesh and dried bones of the mummy had absorbed all of the acid the heavy carboy had contained. Now it seethed scarlet flame from head to foot. Even as they watched it blackened—shriveled—dwindling like a moth caught in a flame. Immune to pain, to crippling blows, the supernatural vitality that animated the mummy's form was helpless against the one enemy to which it was vulnerable—the healing purification of naked flame.

"Look—the thing has the collar!" Thongor croaked, pointing.

And it was true. As it tore loose from Thongor, feeling the bite of the virulent acid, the mummy had snatched its jeweled treasure from Thongor's girdle. Now it brandished the Emerald Flame amid the seething fury that was rapidly consuming it. One hip joint, eaten through, collapsed, and the burning mummy fell to the stone flag, coming apart. An arm dropped, twitching, from the blackened rib cage, sooty claws still scrabbling and scratching. Within seconds the mummy crumbled in the midst of the roaring fire, which died to glowing coals, and then to a heap of white ash where a few lumps of charred bone protruded.

Thongor limped over to inspect the remains of the enchanter's mummy. The skull was a blackened shell, hollow and cracked in the heat. It fell to pieces at his touch. From the pile of ashes, crumbling bits of bone, and scaly, blackened gristle, he drew forth the jeweled collar, smeared and dull with ashes. He wiped his hand across the glistening crystals.

They were dead and dull. No longer did the dancing emerald flames inwardly illuminate them. Mere lusterless bits of smooth crystal now, devoid of beauty or value. Obviously, when the life force of the mummy was extinguished in the flames, the spell was broken whereby the souls of his murdered victims where chained within the gems. Thongor dropped the dead crystals with a little grimace of disgust.

* * * *

By mid-morning they had reached the ring of hills that enclosed the vast, bowl-shaped depression. Thongor reined in his *kroter*, and turned for one last look at the black citadel that thrust its wilderness of turrets and cupolas skyward from the rocky knoll at the centre of the valley of death and desolation. Rarely had he been so glad to shake the dust of any place from his heels.

Where she lay in his arms, seated before him astride the *kroter*, Zoroma trembled at the memory of the horrors they had endured in that ghastly ruin.

Grinning, Chelim reined up beside his chieftain. "Where now, Thongor?"

The young barbarian flexed his powerful arms as the girl lay back against his chest, her warm cheek laid trustingly upon his mighty heart.

"Anywhere at all where we can find water and game—due north along the coast, I think; the sooner we get back into Chush, the happier I will be!" he said.

The massive Zangabali grimaced and spat. He turned his gaze to where the fortress of Shan Chan Thuu loomed in the distance. "After the nights of fear we spent in that haunted mausoleum, I'll be glad to face Dorgand Tul and his spearmen again," he laughed. "They, at least, are mortal! Give me a foe you can kill with the thrust of good, clean steel, and I will stand against any enemy. But this battling against shadowy sorcerers is not for the likes of me!"

Thongor grinned. "Aye, but still, we did not come away empty handed," he growled.

Chelim blinked in puzzlement—then grinned at the girl nestled demurely in the circle of the young barbarian's arms. "Say, rather, that *you* did not come away with empty arms—but what of the rest of us?"

Thongor grinned and dug one hand into the pocket-pouch of his girdle. He held out a fistful of gold coins and glittering gems and laughed at the expression of astonishment that crossed Chelim's heavy features. "In Gorm's name, man, you did not think I came away from that crypt of nameless horrors in such a hurry that I failed to fill my pouch, did you? There's enough loot here to buy you all women and weapons and new mounts at the next city we enter!"

The slack-jawed astonishment faded from Chelim's features and was replaced by a grudging admiration. "Well…perhaps I did underestimate you," he grunted. "I doubt that *I* would have lingered in that gloomy cavern long enough to pick up loot."

"Nonsense," Thongor snorted. "Why fear? The mummy was dead at last. But, come, let us get on. Ahead lie good, comfortable jungles—complete with streams of fresh, cold water, and game.

Game! Gorm's blood, it has been so long since I last had a good steak that my belly has almost forgotten the taste of meat! Tell the men to ride west, Chelim—I'll have a hot meal before I curl up in my pallet to sleep this night!"

He thumped booted heels in the ribs of his *kroter* and rode past the burly Zangabali. Noticing with a grin how the arms of his young chieftain tenderly enfolded the slim form of the jungle girl, Chelim laughed. Thongor was thinking of more things than filling his hungry middle, Chelim knew, and it would be hours before the young barbarian finally slept.

They rode off through the dusty hills, to where the lush jungles of Chush beckoned once more.

Again Thongor's band raids the rich caravans of the merchants of Arzang Pome, Sark of Shembis, until at last the furious ruler finally snares them and consigns them to the slave block. They endure the merciless life of galley slaves until Thongor leads a revolt which frees them and sets them on a new life, as members of the bloody corsairs of Tarakus, the renegade Pirate City.

For two years Thongor rises to notoriety among them, winning his own craft, the Black Hawk; he and his lusty crew sail the dangerous seas in search of riches and new glories.

BLACK MOONLIGHT

1

Uncharted Seas

The red sun sank in a sheet of flame over the dark waters of Yash-engzeb Chun, the Southern Sea. It blazed fiercely, igniting the western sky, and against the flame the jungle isle of Zosk loomed up: shaggy, black, mysterious.

Since noon the pirate galley *Black Hawk* had stood against the wind, lying off the wide lagoon where billows drove snowy foam against a curve of tawny beach. Now a chill wind rose with the coming of night. It rattled the fronded tree-ferns and cycads that stood like a green wall beyond the curve of wet sand: it caught and boomed the scarlet sails of the lean, rakish black galley, and the gusting breeze sent waves slapping against the sharp dragon-prow.

The gusts were dank with wet and chill. On the foredeck of the galley the first mate shivered to the wind's bite, and drew his heavy boat cloak more closely about him. The tall, massive Zangabali, Chelim, with stubbled jaw and shaven pate, shivered in the keen breeze, gold hoops glittering in his ears. It was late in Shamath, the first month of autumn, with a hint of winter on the wind's edge.

A dark shape loomed against the crimson sky; turning, Chelim nodded to his captain. "No signal yet; the lad's lost," he grunted.

The captain of the *Black Hawk* said nothing. The dank wind caught and spread his black cloak, like dark wings on the wind.

Beneath the cloak he was half-naked, his bronze body possessing thews like a young gladiator. Black and thick as a *vandar*'s mane, his unshorn hair blew from broad shoulders, framing his stern, impassive face, strong-jawed, clean-shaven, grimly expressionless. Under scowling black brows his strange gold eyes blazed with sullen, lion-like fires. Few city-bred men could meet the glare of those sombre, burning eyes; fewer still could stand before him in battle. Despite the chill night-wind, his superb body was clad only in a Lemurian war-harness of belted straps, with a heavy ornate girdle about his lean hips and a scarlet cloth about his loins. As a Barbarian from the wintry Northlands beyond the Mountains of Mommur, he found the night sultry.

To the pirates of Tarakus, to his fellow captains of the Red Brotherhood, he was Khongrim of the Black Hawk. But those who had served him since before his pirate days knew his true name as Thongor.

"Lost, or slain," he growled in a deep voice. "Gorm knows what beasts lair in those jungles. And there may be savages…I have heard the captains tell strange tales of such isles."

"I, too," muttered the mate, and if he shivered a little, perhaps it was the cold edge of the wind. But these were uncharted seas, and yonder isle was marked on no chart. Few ever dared sail this deep into the unknown west: the fat merchants of Thurdis or Tsargol clung to the coasts of Kovia or Ptartha, and the corsairs preyed only where there were rich cities to loot and plunder.

But Thongor of the *Black Hawk* would venture down the red throat of hell itself for such a treasure as the jungle isle of Zosk held hidden, if old, whispered legends were true. Somewhere in the dark mass of trackless jungle lay a fortune in pearls, a treasure-trove of the rare flame pearls of Cadorna, worth a kingdom's price in the thieves' bazaar at Tarakus. And the captain of the *Black Hawk* meant to claim that treasure at sword's point, if need be. Since noon the corsair craft had sounded the jungle isle, finding this lagoon, and sending ashore a volunteer to scout for hostile savages. Reckless young Kanthar Kan had won the toss of the dice. Hours since they should have glimpsed his signal, as arranged. What unexpected doom had befallen the gay, laughing young swordsman? They could wait on him no longer.

Thongor tossed back his mane impatiently. "Chelim, take us in and let go the anchor. Trice up all sail. Fulvio!"

"Aye, Cap'n?" A scrawny, wizened little rogue detached himself from the wheel and snapped to alertness.

"Pick a landing party, and see them well-armed. Lower the longboat when ready. We're going in."

2

Death by Fear

A quarter-hour later the longboat was slung over the side on squealing winches. Fulvio's landing party swarmed down the lines to take places in the thwarts—a motley crew of ruffians they looked, ragtag scrapings of the gutters of half the cities of the West. There was a fat, moon-faced Kovian with cold eyes and a placid smile, and a notched cutlass in his sash; swarthy-hued, black-thatched Thurdans, a villainous and foul-mouthed lot, with gaudy kerchiefs knotted about their brows and gems flashing on dirty fingers; even a few tawny-skinned, almond-eyed men of Cadorna, who cursed their mates in sing-song, soft voices, fingering dagger-hilts. Some were marked with slave-brands and some bore the sign of outlawry; all were scarred with sword-cuts from many battles on land and sea. A villainous lot, but loyal to the death, and gallant fighting-men who would follow wherever Thongor led, and serve him to the last drop of red blood.

The longboat pulled away from the lean black hull of the galley and glided in on silent oars. They ran the boat up on the wet beach and sprang out, sea-boots crunching in slick sand, dragging the hull further up the strand where the waves could not reach. It was nearly dark as they entered the dense wall of foliage; the moon had not yet risen, and the dying coals of sunset glimmered on their naked cutlasses and flashed in their eyes as they glanced about uneasily.

The jungle was thick and black and still. *Too* still. The jungle aisles should have rung to the roar of hunting *vandars*, the screech of river-*poa*. But all was silent as death.

Thongor sensed the wrongness in the heavy air from the first. His pirates were city-bred men, their senses dulled from the stench and clamor of the back-alleys that had spawned them. But he had the keen, sharp-honed senses of the wilderness-born—the cruel wastes of the frozen North had cradled him, and his was the hair-trigger sensitivity of the true savage. To have survived in the bitter land of his native Valkarth, he had learned to taste the breeze like a hunting cat, to listen to every whisper, to read the night like a stalking beast.

Once they had wormed through the dense wall of trees, the chill wind died. Blackness lay about them, heavy with the stench of rotting leaves, sour mud, thick with the heady perfume of jungle flowers. And there was something else on the air, as well.

There was the smell of death...

His strange gold eyes searching the gloom to every side, his great Valkarthan broadsword naked in his hand, Thongor took the lead, prowling through the black jungle as silent as a cat. A quarter of an hour later they found the body.

It was Fulvio who came upon it first. The scrawny, one-eyed little rogue almost stumbled across it in the impenetrable gloom. His squawk of alarm brought Thongor shouldering through the heavy bushes. The body lay sprawled half under a towering *jannibar* tree. They dragged it into the open and the bosun, a grizzled old Thurdan named Thad Novis, unhooded the lantern he carried, lighting the man's face with the dim beam of candle-flame.

It was Kanthar Kan.

"Gods, Cap'n, I nigh stepped on him in the dark, and me blind as a *xuth*!" Fulvio whined, shivering. One stifled a cry of surprise as the lantern lit the face of the young swordsman.

Thongor said nothing, but his jaws set grimly. There was no mark on the swordsman's body, no cut or wound to be found. But he was stone dead; and the expression stamped on his face was horrible to view—hideous beyond thought. His eyes stared half out of his skull, frozen in a goggle-eyed stare of incredulous horror. His lips were peeled back from his teeth in a ghastly grin. His features were distorted in a grimace of utter horror that sent a chill up the spine to look upon.

Thad Novis ran his hands gently over the cooling corpse, finding nothing. He raised grim eyes to the questioning gaze of his captain. "'Tis devilish weird," he said in a low voice. "Like the lad died of sheer fright. Not a mark on him, anywhere."

The men muttered at that, casting uneasy glances at the black jungle that crowded silently to every side. Some fingered protective amulets or small images of carved stone that dangled about their necks on chains or leather thongs. Thongor took up the lantern and went to search the ground where Kanthar Kan was found. The lantern-beam disclosed something even more mysterious than a man who died from fear alone. Kanthar Kan had drawn three words in the bare earth with his fingers before death had claimed him—and they had another mystery to solve.

"*Beware...Black Moonlight,*" Thongor read in a grim voice.

"Cap'n, let's go back to the ship an' wait for day," Fulvio whined. "Gods know what that means, but I don't like the sound of it!"

"Nor I," admitted Thongor. "But we go forward, nonetheless."

They shouldered further into the black jungle, leaving the corpse behind. There would be time enough later to lay their dead comrade to rest, if they lived. Gallant, gay young Kanthar Kan would laugh no more: and the mysterious doom that had struck him down in the black jungles of the isle of Zosk lay somewhere ahead of them, brooding in the silence of the night.

3

The Warning on the Monolith

The moon had risen over the edge of the world, the great golden Moon of old Lemuria, flooding the jungle with its silken light. It was easier, now, cutting through the dense foliage with cutlass and scimitar and blunt-tipped Chushan *kunwars*. But they were growing weary by this time, tired of the fetid reek of rotting vegetation, the bite of insects. Tangled vines caught their feet, tripping them; they slipped in slick mud, cursing, grumbling at thorn-edged leaves that raked bare arms and drew blood.

By moonrise they had come as far as they could go. Here the jungle fell away in a stinking marsh of black mud and rotting stumps; snakes thick as a man's thigh slithered fluidly over fallen tree trunks, and the track of monstrous *poa* were visible on the mud-banks.

Thongor gave the signal for a rest-halt. The men sprawled wearily about, wiping sweaty brows with dirty rags, gulping lukewarm wine from skin bottles, glad of a chance to rest aching legs. But the Valkarthan needed no respite: his iron thews seemed invulnerable to fatigue and he could go forward far more swiftly alone. Leaving scrawny little Fulvio in charge, he moved out to the east, skirting the swamp, searching the thick brush with every sense at the alert.

He found the thing by moonlight. A great shaft of gray, lichen-covered stone, thrusting out of the wet earth at a steep angle. The roots of a giant *lotifer* tree had netted the stone pillar, tilting it awry. The clear gold moonlight lit the mold-encrusted monolith sharply.

Thongor paused. Then men *did* inhabit this strange isle of death and nameless, shadowy horror—or had once dwelt here; for the inscription on the stone was in an antique mode of glyphic writing. With the blade of his dagger, he scraped away the crust of lichens, laying bare the deep-graven hieroglyphs. The language of the inscription was known to him from his travels, for once, years before, in a ruined, deserted city in the desert country of the north, he had seen such glyphs. The young Valkarthan was unschooled, but his adventurous career had carried him into strange corners of the Lemurian continent, and he had acquired shards of odd and curious knowledge along the way.

The inscription sent a chill up his spine as he read it by moonlight.
The stone god walks when the Black Moon shines.

His hackles stirred; a tingle of preternatural uneasiness prickled at the nape of his neck, as if he sensed the touch of unseen eyes on his back. He half turned, the steel blade of his great sword, Sarkozan, flashing in his hand; then, with a wry grin twisting his lips, he restrained himself. No puling boy, he, to start and pale at a few words cut on a stone pillar! It took more than an ancient warning to strike fear into the heart of Thongor of the *Black Hawk*—Khongrim of the Red Brotherhood, the terror of the Southern Sea!

He went forward again, but this time with greater care than before, and keeping well to the shadows. Some hand, long ages dead, had cut that warning of the Black Moon on the mould-crusted monolith; but something very alive had struck down gay, reckless Kanthar Kan to death. And he, too, had warned of the mysterious peril with his last strength, digging numb fingers in the wet earth to warn his shipmates when they came on his track…

Thongor glided through the underbrush like a stalking *vandar*. What was the curse that haunted this weird isle of treasure and nameless terror? He would learn the answer sooner than even he could dream.

4

The City of Death

The cold wastes of the Northlands had spawned him, but since he had come down across the Mountains of Mommur five years before, the jungle-girt cities of Kovia and Chush and Ptartha had been his home. So the Valkarthan was no stranger to the tropic wilderness through which he moved silently and swiftly, yet with great care. A mere youth, he had joined a pack of bandits in wild Chush, quickly rising to become their chieftain. He and his legion of cutthroats had been the bane of the fat-bellied merchants of Shembis, whose jungle caravans they had raided time and again, until the vengeful prince of that city, Arzang Pome, had hunted them down.

Then he and the survivors of his band had been sold on the block like animals. Arzang Pome had chained the Valkarthan and his bandits to the oars of the slave-galleys of Shembis, and long did they toil under the singing whips in the blazing sun while the hated Dolphin banner floated lazily overhead and the perfumed merchant-captain who was their master sipped cold wine and fondled his wench under striped awnings while they broke their backs at the oars. Then one hot night they rose with naked hands and broken oars to slay and slay in red, roaring rage—stealing the very galley on which they had slaved—and off to the high seas, to join the fierce corsairs of Tarakus the Pirate City, and to learn a new trade. But piracy was close akin to banditry, and thus Thongor and his comrades had risen in the past two years to a high rank amid the corsair fleet.

It was the dying whisper of an old veteran sailor they had rescued from execution in Cadorna that had put them on the track of the fabulous treasure of the isle of Zosk, deep in the uncharted wastes of the sea. Somewhere in those black jungles a fortune in flame pearls lay hid—"in the place of the great stones" the old sailor had said.

And then Thongor came upon it, stark and cold and dead in the flood of the golden Moon.

The young barbarian came to a sudden halt there at the edge of the jungle. He stared ahead, his blood racing with the thrill of discovery. Was *this* the 'place of the great stones' the dying sailor had spoken of? A few yards from where he crouched in the thick brush, the jungle dwindled away to a rocky plain. The ground fell away beyond, in an immense, circular valley like a vast bowl cut in the rock. Tumbled stone slabs lay about: broken spires of rock loomed and tilted, for all the world like the shattered pillars of some dead, ruined city of time's dawn. Here and there, tremendous blocks of stone lay tumbled, as if scattered about by the careless hands of playful giants.

Thongor searched the wilderness of broken, scattered stone with thoughtful eyes. Surely, this must be the place the old sailor had whispered of. But was it a thing of nature, or the work of men? The monolith he had come upon in the jungle had been cut and set by human hands…and the regularity of these stones was haunted by an uncanny suggestion of human purpose and workmanship.

He went down into the valley and prowled the silent avenues of somber desolation. No sign of life alerted his keen senses. If men had ever dwelt here, they were long vanished. No smoke of cooking fires ascended the moonlit sky, no footstep echoed down the empty avenues of tumbled stone, no human rubbish caught his searching gaze, not a shard of broken pottery, a discarded rag, or the ashes of a dead fire. It was like a city of death, this waste of broken rock: like the gaunt bones of a dead metropolis, eerie and silent and empty in the wash of moonlight, and if anything wandered here, they were ghosts of the long-dead past.

Amidst the trackless ruin, he came upon the pool the old sailor had spoken of. A motionless disc of dark waters, impenetrable to the eye, ringed about with a lip of stone. This surely was the work of men, for the pool formed a perfect circle and the stone margin was cut and dressed and smoothed by skill and not by nature.

In the center of the pool, a stone pillar rose against a tropic sky filled with blazing stars. It was like the monolith he had found in the jungle, and yet different, too. For thirty feet the stone pillar loomed up in the moonlight, tall and straight as an obelisk, but rough-hewn and jagged, and it bore no glyphs that he could see. All about the motionless pool stretched a plaza of tumbled, uneven stone slabs. Thongor crossed the plaza with silent tread and knelt by the edge of the pool, dipping one hand within.

The water was cold and foul, scummy and stagnant, but his hand came up filled with dripping pearls. They were slick and moon-like, with a sullen glow of fire in their sheen and rondure. Flame pearls of Cadorna—he knew them at a glance—of superb and perfect water and extraordinary size!

He held a satrap's ransom in his hand. And the wealth of a dozen emperors slept still beneath the dark waters. A smile lit his somber features. The buccaneer scooped up handful after handful of flame pearls from the black pool, admiring their glistening fire in the cold moonlight. Entranced, he stared down at the wet pearls in his hand. They glowed like little moons.

Then a deep-chested snarl reached his ear—the scrape of callused bare feet on dry stone. He sprang to his feet, thrusting the dripping handful of pearls in the top of his swash sea-boots, and turned.

And then the savages were upon him, a herd of snarling, naked beast-men, broken tusks bared and bloodlust burning in their slitted eyes. The very earth spewed them up: from dark lairs under the tilted slabs of the plaza they came. Troglodytes—cave dwellers! He knew then why he had found no token of human habitation in all these acres of immemorial desolation. And they were upon him, heavy bodies hurled at his back, hard paws clutching his arms, fangs snapping at his very throat.

5

Red Steel!

The young buccaneer shook the hairy-pelted savages from him as the kingly *vandar* of the jungle shakes off a pack of dogs. He drove his booted heel deep in the belly of one snarling foe: the beast-thing grunted, folded and fell.

Then the great broadsword, Sarkozan, was free of its scabbard and singing its cold and eerie song of death as it cut the wind. There were old runes acid-etched down the length of the long, deep blade, and the great gem set in the pommel blazed like an angry eye. The broadsword flashed, a brilliant steel mirror in the Moon, as Thongor whipped it high over his head and brought it whistling down to bite through brain and bone and meat. The clean steel glittered once and when he drew it back, it was washed with red.

For a time he held them, sweeping the great sword in a tireless arc. They feared the cold flash of the edged steel as a witch fears silver. He held them at bay, but they came at him in twos and threes, bounding like jackals, fangs snapping hungrily for his flesh. The Valkarthan at first thought them savages, then beasts, finally men. They went naked like brutes, but walked upright like men. They had hulking, anthropoid bodies, sloping ape-like shoulders, and long arms, knotted with bulging sinews, that hung dangling to their knees. Their heads were bullet-like, sunken deep in massive shoulders, hidden in a tangle of filthy, matted hair through which slitted eyes gleamed redly with mad fires.

But their thick torsos and bowed legs bore but a sparse pelt. The hide that showed bare between patches of stringy fur was the hue of dirty amber and their blazing eyes were aslant, as far as he could judge. The young buccaneer knew but one nation in all Lemuria with tawny amber skin and slanted eyes—the men of ancient Cadorna, westernmost of all the cities of Lemuria. Could these snarling, shambling, loping beast-things be the degenerate remnants of a lost Cadornyana colony, forgotten for ages?

Perhaps. But he had no time to puzzle it out now. He was too busy merely staying alive. They came at him like mad dogs and he cut them down with singing red steel till they heaped the stone margin of the pool with their gore-splashed bodies. Eight, ten, a dozen he slaughtered, but it was only a matter of time until they swarmed over him, battered him down, dragged him to earth under the sheer weight of their numbers.

Now he wished he had not come down alone into the great bowl-like valley, but had gone back to camp as he should have done. O, to have a stout dozen of his brawling buccaneers at his back, with dirk and cutlass and scimitar! But it was too late for recriminations now. He fought on, but now even his iron thews ached with weariness and the breath rasped in his dry throat. He blinked against the red mist that thickened before his gaze.

Then one of the loping beast-things, perhaps less sunk in the red murk of savagery than its fellows, closer to the light of reason and manhood, saw in its cunning that it could not reach the hated man-thing through the wall of red and singing steel. So it squatted on the broken paving, plucked up a heavy shard of rock in one hairy paw, and flung it at Thongor with all the coiled strength of that ape-like arm.

It caught the Valkarthan on the brow—a stunning blow. He lurched, staggered, fighting for consciousness, and the red sword sagged in suddenly nerveless fingers and fell, ringing against the stone pavement of the plaza like a stricken gong.

Then they had him at last. A thickset body slammed into him, chest and belly, and drove him from his feet. In a flash the burly beast-thing was worrying at his throat. Thongor jammed one fore-arm under the creature's jaw and held the snapping fangs away from his jugular. Fetid, stinking hot breath blew in his face. The naked, furry body was rank in his nostrils. Thick-fingered paws closed about his throat, throttling him. He grunted as another heavy body slammed on top of him, and another, until he was buried under a pack of snarling, clawing beast-things.

His mind dimmed as he fought for breath. A haze thickened before his eyes; his lungs were afire; his heart labored within his breast. He fought for air and with ebbing strength to hold those snapping tusks away from his throat.

Then a sharp, imperious voice called out from somewhere be-yond the heap of beast-things. Thongor could not make out the words, for they were in a tongue unknown to him. But the crushing weight that pressed him against the broken stone slabs lessened and the iron grip loosened from about his neck. He gulped air into starved lungs as strong hands dragged him to his feet and bound his wrists behind his back with tight leather thongs that bit into numb flesh. Many men would have despaired then, taken captive by the shambling horde that infested the ancient ruins.

It was not the way of Thongor to despair, but he stared into a grim future, knowing that his life could now be counted in hours; perhaps, in minutes.

6

Night Fears

It was the grizzled old Thurdan warrior, Thad Novis, who was the first to become uneasy over Thongor's prolonged absence. The old warrior had been a stalwart of Jorn's Raiders when the boy Thongor had first joined the pack of bandits he would later chieftain. From the first, the oldest warrior had felt a paternal stirring in his breast as he saw the grim courage and iron strength and utter fearlessness the barbarian boy displayed. Thad Novis had followed his young leader from banditry into slavery, and from thence to a life of lawlessness and adventure on the high seas. His dogged loyalty had never wavered; now he prowled the perimeter of the camp, baffled and obscurely worried, peering into the moon-washed jungle with searching eyes.

At length he sought out scrawny little Fulvio, who sprawled lazily against a log, nursing a fat wineskin.

"Hell's blood, man, what ails you?" Fulvio whined. "The chief can take care o' himself better than any of us. Wait here, said he, and wait here we will. He'll come back, in his good time. Sit—rest—take some wine!"

The older man shook his head determinedly. "It's not like the lad to be gone so long," he growled. "He meant to scout a path around this swamp, not explore the stinking isle himself. Something has taken him, I know…perhaps the same Thing that took poor Kanthar Kan…"

The words hung there in the air. Fulvio licked thin lips with a pointed tongue, and shivered as to a sudden gust of cold. Deep in his heart, the wizened little one-eyed rogue knew the stolid, loyal Thurdan spoke the truth. But the whining little Fulvio was reluctant to stir from this place of safety to plunge into the unknown and silent depths of the waiting jungle.

Fear and loyalty wrestled within Fulvio's scrawny breast. Self-love and the greed for gold were the only passions the little gutter-rat had ever known. But he, too, worshipped Thongor and went in awe of the mighty barbarian. Thongor was what he perhaps could have been, had he been nourished in the wintry wild among strong, stalwart men and noble-hearted courageous women; but Fate had given him a sniveling beggar for a father and a sluttish shrew for a mother, and the stinking back-alleys of the slums of Pelorm for his home.

Fulvio was cowardly at heart, and vicious as only the cowardly can be. But in his heart, where fear wrestled with loyalty, he idolized the strong young buccaneer captain. And, for once, loyalty won out against a lifetime of twisted selfishness.

Spitting vile curses, little Fulvio scrambled to his feet and snarled at the sprawled men of the landing party. "On your feet, you yellow-gutted whelps! We're movin' out, Gods help us. The Cap'n should of been back by now; something may have happened to 'im." He fixed the stolid old Thurdan with a venomous eye. "Gorm help you, grizzled old dog, if the Cap'n ain't in need of us!"

Thad Novis said nothing. Incapable of feeling the cold, sick gnaw of fear himself, he never knew what spark of true heroism he had stirred to fire in Fulvio's breast.

They fanned out when they hit the jungle, keeping well in earshot of each other. Blackness closed about little Fulvio like a clammy hand. Sweating and cursing foully under his breath, the little rogue limped along, lashing out at tangling vines and thorny branches with his cutlass as he went. It was one thing to follow such a man as Thongor into the black yawning maw of unknown peril; it was quite another to do it on your own volition.

The jungle thickened about them, entangled boughs shutting out the rich floods of moonlight. Clumping along through wet darkness, Fulvio thought of the slithering, be-fanged things that perhaps lurked all about him in the night. He envisioned the landslide-rush of the *deodath*, the dreaded dragon-cat of the jungle countries. Cold dew dripped down his scrawny neck—or was it the numbing kiss of the *fathla*, the ghastly, blood-sucking tree-leeches of Chush and Kovia? A heavy vine swung overhead—or was it the horrible, man-crushing coils of the *oph*, the horned serpent of the tropic depths?

Night-fears preyed upon him, nibbling away at the edges of his courage, sapping his resolution. But the little one-eyed rogue limped forward without pause, cursing himself for a foolhardy, reckless madman every long step of the way.

They came to the stony monolith Thongor had discovered earlier, and paused, eyeing its enigmatic glyphs with shuddering apprehension. Dread shapes of night and terror were known to haunt old ruined cities—ghouls and morgulacs, as Lemurian legend named vampires, and prowling ghosts of the dead that could not rest.

Thad Novis hefted his heavy scimitar uneasily. "Which way?" he asked.

Fulvio gnawed his under-lip, glancing dubiously about. Here the jungle aisle parted, one lane wandering deep into the jungle's black heart, the other striking away due east. It was in that direction Thongor had headed an hour before, but Fulvio could not know that.

"Which way, Fulvio?" puffed a fat, moon-faced Kovian named Qualb. The others crowded near.

Fulvio said nothing, chewing his lip in a torment of indecision. Which way? One path led to Thongor, who might even now be face to face with death; the other route led far from his peril, and if they followed it they would become lost in the black jungles of Zosk.

Which way?

7

The Black Moon

The beast-men staked Thongor out to die. They drove four pegs into the earth between the riven slabs of the plaza and bound his wrists and ankles to them with tough thongs. Spread-eagled, his sinews stretched to the limit of endurance, even the Valkarthan's steely strength could not free him of his bonds.

Jaws set grimly, Thongor waited for death.

The leader of the horde of shambling degenerates paid his captive no attention. With the rapt, blind gaze of a fanatic or a madman he stared without blinking up into the cold fire of the golden Moon. He was unlike the grunting horde of savages he ruled: tall, slim, gaunt to the point of emaciation, his lean frame wrapped in tattered, filthy rags of what had once been the gorgeous ceremonial robes of an ancient priest.

He stood on the top of a block of stone, staring beyond the black pool and the rough-hewn pylon of rock to the soaring Moon.

His hair was a tangle of matted witch locks as it fell about the starved skull of his face. His eyes burned through the tangle like sick green fires. He was priest-king of the hulking, naked brutes, the last of a time-forgotten line. But he was only slightly more *man* than they. Beneath the gorgeous, filthy tatters his gaunt body was naked and unwashed. His feet were bare and black with filth. His grime-crusted hands, gaunt like terrible claws, clutched a rod of sleek black *nebium*, atop which a smoky crystal pulsed like a dying coal.

Thongor had seen black rods like his before, and he knew them for Rods of Power. He also knew the black, unholy sorcery men wrought with such relics of ancient wisdom, and his lips pressed together until they paled.

With Thongor securely bound, the shambling beast-men withdrew grunting, squatting in a semi-circle behind the priest and the sacrifice. And the ceremony began...

Scattered rags of cloud fled before the Moon, spreading its light in wandering shafts of cold fire that flickered eerily here and there over this weird scene of stony desolation. The wizard began talking to the half-hid Moon in guttural, clotted sounds that hardly sounded like human speech. The blood ran cold in Thongor's veins as he heard the strange, coughing sounds. He knew *that* tongue from of old; it was the Chaos Litany. The Dragon Kings of age-lost and legend-drowned Hyperborea had learned it from the black gods of madness who ruled beyond the stars. Human lips were never meant to frame such sounds, and to hear them spoken by a man was blasphemy against human kind.

The alien speech droned on, and suddenly a thrill of superstitious awe ran through Thongor. For the shifting, flickering rays were changing hue. He stared up, scalp prickling with chill premonition. *And the Moon turned to blood.*

Shafts of weird crimson light wandered about the scene of primal desolation. It was uncanny—horrible. The Moon glared down at him like the red, burning eye of some maddened god. Behind him somewhere, the beast-things groaned and whimpered, groveling before this awesome display of supernatural power. On the stone block, the wizard stood like a stone-carved image, rapt in unholy ecstasy, as the abominable litany spewed from his writhing lips.

Then Thongor sensed a tension in the air. Nature seemed to hold its breath, awaiting some dark miracle of evil. An aura of force tingled along the nerves of the young buccaneer. And the sky, which had been velvet-black, flushed with cold, dead white radiance.

As the heavens reversed their coloration, the very stars did so as well. Now, through weirdly-colored, ragged clouds the stars burned like black diamonds. The scene was such a mingling of incredible terror and wonder, that it wrung a cry from Thongor's grim lips. "Gorm!" he groaned, calling upon the god of his savage homeland. And it was as much a prayer as a curse.

And then the Moon turned black, and even the gods could not help him now.

8

It Walks by Moonlight

From a disc of evil crimson, the Moon's brilliant fires curdled, darkened, became utter blackness like a pool of ink. Weird, weird, to watch a Black Moon blaze in a sky of dead white flame. In his wildest nightmares, the Barbarian had never dreamed of a spectacle so awesome and unreal.

But the ultimate abomination was yet to come.

For still a ragged drift of torn and tattered cloudlets hung before the orb of ebon fire, scattering its rays. The shafts of dark light floated here and there about the plaza, blackening the crumbled stones which otherwise lay bathed in the strange, sourceless luminescence of the glowing sky.

Now, shaft after shaft of black moonlight flashed across the massive pillar of dark, jagged stone that loomed from the center of the pool. And as the uncanny negation of light blackened the rugged monolith, it began to *change*.

It softened, slid and clotted like hot candle wax; it was as if the kiss of the black rays awoke the dormant spirit within the stone pillar, which struggled to regain its lost shape. As Thongor watched in unbelieving amazement, the stone flowed like wax, melting and reshaping itself in the dark radiance. The pillar cleft at the base; two shards split from its flanks; a rough sphere melted into being at its crest. The new shape the monolith assumed under the weird influence of the moon-rays bore a loathsome yet haunting familiarity. It was a botched, obscene caricature of Man—a hideous, twisted, distorted semblance—but a semblance, nonetheless.

The melting stone solidified now. Like a grotesque idol hewn by a gibbering madman, the stone thing stood amidst the dark waters. And lived. And *walked*.

One stone limb thrust forward, lurching. At the knee—or where the knee would have been, had the stone thing possessed one—rough stone rubbed against stone with an incredibly horrible *grating* sound. Then, jerkily, the other leg thrust forth dripping from the dark pool. The misshapen paw that was the thing's foot or hoof crunched on the stone paving, which squealed under its many tons of ponderous weight.

Behind the spread-eagled buccaneer, the beast-men moaned and babbled in an ecstasy of fear and gloating anticipation. And globules of cold sweat burst forth on Thongor's brow: he knew now the death decreed for him. *He was to be trampled to red slime beneath the stone paws of the walking god!*

But it was not the way of Thongor to lie supinely, waiting for death. Savage rage surged up within him, crushing out his cold fear. Black fury boiled in his veins. His brows contorted in a spasm of berserk, fighting wrath. Suddenly he split the air with a bellow of inarticulate anger. The roar of a cornered *vandar* burst from his snarling lips. And down his wide-stretched arms great thews swelled in a vain attempt to wrench his arms free. Mighty bands of solid muscle stood forth in knife-edge relief on his magnificent chest. His face blackened with effort as he threw every ounce of iron strength his splendid physique possessed into one colossal surge of power—

And failed!

Though he tore his wrists raw, the leather thongs held and the deep-driven stakes did not budge. Again and again he threw the coiled strength of back and arm and shoulder into a terrific effort to burst his bonds. His deep-chested roar of challenge made the night hideous: booming echoes bounced from rock to rock. But nothing sufficed to free him from this death trap. And step by ponderous, shuffling step the weirdly animated stone thing advanced upon him. Its blind, ghastly caricature of a face stared stonily down at him now from what seemed a tremendous height. Another instant—another slow, dragging scrape of stone against stone, and it would be upon him.

Then—somewhere behind him, beyond the edges of his vision—*riot*.

The beast-men exploded into squeals of pain. The ring of blades—the patter of many running feet. A spear went whizzing over Thongor's prostrate form to clatter off the pitted breast of the now-immobile stone thing. Slowly, hideously, the blind featureless face of jagged rock twisted to as if to stare beyond Thongor to the source of the inexplicable interruption. Due to a trick of light and shade, the mask of stone bore a momentarily quizzical expression.

Then, from behind Thongor, a hand grabbed at his arm and a steel dagger-blade flashed downward toward his flesh.

9

Night of Hell

The flashing blade slashed through the thongs that bound his wrist. The leather snapped and his arm was free. He looked up, relief flooding his features, to see the plump, anxious face of the moon-faced Kovian, Qualb, as he bent puffing to cut free Thongor's other arm.

"Damn your hide," Thongor growled, "I thought you lazy dogs would never come!"

"Bless me, Cap'n, an' we might not yet be here, lost in this cursed maze of tumbled stone, had it not been for you a-yellin' like to wake the dead!" Qualb wheezed, chuckling, as he slashed the thongs that bound his feet. "Once ol' Thad Novis heard that bellowing, he knew 'twas you, and we came straight!"

Thongor staggered to his feet, grunting at the pain of circulation gnawing at his numb flesh. His hands were black and swollen, almost useless, like blunt paws. But the heavy sea-boots had protected his legs from the worst punishment, and he could stand. He turned, taking in the situation with one swift, all-encompassing glance. His stout band of rogues was cutting the shambling savages to ribbons. In another few moments, the beast-herd would break and flee for their subterranean burrows—

A screech of fury—

The gaunt wizard, his uncanny trance broken, stood on top of the great rock, glaring down at them with mad eyes of scarlet wrath. One starved, skeletal arm brandished aloft the Rod of Power. From writhing lips burst forth again that hellish litany of black sorcery.

And the stone thing moved again!

Slabs squeaked under its shifting weight as it lurched forward, heavy, clubbed arms raised threateningly. And directly in its path, Thongor's gallant little band of buccaneers stood holding off the horde of grunting savages. A few more sliding steps and the walking idol would be among them. Feet like boulders would crush and slay, trampling the men down as a man might snuff out the lives of crawling insects under his heel.

There was no time to shout the warning—no time even to think. Thongor was triggered into a rush of instant action by some instinctive thing quicker and simpler than thought itself—the killing fury of a maddened beast. A growl of challenge burst from his lips, which writhed back from his white teeth in a fighting grin. And he exploded into action.

One fantastic, superhuman bound carried him to the crest of the towering rock where the warlock stood, arms lifted in imprecation. Thongor was upon the crazed witch-man before anyone even saw it. His hands were still numb and useless, but they were callused and hard and heavy. With the back of one he clubbed the warlock across the mouth and knocked him to his knees, spitting broken teeth and dribbling blood. With the other numb paw Thongor ripped the crystal-tipped wand from his hand—then kicked him full in the face, hurling him backwards off the rock to thud sprawling and astounded on the pavement below.

Directly in the path of the stone monster.

Dribbling blood and the foam of maniacal rage, the warlock staggered to his feet, eyes burning like hell-moons through tangled locks. Then his fury ebbed—his swarthy features paled milky-white—his eyes goggled in unbelieving horror—for his own god was about to trample him down underfoot.

Thongor whirled, poised, and flung the *nebium* wand like a javelin. Straight and true it hurtled against the pitted breast of the walking thing it had roused to a hideous travesty of life. The flashing crystal struck the stone breast first—and exploded in a dazzle of diamond dust.

And the Black Moon died...

Swift as waking from a dream, the haunting spell of evil magic faded from the night. The uncanny, incandescent heavens dimmed—darkened. The evil Moon glowed red—then bright, pure gold again. No more did black stars blaze in an enchanted sky: now the familiar stars of old twinkled down from dark and friendly heavens once again.

There came a creak of stone rasping against stone. The lurching, dragging thing froze into immobility as the evil spell which had for a time flogged it to a ghastly semblance of life perished with the splintering of the crystal. And the stone god became... only a thing of stone.

But when the spell that had animated it was broken, it had been off-balance, lurching forward to trample Thongor's embattled pirates. Now, like an avalanche, it came crashing down to smash asunder against the paving. The thunder of tons of stone against stone was deafening. But even above the clangor of the fallen image, as it shattered into a thousand bits against the floor of the pavement, one sharp, agonizing screech of unbelieving horror pierced the thunderclap of noise.

It was the gaunt warlock. The wizard-priest of the troglodytes had been directly in the path of his toppling god. Tons of falling rock buried him from sight and his last cry was cut short. Then the beast-men broke and fled with whimpers for their holes, while Thongor's weary pirates rested on their crimsoned swords and watched them go, panting. The troglodytes' spirit was broken, but then few men can endure to stand and watch the death of their god. And they were not quite men.

In the ringing silence, Thongor sagged, relaxing, and began to rub feeling back into his hurting hands. He was grey with rock-dust from brow to heel, and devilishly thirsty, but he was alive and whole. And this night of hell was over.

10

High Seas

Dawn burst flaming up over the edges of the world and drove away the shadows of the night. With dawn came a quick, freshening breeze that caught and boomed in the scarlet sails of the lean black galley. Taut rigging thrummed like a great harp in the rising wind. The deck swayed and the prow rose sharply.

Wrapped in a warm cloak, Thongor leaned against the rail, pouring cold red wine down his gullet. When he came up for air, bald, glum-faced Chelim was at his side.

"The burial-party are all aboard now," the Zangabali grunted heavily. "Kanthar Kan sleeps with his fathers now—or drinks the morning cup in the Hall of Heroes, if the priests tell it true."

"Aye," Thongor nodded. "And is that why you've such a long face? He died like a man, writing a warning to his shipmates with his last dregs of strength. There's naught to mourn in a brave man's death. Pray Gorm we all meet our end so gallantly!"

The first mate rubbed stubbled cheeks, his expression sour.

"'Tis not that, Cap'n—but this cursed voyage, come to nothing! All this way, and lose a good man, and for what? No treasure… only black jungles, stinking savages, and sorcery to boot. Perhaps we'll greet a fat merchantman on our way home to Tarakus and lighten his cargo a mite, but I cannot help but wish it had been…"

His words trailed off. His eyes widened and a look of blank stupefaction passed over his face, giving him a singularly ludicrous expression. For without a word, face solemn, Thongor had bent and dug one hand deep in his high sea-boots, and brought up a handful of glistening ruddy pearls. And another. And another!

"The brutes surprised me at the pool, just as I was admiring their pretty pearls," the young buccaneer explained. "I just had time to stuff a few handfuls in my boots—devilish uncomfortable things to walk about on, pearls are. But there should be enough pretties here to warm the heart of the coldest trader in the thieves' bazaar back in Tarakus…and enough to split among the crew so that any that want can retire to a life of ease, after this voyage."

The look of astonishment passed from Chelim's face and was replaced by a wondering, beaming grin. "Hoy, Fulvio, lads, come here!" he boomed. "See what the Cap'n fetched back from that cursed land. Lad," he said frankly, "my heart goes out to you: with a pack of howling savages just leapin' on your back, you take time enough to shove a prince's ransom down your boots before turning to fight for your life. Now *that's* what I call thinking like a born pirate!"

Dog-tired from the night's perils and exertions, the crew ambled over to the rail to find out why their captain and first mate were whooping with laughter in so odd a manner. Needless to say, once the cause of the hilarity was made clear to them, their hearts lifted at one glimpse of the fabulous flame pearls of Cadorna. A pirate, like a man who follows any other trade, likes to turn a tidy profit from a day's toil. And not long thereafter, as the lordly Sun ascended the clear blue sky, the pirate galley *Black Hawk* drew up her dripping anchor, turned about into the wind, and pointed her dragon prow to the high seas and whatever new fortunes awaited her.

Thongor's feats among the corsairs of Tarakus become legendary until, finally, he falls foul of their King and, after a bloody duel in which Thongor slays him, the Valkarthan is forced to flee from the navy of his erstwhile companions. During the next year he battles through the jungle Southlands, enlists in the services of the Sark of Zangabal as a mercenary swordsman, then falls back on his old trade of thief.

It is the year 7007 of the Kingdoms of Man and Thongor is now twenty-five years old.

THIEVES OF ZANGABAL

1

In the Hall of Seven Gods

The priest Kaman Thuu was old and gaunt and skeletal, his lean body wrapped in a robe of crimson velvet whereon the symbols of the Seven Gods of Zangabal were worked with stiff gold thread. Jeweled rings flashed and glittered on his clawed fingers, and his eyes burned keen and sharp in his shaven, skull-like head.

"We are agreed then," he purred. "For twenty pieces of gold you will rob the house of Athmar Phong the magician and fetch back to me the mirror of black glass you will find in his workshop. And this task you will fulfill this very night."

"Aye," the bronzed young giant grunted sourly, "but I do not like the task."

"I have already explained that you have naught to fear at the hands of Athmar Phong," the priest reminded him silkily. "This is the first day of Zamar, the first month of spring. On this night the magicians of the Grey Brotherhood, to which Athmar Phong is sworn, meet on a mountainous plateau far to the north of here for their vile and sorcerous sabbat. Thus will the magician be absent tonight, and thus you may thieve the mirror for us in utter safety."

"So you claim," the youth growled, "and so it may well be. But it is never wise to meddle in the affairs of wizards, and their houses go seldom unguarded. What if this Ptarthan sorcerer has left behind a demon to watch over his treasures?"

Cold amusement flickered in the cold eyes of the gaunt priest. He ran his gaze over the broad shoulders, the long and powerfully muscled bare arms, and the deep, heavy thews of the chest of the young barbarian who sat before him in the veiled antechamber of the temple. And he let his gaze linger on the massive hilt of the great two-handed Valkarthan broadsword that hung at the lean waist of the young thief in its long scabbard of dragon-leather.

"Surely you are not…*afraid*?" he suggested slyly.

The young barbarian flushed angrily. His strange gold eyes, that burned with sullen, wrathful fires under scowling black brows in his tanned face under the thick, unshorn mane of black hair, blazed with sudden temper. Then they cleared, and the youth threw back his head and laughed.

"Gorm!" he rumbled. "You sit here safe and secure in your silken nest, a pure and holy priest of the Gods of Zangabal who would never sully his sanctified fingertips with blood or crime—and pay another man to take risks and dare the perils you would shudder to face—and then taunt him with a hint of cowardice!" The burly young barbarian laughed again, and spat on the fine Pelorm carpet. "Wizards and priests! You are alike, the both of you—and I would have dealings with neither, if I had my way!"

The gaunt skull-face of Kaman Thuu tightened and his voice grew harsh and contemptuous. "Would you rather starve like a whining beggar in the back-alleys of Zangabal, barbarian? Because that you will do if you refuse the task I have set you. Remember, the Thieves' Guild is powerful in our city: to make your living as a thief here, you must join the Guild, or fight both your brother thieves and the city guard each time you attempt a robbery. And to enter the Guild, you must pay a heavy fee in gold. For weeks, by your own account, you have fought over scraps like a half-starved animal, stealing from the bazaar, lifting a fat purse, scrabbling like an *unza* for a bare subsistence. I alone have offered you gold for a task: reject my offer, and you perish miserably either of a starved belly or at the hands of the Guild—"

Thongor—for it was he—waved away this cloud of words with a grunt of surly acknowledgement. "I know all this, priest. And I also know why you come to me, an outlander, with your offer—because the self-respecting thieves of Zangabal have already re jected you! By Gorm the Father of Stars—even the cunning thieves of Zangabal dare not steal from this Ptarthan mage! But I must do it or starve, so save your breath. But I still ask: what if this Athmar Phong has left a demon to guard his house while he is absent? I have fought beasts and men before now, but no warrior can pit naked steel against hell-spawn and live!"

The priest narrowed thoughtful eyes. "There is some truth in what you say, barbarian. Athmar Phong *is* reputed to hold a familiar spirit or elemental bound to his service. That is why we of the temple are willing to entrust to your hands a rare amulet which is one of our treasures."

He dipped one bony, bejeweled hand into his crimson robes and brought forth a small object of curious workmanship which he set gently on the tabletop between them, moving to one side the empty wine bottle and the remains of the meal of broiled *bouphar*-steak with which he had somewhat appeased the ravenous appetite of his surly guest.

The thing was as long as a man's middle finger and made of colorless crystal. It glittered in the orange light of the candelabra. Thongor picked it up gingerly, turning it so it caught the light. He scrutinized the amulet but could make nothing of it. The surface of the lucent crystal was engraved with a pattern of tiny heiroglyphs in some unknown language. He grunted sourly. A simple barbarian, bred in the savage wilderness of the frozen north, far from the perfumed cities of silk-clad men, he had a healthy warrior's contempt for all this foul, sly witchery. Still, there was an odd glitter to the thing: and his fingers tingled with the faint currents of some uncanny force locked within the very structure of the crystal...

"What does this gewgaw do?" he rumbled mistrustfully.

"This amulet is called the Shield of Cathloda," the priest told him in a severe tone. "It is a rare protective amulet which diverts and absorbs the attack of magical forces, and it was made a thousand years ago in Zaar the Black City far to the east. It can rechannel or cancel anything up to ninth-order forces. Fear not; even if Athmar Phong has left magical traps or a guardian familiar of some kind, you will walk safely and unharmed."

Thongor studied the crystal cylinder for a few moments. Then he stood up, slipping the amulet into his pocket-pouch and drawing an immense hooded black cloak about his brawny shoulders. "Very well, priest," he growled. "I will chance it for your gold…although something tells me it is a bargain I will yet live to regret—*if* I live!"

2.

Black Catacombs

The priest then led Thongor from the veiled antechamber and into the central nave of the colossal temple. At this hour of night there were no worshippers in the vast gloomy domed chamber, which murmured with whispering echoes.

At the far end of the hall, which was lined with titanic pillars of pale marble that loomed up into the shadow-thronged darkness of the vault above like stone sequoias, stood towering idols hewn from seven kinds of stone: the Seven Gods they worshipped here in Zangabal on the Gulf. Thongor eyed them grimly, unimpressed. The winged colossi, bearing mystic attributes and symbols in their many arms, tridents, stylized thunderbolts, crowns, swords and less-recognizable accoutrements, glared down at him, their stone faces shining in the dim gleam of coiling blue flames which glided heavenwards from a vast bronze bowl on the alabaster altar. The superstitions of the barbarian were bred deep in him, stamped in blood, brain and bone: but he knew them not, these alien gods of the tropic, jungle-clad Southlands: he swore only in the name of Father Gorm, the grim God-King of the dark northern wastes of ice and snow.

The priest led him around to the rear of the sevenfold dais where the stone colossi reared up. There he touched a hidden catch. A panel of thick marble sank from view, soundless and sudden as a feat of magic, revealing the yawning mouth of a black cav ern. Thongor growled, nape-hairs bristling at the thought of entering the ominous portal.

"This hidden route will carry you to the house of Athmar Phong," the priest said smoothly. "You will follow the yellow symbols only: they are shaped like the Yan Hu glyph—you know the characters of our Southland language, do you not?"

"Aye," he nodded curtly.

"Then follow only the yellow Yan Hu, and it will lead you to the pits under the magician's house. Let me caution you not to stray from the path thus delineated, for other characters mark other routes, such as for example, the Shan Yom glyph, marked in red, which leads to the waterfront. You will come up beneath the house, and will thus avoid the many magical traps or defenses the Ptarthan wizard has doubtless set over his walls, his doors and his windows."

Despite the soothing words of the gaunt priest, the brawny young warrior still hesitated at the threshold of the black tunnel's mouth.

"What are these cursed caverns—how did they come to be here?" he demanded. "Since I bear your crystal toy, why should I not take my chances with the front gates and walk the streets under the open skies like a man? I am no skulking *unza*, to slink through your stinking sewers!"

The priest answered smoothly: "These cavernous passageways are very old; indeed, their origins are lost in the dim mists of the ancient past. But the chronicles of our temple tell that at the end of the Thousand-Year War with the fall of Nemedis in the east, the children of Nemedis came thither to found the nine cities of the west. It was Yaklar of the House of Ruz who was lord of the founding of Zangabal, and it is written that the hidden ways were here even before the walls of the city were first raised. More than this we know not, but by means of this secret the temple is mighty in Zangabal, and even the Sark in his mighty palace is not beyond the reach of our eyes and ears, for the tunnels extend even under the royal precinct. But come, barbarian, you must linger no more: night passes swift-winged, and you must accomplish the theft of the black mirror before dawn or be surprised in the midst of the task by the returning of Athmar Phong."

The gaunt priest stood by the open portal until the grim-faced young warrior had vanished in the darkness of the tunnels; then he released the secret spring and closed the hidden door again. He stood for a moment, fingering his lean jaw with bony fingers. With luck, the mirror would be in his possession before the first hour of morning, and with it—*power*! Power to bend even the strong will of Athmar Phong to his bidding. Power to command the secret of the mirror itself, by which he saw a clear path from this place to a higher…to the throne of Zangabal itself! He smiled a slow, evil smile at the thought.

And, as for the barbarian—well, why should he squander even a portion of the gold his wiles had wrung from temple-worshippers? The youth could be disposed of without loss: he was not even a member of the Thieves' Guild, which was a stroke of good fortune, as the Guild took a disquieting degree of interest in the disappearance of its members. But no one would even miss the Outlander.

His hand went to the small glass phial concealed in a secret pocket of his robes. There was enough powder of that deadly narcotic called Rose-of-Dreams within the small phial to destroy a dozen such as Thongor of Valkarth.

* * * *

Thongor strode through the darkness, his strange gold eyes questing about distrustfully and one hand at the hilt of his mighty broadsword. The cavernous passage was black as the depths of his savage northlander hell, and it reeked of dead things long unburied.

Dangling stalactites hung from the arched roof overhead, glistening wetly in the dim, faint light. The very presence of the hanging spears of stone denoted the awesome and incredible age of this network of secret passages beneath Zangabal, for Thongor understood that such were slowly built up over weary aeons of sluggish, calcareous drippings. He would almost have assumed the passages to be the work of nature from such evidence, but the walls and floors of the tunnels clearly showed the handiwork of the builder. For although obscured by centuries of neglect and decay, the ancient marks of stone-working tools were still visible along his path. He wondered grimly what unknown people of earth's remotest dawn had built these subterranean ways, and for what mysterious purpose. Often he had heard whispered myths of the pre-human Dragon Kings of lost and boreal Hyperborea, buried countless ages ago under the fathomless snows of the ultimate polar north. Legend told that the mystery-race of lost Hyperborea, sprung from the gliding serpent and not the jungle ape, as were the races of men, had ruled all of old Lemuria before the creation of Phondath the Firstborn, the Father of All Men. Could it have been the shadowy Hyperboreans who cut these passages through the depths of the world?

Shrugging, he put such questions aside. It would be futile to puzzle over such mysteries, since he had no answer to the riddle. He strode forward, his black leather boots crushing the mold and pooled slime which covered the stony floor.

And then he came to the branching of the tunnel. One offshoot led away to his left, but it was marked with the Shan Yom symbol painted on the wall in strange pigments that glowed with cold, crimson fires. The other passage, to his right, was emblazoned with the phosphorescent yellow glyph of Yan Hu. He took the right hand way.

Cold water dripped from the roof above, slow drops splashing in black pools, beslimed and foul. Small sounds came to his ears as he strode forward: the squeak and scurry, the rattle of tiny claws rasping over wet stone; the tunnels were a-swarm with *unza*, the hideous, naked scavenger-rodents of Lemuria. He could see the gemlike wink and glitter of small, red eyes from the black mouths of side-tunnels as he moved forward. He ignored the scrabbling rats, but his hand tightened on the hilt of his broadsword: the *unza* were eaters-of-flesh, and where they slithered thick could also be found larger and more dangerous creatures.

Once a black serpent slid across his path and he recoiled, choking back a curse. But the viper glided on, ignoring him even as he ignored the rats. Then the foaming torrent of a subterranean river cut across his path. He crossed it by means of a narrow, arched bridge of stone. Icy spray splattered him from the black waters as they rushed by beneath his heels, and his feet slipped on the treacherous slimy mold with which the stone arch was crusted, but he plodded forward grimly.

He sullenly cursed the ironies of fate that had cast him up on this shore. Nine years had passed since he had found his way down across that mighty mountainous spine of the Lemurian continent, the Mountains of Mommur, from the frigid wastes of his homeland. Since then, in his wanderings in these Southlands, he had been an assassin, a wandering adventurer, a thief—the last profession ending on the slave-galleys of Shembis from which he had escaped, leading a slave-mutiny and stealing the very galley on which he had toiled under the overseer's singing whip.

Thence he had sailed south to Tarakus, the pirate city that lay at the foot of the Gulf of Patanga, where it mingled with the wind-lashed waters of the Yashengzeb Chun, the Southern Sea. The youth had brawled and battled his way to power in the red, roaring Kingdom of Corsairs: as one of the proud Captains of Tarakus he had swaggered through the narrow, spray-swept streets of the little seaport draped in costly brocade, emeralds and rubies blazing about his corded throat, and the wealth of a dozen fat merchant ships piled in the basement of his great stone house. But, alas, his hot Valkarthan temper had been his doom, and he had slain the Pirate King in a duel still legendary among the wild rogues of the Corsair Kingdom. He had fled with half the Tarakan navy at his heels—of his golden treasure-trove, he bore off only the rags on his back and the mighty broadsword of his kingly sire. Thus, during the year past, he had fought his way through the jungles of the Southland to the quays and docks of Zangabal, hoping to enter the Sark's service as a mercenary swordsman. But, that failing, he had fallen back on his old profession of thievery, and thus had come to the present perilous impasse—serving a black-hearted priest by robbing a dangerous and potent magician.

Suddenly a black wall swung up before his very face, and Thongor jerked his attention away from his wandering memories. His underground journey was over, and the house of Athmar Phong lay before him.

3.

Soft Lips

Thongor ran his hands lightly, questing, over the wall of black stone that confronted him. The marked path ended here, that much was certain: behind this wall, then, must lie the pits below the house of the Ptarthan mage. But how to pass the wall?

Growling a curse on that smirking priest, who had not forewarned him of this barrier, he fumbled about in the dark and at last—more by happy accident than by careful plan—his fingers found the hidden spring and depressed it. The smooth wall of black stone sank soundlessly into the earth and the warrior stepped forward into a gloom-drenched room cut from smooth, heavy stone.

He did not, as of yet, seek to close the opening thus made. One could never be certain how swiftly one wanted to leave the house of a wizard, and a smart thief never closed a door behind him if he could help it.

The basement was piled with crates, bales and barrels. Thongor did not waste time looking them over; he prowled through the darkness of the room, every sense at the alert, the great broadsword naked in his hand. Soon he encountered a stone stair against the further wall, and followed it up to the next floor on silent feet. Pushing through a heavy hanging of purple cloth, he found himself in a room so weirdly furnished that at first all he could do was blink and stare and blink again as he stood in the doorway.

The walls were of smooth stone faced with gray plaster and lined with shelves of dark wood. Along these were stacked and piled a jumble of curious things. Bottles and jars and flasks filled with colored liquids and nameless powders, bundles of dry withered leaves and grotesquely shaped roots, little cloth bags tied with a drawstring and filled, perhaps, with strange drugs and deadly powders.

And books—more of these than Thongor had ever seen before. Huge, thick, ponderous tomes made of crinkled sheets of rough parchment, crudely bound in heavy leather or carved wood or painted ivory panels.

This, he knew, must be the magical workshop of Athmar Phong. A massive desk of oily black wood, carved all over with grinning devil-masks stood to one end of the room, its top littered with hieroglyphic charts and curious instruments of brass and crystal. A man's skull of browned bone stood as a paperweight on one corner of the desk, and rubies were set in the sockets of the skull-like eyes. They glinted with malign, small lights that seemed to follow his movement as he crossed the room.

A monstrous, stuffed dragon-hawk, a winged and terrible flying dragon, hung from wires suspended from the rafters. In a globe filled with milky fluid, a human brain floated.

Thongor noticed that this room was well lit, although he could not discover the source of the illumination. Gazing about, he could see no windows, nor were there any lamps, candles or torches to be seen: nevertheless the chamber was bathed in a harsh, gray, sterile light that leached most of the color out of things. A prickle of unease crawled down his spine, and, as he could not see the black mirror the priest had sent him here to fetch, he hastily quitted the silent room and pushed through a velvet-hung doorway into an adjoining chamber.

Whereas the first room had been cold and grim and workman-like, with its harsh gray illumination and bare stone floors, this second chamber was a nest of silken luxury. The air reeked with heavy perfumes from a fat silver incense-lamp on a low tabouret of sleek blond wood inlaid with small panels of delicate ivory, exquisitely sculptured with shockingly detailed pornographic tableaus. A long, low divan lay along the further wall—and there, languorously coiled amidst a nest of bright-colored fat cushions, a young girl of breathtaking loveliness watched him from dark almond eyes.

The shock of discovering that the room was occupied by another stunned Thongor for an instant—but no longer. The hair-trigger reflexes of a barbarian warrior took over. The keen point of the great broadsword came up and hovered a half-inch from the base of the girl's throat.

"One sound—one word—!" Thongor growled.

The girl smiled slightly and continued to regard him from under thick, sooty lashes. Thongor looked her over curiously. She could have been eighteen, but no older, for her sleek, soft body was as slim and graceful as a young panther. A thin sheet of green silk was drawn partly across her white body, leaving bare one arm and one long, slender leg, with a silver disc upon the tip of each of her young breasts. Her long, thick hair was fire-red with gold gleams shot through the silken tresses. Thongor had never seen a redheaded girl before, but he knew that some of the slave women in the harems of the Southland kings used color dyes, which may have explained the dazzling shade of her tresses, which were woven into one thick braid with strands of glowing pearls.

Her face was filled with fresh young beauty. Dark, tip-tilted eyes under thick black lashes, a full-lipped, warmly crimson mouth; and soft delicate skin of flawless pallor.

"Thank the Gods you have come!" the girl breathed in a low, quiet voice, deep and husky. She writhed a little on the silk divan, and the thin covering of green silk slipped awry a trifle, revealing the naked curve of her thigh and slim hip. Slowly, so as not to trigger him into action, the girl lifted into view her slim, bare arms:

they were bound at the wrist with manacles made of small gold chains.

"Who are you, lass? The wizard's concubine?" he demanded roughly, still holding the great sword at her warm throat.

"The wizard's slave," she sighed. Then, before he could speak, she continued in a rush of words: "Athmar Phong stole me from my people when I was eleven; for seven hideous years I have been his helpless slave, the subject of every vile whim and loathsome fancy that came into his black, putrid heart!" Her shallow young breasts rose and fell, straining the green silk of her covering taut with every breath.

"For seven years I have dreamed and prayed that someone would come to free me from this hideous bondage, and at last *you* have come to break my chains and set me free!"

Heedless of his lifted sword, the girl slid from the couch and knelt before Thongor, the heart-shaped oval of her face lifted to him, tears trembling on her sooty lashes.

"Free me...free me, warrior...and I will gladly be *your* slave!" she whispered.

Thongor was young, and he had been without a woman since leaving Tarakus a year before, so it was not surprising that the blood rose hotly within him. Growling a calming word or two, he sheathed his sword and bent to snap the slender golden chains that bound the wrists of the helpless girl. Then he lifted her from her knees in his strong arms. She curled languorously against him, her slim arms sliding around his waist, her naked legs smooth and soft against his bare thighs. The pulse thundered in his temples as he felt the resilient warmth of her breasts pressing against his bare chest through the thin silk covering that was all she wore. She lifted her soft, trembling mouth to his lips. Another instant and he might well have forgotten the dangers of this place, and the perilous mission that had brought him...another instant and he might have lost himself in the warm softness of her...

But even as her panting kiss seared his mouth, even as his brawny arms encircled her slim hips, one sly hand slipped into his pocket-pouch—and the girl sprang halfway across the room and turned to laugh mockingly at him—with the Shield of Cathloda clenched between her slim, white fingers.

4.

Spawn of Hell

For a moment he stood frozen with shock, his senses still tingling with the warmth and softness of her slim, young body. She stood across the room, her lips parted—and laughed.

But it was not the soft laughter of a young girl. Peal after ringing peal boomed and roared from her soft, warm lips—and even as he stared uncomprehendingly, dazed with the swiftness of the change, hellish fires blazed up in her almond eyes. They flamed like pits of burning sulfur. And now that she laughed, her lips were drawn back, revealing hideous yellow tusks, like those in the black, blubbery, bristling jaws of the savage Lemurian jungle boar.

She began to...*change*.

Her limbs blurred, then grew transparent as smoke, then re-molded themselves. A ghastly parrot-beak thrust from the warm oval of the girl's face. Blazing orbs of yellow fire seethed with hellish mockery beneath her arched brows. Her hands became scaly bird-claws, armed with ferocious talons.

"Fool of a mortal," the bird-demon croaked in a ringing metallic voice, "I knew of your presence within the house of my master from the first moment you set foot herein, and I chose a form that would lull your suspicions—"

Thongor struck.

The girl-thing had fooled him for a few moments—but now the fighting instincts of a northland warrior turned him into a battling engine of destruction. One hand flashed out, scooped up the fat, round, silver incense-lamp and hurled it straight as an arrow into the demon's half-transformed face. The thud of heavy silver against flesh was audible the length of the room. The monster, its body still a hideous blend of exquisite human female and grisly bird-thing, staggered back from the impact.

The silver lamp broke open, and glowing pink coals splattered the half-changed body of the demon guardian. In an instant, the disarranged piece of green silk the devil still wore went up in a flash of flame. Blazing coals dribbled down between the white, soft breasts of the girl-like torso, raising terrible weals and blisters. The parrot-beak gaped open, screeching with agony and fury.

Thongor had not paused, as would a civilized man of the southern cities, to use reason; instinct alone told him that if the demon still wore flesh, that flesh could feel pain. He followed the flying brazier with the small tabouret on which it had stood. This he hurled like a powerful catapult straight at the ghastly scaled claw that clutched the protective talisman. The blunt edge of the wooden tabouret caught the slim girl's wrist, which had only partly changed into a demon's claw. The bone snapped with the sound of a dry branch cracking. The claw sagged limply as the demon howled—and the amulet fell.

Thongor dove across the room. His flying body crashed against the tender girl-legs of the monster and sent it reeling back against the further wall, while he scooped out one hand to catch the talisman. Luckily the fragile crystal thing had fallen on thick, soft carpets—had the floor been of bare stone, like the workshop through which he had recently passed, his only hope of escaping from this den of hell alive would have smashed to a thousand tiny shards.

Swift as he was, the demon was swifter. Even as he went crashing back against the wall, it—*changed*. The body crumbled into a coiling length of smoking stuff, and one arm snaked out, inhumanly long, to snatch the fallen amulet almost out of Thongor's very fingers. The young warrior came to his feet in a rush, steel singing as he tore his sword from its scabbard.

The demon melted before him, reassembling itself across the room. Only the hand which grasped the all-important amulet had remained solid on this plane as the demon moved. Thongor took a swipe at it, but missed. Now he lunged for the monster, swinging up the mighty broadsword, deep chest thundering forth his primitive challenge. The great sword swung glittering up and came hissing down to clang against the scaled, reptilian body of the demon, by now fully transformed to its normal appearance on the earth-plane.

It was like swinging at a wall of solid steel. The shock travelled up Thongor's arms to the shoulders, numbing and paralyzing even his mighty thews. The demon's breast was solid as iron. It was astonishing that the blade of the sword did not shiver to fragments from the impact. But they had wrought well, those wonder-smiths of age-old Nemedis from which the ancient sword had come: potent spells and powerful runes had filled the crystalline structure of the great steel sword with terrific power. The blade held, although nicked: but the ringing shock numbed Thongor to the shoulder and the great sword fell from his nerveless fingers to clang like a struck bell against the stone floor that lay beneath the carpets.

His arms temporarily helpless, Thongor lashed out with a boot-ed foot. Howling with harsh mockery, the great yellow beak of the demon was open, and Thongor's foot crashed into its mouth, crushing the beak to gory ruin. Green hell-blood spurted from the crushed face of the devil, and again it went reeling back against the wall.

Thongor began to understand the limitations of the thing. It had complete control over its body and could doubtless transform itself to the likeness of any creature in earth, hell or heaven, but it was slow of thought. Anticipating a blow from the great Valkarthan broadsword, it had increased the density of the matter of which its breast was composed until it reached the hardness of solid metal— but had not thought to extend the same protection to the rest of its body.

Thus, if the young barbarian could keep it off balance, he might yet defeat the creature, or at least wrest the powerful talisman from its clutches. He dove after the monster as it fell squealing to the floor, its face a bubbling, gory wreck. He landed squarely upon it, both boots crashing down in its groin with crippling weight.

It was naked now, the green silk covering of its girl-guise burnt away by the scattering coals, and sexless as a stone to the eye, at least, but still vulnerable to such a brutal blow. He came crashing down with both feet and heard it voice a shrill shriek of bestial agony. Alien organs crunched and popped under his weight, and more of the green gore splattered from pulped flesh.

But it availed him little. For a second only it squalled and flopped in pain—then it hardened its body to the density of steel all over. He could feel it happening even as he grappled with the wriggling thing. They were both on their feet in a moment, battling lustily. Thongor swung balled fists into the thing's gut and groin, but only tore the skin from his brawny knuckles and numbed his hands again. He shouldered it with terrific force, hoping to break free, and for a moment he took the monster-thing by surprise and shoved it off balance. He heard bird-clawed feet rip through the soft carpeting and squeak against naked stone as it fought to regain its balance.

Then two great hands like twin iron vices closed about his throat and *squeezed*. Blood roared in Thongor's ears like pounding surf. A red haze thickened before his eyes, obscuring his vision. Dimly he could see the snarling visage of the demon's beaked face—now repaired and whole—screeching into his own. But the crushing and intolerable pressure on his throat sent needles of unbearable torment lancing through and through his brain like thrusts of pure, blinding flame.

He fought desperately with every atom of strength in all his mighty form. Lashing out with strong legs, he sought to crush the clawed feet of his foe or entangle its legs and knock it off balance, but to no avail. The demon increased the density of its body, and thus its weight, till it stood as unmovable as a pyramid of solid stone. Thongor rammed his burly shoulders into its chest, thudded balled fists into midsection and groin—but again, to no avail.

He could not breathe. The iron strength of the howling brute was crushing the very life out of him. Strength drained from his knees; he sagged toward the floor, still battling like a titan. His vision had darkened now, so that he could barely see. His knew his face must be black from congested blood, a snarling tiger-mask of grim ferocity. The blood roared in his ears like a thousand seas plunging over the edges of the world to shatter like a thunderclap against the foundations of eternity.

He fought on, as consciousness ebbed and darkness closed around him like black rising waters. He passed into utter blackness, still fighting...

5

Ald Turmis

Thongor came awake like some great jungle cat. His savage heritage had honed his reflexes to exquisite keenness. He did not come awake through slow, foggy transitional stages, as softer, city-bred men awaken, but all at once—from total unconsciousness to full, tingling alertness, like a jungle predator whose slumbers are disturbed by the faint, distant snapping of a twig.

A dim, remote light beat about him. Cold, rough, wet stone was against his naked back and his numb wrists were stretched against the wall of rock, clamped helpless with thick bands of icy metal.

He was in a large, empty chamber cut from naked stone. This his hearing told him instantly; he could hear the faint echoes of water dripping down through the foundations of the building above. From the darkness, the moisture, the foul stench, he reasoned that he must be in some dungeon cell beneath the house of the Ptarthan wizard. His cloak was gone, his sword and other weapons and accoutrements—even the pocket-pouch at his waist, where a few lonely coins were stored against hunger.

But these things mattered little. He was surprised to find himself still alive. And alive he was, or all the myths were wrong—for surely no disembodied spirit could feel such pain as went throbbing and pulsing through every nerve in his body. He took a deep breath, and felt the red waves of pain beating against the very citadel of his mind. His body felt as if every inch of it had been beaten all over with leather clubs. But he still lived.

"I wasn't sure whether you were alive or not," drawled a young man's lazy voice very close to him. Thongor felt the icy drench of shock go through him, and twisted his head about—ignoring the blaze of pain from sore, bruised muscles—to find he had a cell-mate.

His companion was a slim, dark young man, Thongor's age or perhaps a year or two younger, who wore the simple red leather harness of a lone fighting-man unattached to the service of any house or lord. The youth wore a scruffy beard of perhaps two weeks' growth, and was somewhat soiled and stained from the filthy dungeon.

Thongor took him in in one swift, measuring glance. The young man was well bred, with intelligent, dark eyes and a not-unpleasant smile, if a trifle dispirited and sardonic, and he had about him the trim, supple, hard-muscled look of a good fighting-man.

Thongor relaxed, grunting. "I live," he said simply. "Why are you not bound, as I am?" he asked immediately, for his companion was secured by a single chain about his booted leg which was fastened to a ring set in the wall.

The young man grinned faintly. "Because Athmar Phong's pet devil had no trouble in knocking me witless, in contrast to the battle *you* put up. I gather he doesn't consider me of any particular danger. Unlike you—he must judge you a worthy opponent, even for a demon. I could hear the fight all the way down here: it must have been a magnificent brawl!"

"It was," Thongor grunted, "but I lost it. Who are you, and why are you here?"

The dark youth cocked a quizzical brow. "For that matter—I might ask the same of you, my friend!"

The barbarian grinned. "Just so: I am Thongor, a warrior out of Valkarth in the northlands. I sought to steal a magic mirror from this Ptarthan sorcerer, but it seems I have yet a few things to learn about the profession of thievery. And you?"

His companion smiled wryly. "I am named Ald Turmis, and my city is Zangabal. *Belarba*," he said, and Thongor returned the familiar Lemurian word of greeting. The dark young Thurdan regarded him closely.

"Our sanitary facilities are somewhat limited, but I used most of what water we have to clean you up a bit," he said. "There is still a little, if you thirst."

"I thirst, but also, I hunger," Thongor admitted. "I don't suppose there is any—wine?"

Ald Turmis laughed. "A man who has just escaped alive from a barehanded battle with a demon deserves wine aplenty! Alas, we have none. But there is a jug of ale, and some meat."

Since the barbarian was bound in such a way that he could not use his hands, Ald Turmis had to help him eat and drink. Thongor downed the strong, sour ale in great gulps, and felt his head clear and new life spread through his battered body. The meat was cold and dry and tough, but it was meat; he ate until his hunger was appeased, then he lay back with a grunt of contentment. With a full belly, a man could face the future on its own terms.

Ald Turmis had been looking thoughtful. At last, when the barbarian had eaten, he spoke up. "I don't suppose," he began carefully, "that it was a certain Zangabali priest named Kaman Thuu who hired you to rob this house…"

Thongor blinked. "How did you know?"

Ald Turmis shrugged. "I, too, am down on my luck, Valkarthan. I have been travelling about the cities of the Gulf, seeking a place to sell my sword. I should have gone to Thurdis, it seems, for the new Sark of that city, Phal Thurid by name, has ambitions of conquest and empire and is hiring an enormous mercenary army. But, at any rate, I have thus far failed to find a sinecure, and turned to slavery. This same Kaman Thuu offered me gold to steal a certain mirror from the house of Athmar Phong. That was half-a-moon ago, and I have been languishing in this cell ever since."

"Gorm's Blood!" Thongor rumbled. "That sneaking pig of a priest! He didn't tell me there had been others!"

Ald Turmis smiled narrowly. "If he had, you might not have followed his wishes."

"There is truth in that," the barbarian growled. "Why does he seek so diligently for this cursed mirror? It's not a wench's vanity, that's sure; he is as ugly as a skull."

"Oh, but it is a very famous mirror—the mirror of Zaffar, as it is called. He was a mighty wizard of Patanga in ancient days, and this magic glass holds imprisoned within it a great Demon Prince, who must obey him who holds Zaffar's mirror. All the secrets of time and space, all the wisdom of past ages, all the cryptic lore of age-lost and legend-filled Hyperborea is his who possesses the mighty mirror. Doubtless our priestly friend seeks power, as was ever the way of priests."

Thongor's gold eyes blazed under black, scowling brows. They burned amber and fiery as the eyes of lions. "Well, if ever I get free of these chains, I will smash his cursed mirror over his shaven pate for not giving me warning I was walking into a trap," he growled.

6

Naked Steel

For a time they slept, the two of them, their talk done. Food and drink and rest did much to restore the animal strength of Thongor's battered body. When he awoke again, rested and refreshed, he tugged at his bonds restlessly. "Enough of snoring our time away," he rumbled, nudging Ald Turmis to wakefulness with one foot. "This Ptarthan mage will return hither with dawn. It must be near that now, an hour or so hence, perhaps. If we are ever to free ourselves, we must do it soon, for once the wizard has us in his grasp, we are doomed men. Naked steel cannot battle against blasts of magic."

"We are already doomed men," Ald Turmis yawned. "For bare hands cannot battle naked steel, and I have long since given up trying to break my chains."

"But I have not yet tried," Thongor said quietly, and there was something in the level quality of his voice that made Ald Turmis feel a thrill of hope.

"You have the body of a gladiator, Thongor, and the thews of a god. But surely even you cannot burst our chains?"

There was a note of question in his voice, but Thongor merely grunted and turned to examine his bonds. His arms were spread against the stone wall at his back, and his wrists were held flat against the wall by bands of iron riveted to the stone. The position was cleverly thought out: thus bound he could only employ a portion of his strength towards freeing himself, and could use little, if any, leverage. Still, a man could try.

He took deep breaths, his massive chest swelling with power. Great ropes of sinewy muscle writhed across his naked shoulders and down his mighty arms. He set his back firmly against the wet, rough stone, and strove against the bonds. Although his face blackened with effort and the thews of his torso hardened like solid rock, the bonds held. He relaxed, breathing deeply; then he threw every ounce of surging strength in his terrific body against the bonds once more. Ald Turmis watched with growing fascination. The primal, brute-strength of this half-naked barbarian was something beyond his experience.

City-bred men are for the most part shielded against the raw world of nature—for this is the purpose of cities. Raised behind walls, guarded by armies, they but rarely are forced to pit their naked strength against the savage wild.

But Thongor was born on the wintry steppes of the most terrible wilderness on all the earth. The child of wandering hunters, born to bare rock and numb snow and howling winds, in a cruel land surrounded with merciless enemies, men, beasts and the hostile forces of nature, he was driven to battle for survival almost from the very hour of his birth. At an age when most boy-children can scarcely walk, Thongor had fought with his brothers against hungry wolves, knee-deep in frozen snow, with only a piece of rock for a weapon. Hunting the great white bear of the north, he had lived for days alone on the mighty glaciers with no nourishment but the hot blood of his kill to sustain him. The struggle for survival in the savage wilderness was brutal and fierce; the weak died swiftly and only the mightiest of men survived. Thongor had survived the cold, the harsh winds, the ferocious competition, and the cruel years of his boyhood had driven the hard iron of barbarian manhood deep within him.

The iron band—*broke*.

* * * *

Like twin shadows, Thongor and Ald Turmis prowled through the darkness of the secret passage within the walls of the wizard's house on silent feet. They went armed with lengths of chain, since both the great Valkarthan broadsword and the Zangabali's slim rapier had been wrested from them when they were captured. But a length of iron chain was better than no weapon at all, and in this dark house of magic and mystery a man needed a weapon in his hands.

Privately, Ald Turmis thought they were fools not to flee when they had the chance. But Thongor could be grimly stubborn: he sought his great sword, and would not leave without it.

It had been comparatively easy, with one shackle broken and one arm freed, to break loose of the other. Then, with his bare fingers, the mighty Valkarthan had pried open a link of the chain that bound Ald Turmis to the ring set in the wall. Arming themselves with lengths of the very chains that had bound them, the two young warriors stole silently from their cell and into the depths of the cellars of the house. Their first thought had naturally been of escape, for the concealed door to the network of underground tunnels still lay open. But soon they discovered the tunnels had extended directly into a secret passage within the very walls of the house itself, as well as into the basements. Thus the Valkarthan had refused to flee like a thief in the night, and insisted they use this rare opportunity to recover their weapons, at least. Ald Turmis had argued, but to no avail. To the civilized Zangabali, his sword was little more than a tool, and easily replaced. But to the grim barbarian, the mighty broadsword was like a part of his body: he had lived with it by his side too long to abandon it now through fear.

The wizard's house had many rooms and many floors. Cleverly concealed eyeholes, hidden among the wall-decorations, permitted them to spy on the contents of these chambers.

The first room they inspected in this manner was a laboratory given over to alchemy. A great stone fireplace covered most of one wall, and upon its hearth a magic fire of yellow and purple flames crackled, heating the shimmering contents of strange glass spheres. A profusion of chemical equipment cluttered long, low tables of porcelain and steel. Glass and ceramic containers of bewildering design bore colored fluids of unimaginable nature. And strange instruments of the alchemist's science loomed in the wavering, twilight of the mystic fire: crucibles and athanors, curcubits and aludels, and all manner of peculiar devices beyond their knowledge even to name.

The next room was given over to an even more terrible purpose. Herein stood huge vats of milky crystal, filled with thick, soupy fluids. Naked bodies lay within, immersed in the cloudy depths of these vats. They could not tell if these were the bodies of human beings or of animals—all they could see was the gleam of pallid flesh. But Thongor guessed the loathsome purpose of the equipment, and his hackles rose along his nape.

"Breeding vats!" he growled. "Look against the farther wall!"

And indeed it seemed that the Ptarthan wizard was engaged in the ultimate blasphemy itself, the attempt to duplicate the miracle of life. For steel-barred cages ran the length of the further wall, and therein resided the grisly results of the wizard's experiments, or those of them that had gone awry. After one fascinated look, Ald Turmis spat a heartfelt curse and turned his eyes away from the hideous, deformed hybrids that wriggled, slithered and mewled behind the steel bars. There was one creature whose pink, glistening body was almost covered with eyes…eyes that wept with unutterable sadness, as if the thing had brain and wit enough to realize its own loathsomeness.

Another was a horrible blending of naked young girl and monster plant. Her bare body glistened wetly, pallid and unhealthy, although beautifully and perfectly formed. But her wrists and ankles ended in hairy, thick roots, and her bald head was faceless—a thick profusion of pink, fleshy flower petals.

"By the Nineteen Gods," Ald Turmis cursed sickly, "why does he let the pitiful things live—they should be put out of their misery with clean steel and burnt!"

"Come," Thongor growled, "there are other rooms." They went on and came to a chamber whose walls were hung with silken hangings that rippled with black and crimson like leaping flames. From the vast, complex pentacle traced with glowing chalks against a floor of black marble, the nature of this third chamber was easy to guess. They needed not the stench of brimstone that permeated the air, to know that this room was given over to the wizard's conjurations. Here he performed those forbidden rituals whereby one might summon up demons from below or spirits from beyond. The very air tingled with unholy magic. They passed on, unhurriedly.

Many other rooms were thus inspected, and they saw these were given over to wizard's arts almost beyond conjecture. There was one that was completely lined with mirrors. Walls, ceiling and floor were one vast, glittering sheet of reflecting glass. Mirrored wall reflected mirrored wall and thus on to infinity. The purpose of this mysterious chamber was beyond the comprehension of the two swordsmen, but something about the room was unsettling. It was as if space itself was twisted and distorted among those endlessly reflecting, self-mirroring walls. They caught a weird glimpse of an endless nothingness that lay beyond the stricture of space…yawning gulfs of glittering emptiness stretched away forever.

From this terrible glimpse into the abyss they tore their gaze with difficulty. The echoing vastness of dim, shadowy light caught and held their attention with a fascination almost hypnotic. In this room of mirrors, a man could lose himself, could become forever lost in rapt contemplation of endless infinity, his wandering mind trapped and helpless between glittering planes of nothingness…

They came at last to the central hall of the wizard's house, and Thongor stifled a grunt of satisfaction. A stone dais of many steps supported a sparkling crystal throne, and there on the topmost step lay their two swords.

"Come!" he grunted, fingers questing for the spring that would release the secret door. The hall was untenanted; the guardian demon nowhere in sight. The door slid open noiselessly and they stepped forth into the hall.

And the demon laughed.

7

Swords against Sorcery

The hall was broad and high. Stone columns worked with weird runes and glyphs rose to support a cupola of scarlet crystal high overhead. A floor of polished stone tile rang underfoot. Tall stands of glittering brass held up enormous branching candles of perfumed wax, which cast a wavering gold light over the dark emptiness of the wizard's seat of power. Hangings wrought of curious fabrics, depicting nightmarish visions drawn from ultimate chaos, hung between the columns; in the flickering light, distorted demoniac figures leered and grimaced and beckoned from these tapestries with the illusions of life.

Thongor spared but a swift, all-encompassing glance at the décor. He spun to confront the devil-guardian whose mocking laughter pealed through the vaulted hall in a thunder of echoes.

"There!" Ald Turmis yelled hoarsely.

Thongor turned, iron chains swinging in his hands. The demon had fooled them by rendering itself invisible to sight. Now it melted into being on top of the dais where the sparkling crystal throne of its master towered.

It stood seven feet tall, straddling their swords, which were laid at the foot of the throne like an offering. The heart of Thongor grew cold at the appearance of the thing. Now it had taken on its normal form for this plane—a scaled and reptilian thing with a bird's beak and hooked claws. A jagged scarlet crest adorned its flat, blunt, triangular skull, and a serpent's tail lashed the stone steps. Burning eyes blazed like sulfur down at them with cruel triumph.

"Foolish mortals, not to flee when you had the chance!" it roared in a brazen voice. "For now you perish! I had hoped to spare you for my master's pleasure, but now—*die!*"

Thongor crouched, knees bent, the chain swinging loosely, ready for whatever might occur. Ald Turmis backed across the hall towards one of the tall, towering brass candelabra as the demon launched itself at Thongor. It sprang like a dragon-cat of the jungle, claws barred and glittering in the fiery light. But in the very middle of its incredible leap, it *changed*. A sheet of flame enveloped the hurtling form, and it shrunk into a ball.

The globe of flame hurled directly toward Thongor.

At the last possible moment, the barbarian leapt aside with a lithe, tiger-like bound. The globe of fire flashed through the space where he had stood a half-second before. And, as he leapt aside, Thongor swung the heavy iron chain with all the strength in his mighty arms and shoulders. The iron links whistled through the air and caught the flaming sphere a terrific blow.

Thongor had learned something of the demon's nature. While its powers were great, the limitations that were imposed upon it by nature on this plane gave him a certain degree of hope. True, its ability to change shape and substance was Protean—but while in any specific form it was bound by the natural limitations of that form. For example, as a flying globe of flame the thing was virtually without substance, light and flimsy. It could not have, simultaneously, the lightness of flying fire and the iron-hard density of its devil-bird form.

Hence the smashing blow of the heavy iron chain burst the burning globe into a shower of flying fragments. Bits of flame splattered over the floor. Of course, the demon could re-form—but that would take a few seconds of time.

Thongor seized that momentary advantage. In three lithe bounds he had cleared the steps of the dais, snatched up his mighty sword and tossed the slim rapier to Ald Turmis.

Rivulets of flame snaked over the floor and merged into a burning globe again. But now Thongor was doubly armed: the great broadsword was clenched in his right hand and the heavy length of iron chain dangled from his left. He was ready to pit himself against the demon now—as ready as he would ever be. If it came at him in its fire form again, he would again smash it to flying sparks.

But the seething sphere of flames darkened, blurred. It became a monstrous, shadowy form that congealed and hardened. Birdlike wings branched from hunched shoulders, but they were wings of steel. The neck elongated and a long beak pointed, thrust forth. The demon shaped itself into the likeness of a fantastic bird of metal. The feathers that clad its form and its mighty wings were hard, cold metal, like dagger blades. The long beak thrust forth like a spear-point. Clad in glittering metal, the bird-thing rose into the air and sailed at Thongor where he stood on top of the dais. Wings of glistening steel beat with a clangorous din, heavily, but they supported the clumsy monster aloft. And Thongor's blade and chain would prove feeble weapons against the steel-clad flying monster—

Then, unexpectedly, Ald Turmis struck. The demon, whose intelligence was limited, had almost forgotten his presence. Concentrating on its primary foe, the giant barbarian, it had neglected to attend to the young Zangabali swordsman who stood in the shadows of the column-lined wall. The youth turned and seized the heavy brass candelabrum. Seven feet in the air it loomed, and it was heavy as a man—but desperation lent Ald Turmis new strength, and with a mighty heave he tugged it up and hurled it square against the steel bird as it lurched heavily in flight.

The crashing weight of the massive brass stand brought the steel bird down. It clanged thunderously against the marble pave, and the steel-sheathed wings cracked. The long serpentine neck broke and the spear-beaked head went rolling and clattering against the tiles.

"Well thrown!" Thongor boomed.

Ald Turmis flashed a grin and sprang from his place by the wall to snatch up the severed head. Perhaps he had some wild hope of preventing the demon from re-forming somehow. If so, the hellish powers of the monster were too swift for him. The heavy, cold metal of the head melted into smoke in his very hands. A cloud of green vapor leaked through his clutching fingers and floated across the floor. The broken bird of steel now collapsed into a swirling mass of emerald smoke into which the head-portion mixed and mingled.

A bodiless streamer of dense green vapor, the demon rose. It floated through the air like a cloud of smoke borne by the gusts of the wind. Straight for the place where Thongor stood astride the high dais it drifted…to settle about his throat.

8

The Shield of Cathloda

As the smoke-serpent floated towards him, Thongor struck. His great broadsword swung through the vaporous body of the thing, but did not harm it. The drifting banner of vapor was momentarily broken by the passage of his sword blade, but it melted together almost instantly. It swirled about him, and for a moment he was hidden in the cloud of green smoke. Then two vapor tendrils uncoiled from the mass and lashed about the throat of the young warrior. As the clammy fingers of vapor touched his flesh, they congealed—hardened—took on weight and density. Slithering tentacles of tough, leathery flesh tightened in a stranglehold, cutting off his air.

Thongor's weapons clanged against the steps of the dais as he snatched at the tightening tentacles of the smoke-thing. His iron fingers tugged to loosen the crushing coils. Green vapor seethed about him. Starved for air, his lungs strained, his mighty chest heaved.

The sinuous tentacles sank into his flesh with incredible strength. He fought on, as more and more portions of the green cloud solidified into slithering tendrils which slapped into place about his struggling form. One curled about his narrow waist, squeezing with a crushing grip. Another lashed about one booted foot, seizing a firm hold, and then snaked out and coiled around his other leg—and tightened, toppling him off balance and sending him crashing against the top of the dais.

Ald Turmis came yelling across the room, brandishing his slim rapier, to aid him in his heaving struggle against the kraken-form. But before the gallant young Zangabali could spring to the aid of his embattled comrade, chance, or fate, intervened. Thrashing about, striving for a firm handhold on one of the green tentacles that were slowly crushing the life from his body, Thongor's hand slid along the surface of the topmost step of the dais—and closed about the glassy roundness of a slim ovoid.

The demon exploded.

One moment Thongor lay tightly enmeshed in a tangle of writhing emerald tendrils, which were slowly tightening with steely strength, and the next instant the tendrils disintegrated into green vapor. The whirling vapor was flung from him by some tremendous power. It was as if, out of nowhere, an invisible wall had sprung into being about the half-strangled warrior, and, thrusting in all directions outward from his body in unconquerable force, shattered the very substance of the tentacled demon—sundering it atom from atom with a burst of unthinkable power.

At the moment of the explosion, there came as well a thunderous cry of indescribable torment, a bellowing howl of agony that shook the hall and sent the flames of the tall brass candelabra flickering. Ald Turmis had just reached the base of the nine-tiered dais when this inexplicable event took place. The buffeting wind of the explosion knocked him to his knees. Openmouthed with astonishment, he stared about. Scudding wisps of green vapor were flying in every direction from the proximity of the barbarian, who lay prone and gasping for breath at the foot of the crystalline chair of thaumaturgy.

Even as he watched, Ald Turmis became aware that the demon was unable to re-form into a single wholeness again. For the shredded smoke was melting into emptiness even as it floated about the hall. Wisp after coiling wisp dissolved slowly. And, even as the last gobbling echoes of that demonic bellow of unbearable agony faded, the last wisps of vapor disintegrated.

And the demon was gone.

On top of the dais, Thongor stumbled to his feet, dragging huge gulps of air into his starved lungs. He, too, peered about uncomprehendingly. Then, recalling the smooth, cold cylinder his fumbling hand had chanced to grasp, he looked down at what he held. And he burst into croaking laughter.

"It seems I owe that foul toad of a priest, Kaman Thuu, a debt of thanks after all," he grunted hoarsely. And he held up his hand for Ald Turmis' inspection.

There in his palm lay—the Shield of Cathloda!

9

The Return of the Sorcerer

Thongor rejoined his comrade at the base of the dais. Despite the ferocity of the tentacled assault, and the steel strength of the constricting, snaky limbs, Thongor's massive body was unharmed. A few bruises, a few more aching muscles, a smear or two of blood where rasping, tightening ropes of sinewy tendril had torn away a few square inches of his tough hide—but nothing more serious than that.

"It was the talisman," he explained to Ald Turmis, "the protective amulet the old Zangabali priest lent me when I first entered into this cursed and devil-haunted house. It's proof against every sorcery—it nullifies every spell—drives away every magical or demonic thing that comes near. Now that I think about it, the demon was helpless to harm me when I first encountered it. With devilish cunning, the hell-fiend assumed the form of a mortal wench, to beguile me. And once it had distracted my attention, it stole the talisman—the Shield of Cathloda, as old Kaman Thuu called it—from my pocket-pouch."

"But—I don't understand," Ald Turmis said in a puzzled voice. "Why should—"

"If I had not borne the Shield on my person, the demon could have simply fallen on me the instant I entered the wizard's house and torn me apart—or tried to. But it was unable to hurt me, armed with the protection of the amulet…at least until it had seduced me with its girl-form and distracted my attention from the amulet."

"I begin to see," the youth said slowly. "So it fetched the Shield of Cathloda here and set it beside our swords at the foot of the throne, an offering to its master when he should return from the sabbat."

"Aye," Thongor grunted. "And in my threshing about, I chanced to grasp the amulet, which automatically invoked its protective powers. The thing is small and glassy—I did not even notice it when I grabbed up our swords…"

"So when you seized upon the amulet, it tore the demon asunder. But why—how?"

Thongor shrugged impatiently. "How should I know? I know nothing of sorcery and suchlike. Perhaps it formed an invisible barrier about me, repelling the devil-thing. But it happened so swiftly, that the demon was blasted apart…and, since the amulet destroys the magical power of whatever ensorcelled thing it touches, the demon itself was demolished. For it must have been held present on the earth-plane by a powerful spell of black wizardry: it's abnormal for hell-spawn to gain entry into this plane of being; their natural home is far from here."

"So," mused Ald Turmis, "when the touch of the amulet canceled the spell which gave the demon freedom of movement on this plane, it disintegrated, returning to whatever crimson pit of hell was its natural place. And lucky for us it happened as it did, for the vile thing had well-nigh strangled the life out of you—and would have made short work of me, soon after."

"Aye!" Thongor grunted, touching his bruised and swollen throat with tender fingers, grimacing with a wince of pain. "Thank Gorm I blundered on the crystal thing when I did. But, now, Ald Turmis, let us leave this accursed place, and swiftly. We have our swords, and here lie our cloaks and warrior harness. Let us shake the dust of this place off our heels, and repair to the nearest inn. It will take a jug or two of strong red wine to wash the stink of magic from me, and I can taste it already!"

But Ald Turmis, looking past him to the top of the dais, made no answer. Instead he went pale to the lips and clutched Thongor's arm mutely.

Thongor grunted questioningly, and turned to see what had alarmed his comrade. And he saw—

Even as the ruddy glow of dawn lit the crystal dome above them and bathed the shadow-thronged hall with tremulous, bloody radiance, whirling darkness grew about the empty throne on the top of the tier of stone steps. Was it the hell-spawned guardian, returning to this plane? Or was it has master?

10

The Living Statue

Like a churning cloud of dust motes dancing in a skirl of wind, particles of darkness seethed about the sparkling crystal throne. Gradually the whirling motes drew closer together, forming a shadowy pillar of darkness. Seven feet tall the blurred shadow-shape loomed. The vaporous fabric of its substance grew slowly solid. The tall, massive figure of a man melted out of the dense blackness. He was tall and powerful, with a strong-boned, swarthy face, wrapped from head to heel in a long black cloak whose collar lifted to peaks like horns beside his head.

"Gods of Hell!" Ald Turmis swore—"*The sorcerer returns!*"

And it was even so. As they watched, the heavy form became solid flesh. Still wrapped from throat to toe in the stiff black cloak, whose strange fabric glittered with tiny star-like points of light, the huge man stood. He seated himself in his chair of power and let long, naked hands go out to clutch the arms of the chair. These arms ended with great knobs carved from the sparkling crystal from which the throne-chair was hewn, and each facet of these knobs bore inset a potent talisman of magic. Enthroned in his high place, touching with his naked hands the sigils which commanded unseen sources of power, the wizard was enshrined, invulnerable—a pole of power—the connecting node between the universe of matter and the unseen half-world of tremendous forces which lay behind the structure of the cosmos.

Robed in power, beyond the reach of mortals, Athmar Phong gazed down at them calmly. He was a veritable giant of a man. Had his towering height been less, he would have seemed a grossly fat man: as it was, his abnormal tallness made him seem less obese. But massive flesh lay on his giant bones. His weight must have been twice that of an ordinary man like Ald Turmis.

His face was a gross caricature of cold, cynical command. Hairless, massive-boned, he gazed down at them like some colossal buddha. His impassive, unlined face was a passionless mask of heavy flesh. Cold, slitted eyes ringed in fat looked down at them with a placid contempt. There was callous cruelty in the set of his thick lips, brutal virility in the arrogant thrust of his hooked nose, remorseless and superhuman intelligence in the huge, bulging brows of his naked pate.

"Thieves in my house," he said calmly, "and clever ones at that. For, whether you know it or not, mortals, the guardian of my treasures was a demon of the seventh circle. I am amazed that mere men of brawn such as you had the cunning and the wit to destroy so mighty an entity of the transmundane."

His voice was like his face: heavy, slow, soft and cold. The words glided, oily and thick and sluggish, from almost motionless lips. "Whoever sent you here, must have armed you with a potent name of power. Let me warn you, then, do not think to employ such a name against Athmar Phong. Enthroned, I sit at a nexus of the unseen forces, shielded from such powers as you might bear against me by currents of the ineffable. The name would rebound against yourself, leaving me unshaken. But let me see…"

The heavy, hooded eyelids lifted, baring orbs of utter blackness. No whites were visible about those blazing pupils: nor did they look like the eyes of a fully human creature.

Thongor stiffened, his senses stirring with an eerie chill of superstitious fear. The cold gaze of Athmar Phong thrust at him like needles of steel. His own gaze was locked and held in the grip of a superior will. He felt a weird sensation within his skull, as if cold tendrils of thought were prying through the secret places of his mind. It lasted an instant only, and the tendrils were withdrawn.

Ominous satisfaction curved the lips of Athmar Phong in a slight, subtle smile.

"So it was my old friend, Kaman Thuu, sent you here, dog of a barbarian. I shall repay him trebly for this deed! Yonder youth also, as I recall, came here at his urgings: him we took captive half-a-moon ago, and I thought him well secured in certain cellar chambers set aside for uninvited guests. I see the lad had cunning enough to force an exit from there—or did you aid him with those great brawny arms, eh?"

Beside Thongor, Ald Turmis snarled an oath and his knuckles whitened on the hilt of his rapier.

The Ptarthan wizard smiled cynically. "I read your thoughts as well...rash, impetuous youth, it is best that I immobilize the two of you before you cause hurt to yourselves—"

Before either Thongor or Ald Turmis could think or move or speak, the wizard's hand tightened on one of the talismans set within the handgrip of his throne. A shaft of scintillating azure light speared from the crystal throne. The two young swordsmen stood bathed in the shaft of cold blue light, and the wizard smiled as Ald Turmis cried out sharply and Thongor growled an astonished oath.

"I—cannot—move!" the Zangabali cried in a voice of anguish. His face gleamed wetly white, and as Thongor looked he saw an unnatural pallor sweep over the lean, strong body of his comrade, who was naked but for a ragged clout.

"Numb...cold," Ald Turmis groaned. His voice sounded hoarse, constricted, as if the muscles of his throat were half-paralyzed. The wizard chuckled above them, a gloating sound that roused a warning growl in Thongor's deep chest. He, too, felt a momentary chill pass over his body as he stood in the path of the shaft of scintillating blue light. But then his fingers tightened over the cold, ovoid shape of the Shield of Cathloda, which he still clutched in his right hand, and the brief sensation of numbness vanished instantly.

The blue ray dimmed and died. The wizard withdrew his fingers from the circular sigil of blue metal.

"The immobilizing ray," he said softly. "Your flesh will slowly grow harder and more dense until the two of you will turn to stone. Lovely statues to adorn my hall…yet statues that live and think, for your souls will be held captive within your petrified flesh for all eternity to come. Fit punishment indeed, for the tools of that treacherous priestling, Kaman Thuu."

The giant wizard shifted in his throne. He stretched out one hand towards empty air. "Poor mortals!" he said mockingly. "You searched my halls in vain, for that which you sought but could not find was here beside my place all this while, though shielded from the gaze of uninvited guests. Behold—the mirror of Zaffar!"

One great naked hand clutched out at empty air and whisked aside a blur of bright cloth from a pedestal of glistening silver. At the top of the silver stand an oval disc of thick black glass caught the dim radiance of dawn with sullen, shifting fires. Thongor stared.

The mirror had been covered with a strange cloth whose stiff fabric, bright, blurred, was oddly difficult to see. The eye would not quite focus on it; something about its blurred brilliance was eye-twisting, as if the sight slid off it. So the mirror had been beside the throne all the while!

Beside him, Ald Turmis moaned in anguish. His weird pallor was more visible now. The surface of his bare body, ashen white, looked rough and dry, almost…like stone. And Thongor grimly knew that if he did not act, and soon, the young swordsman of Thurdis who had befriended him in the pits below this house of hell would turn to enduring stone—a living statue, imprisoning the tortured soul of Ald Turmis for all time to come.

11

The Breaking of Spells

The slow, heavy voice of Athmar Phong was speaking again, like the dull tolling of a leaden bell under thick water. Waves of words beat against them as the wizard droned on.

"Behold, O fortunate mortals, that which few eyes have ever looked upon—the supreme magical treasure of all the ages! Zaffar the Great, the mighty thaumaturge of Patanga wrought this mirror, and seven generations of time—as mortal men measure time—went into its making! Seven thousand potent spells of power are sealed into the substance of this black mirror. Zaffar fashioned it from perdurable adamant, the strongest substance known to sorcery. Now it is fragile as glass…and bound helpless and raging therein, lie forever imprisoned the very self and substance of Aqquoonk-agua, one of the nine thousand princes of the infernal pit! Aye, a mighty and eternal prince of hell, older than the very universe of stars itself—a fragment of elder chaos and old night—caught and held within the magic mirror of Zaffar the Great! *Behold*—"

The black mirror was about the size of the *cherm*, the small, lightweight buckler the Lemurian warriors wore strapped to their left forearms. It was black as the heart of darkness itself, a disc of shimmering crystal, thick as the breadth of two fingers.

As Athmar Phong touched it with his naked hands, it stirred with strange life. Thongor felt his hackles rise upon the back of his neck. *Within the shimmering darkness, a crimson shadow moved!*

For a moment Thongor glimpsed a great triangular head. As he watched it, it shouldered into view, peering through the mirror as through a black window. He saw one great, glaring eye—a pit of blazing hellfire—and a wide, fanged maw open, working, scream-ing with silent fury. Then the red thing that was a captive Prince of the Pit slunk back into the darkness of its shadowy home and was lost to view.

"Gorm!" the barbarian grunted, feeling sweat trickle down his sides and moisten his brows. Strange and terrible were the ways of wizards; dark and dreadful were their uncanny arts. The mighty, crimson demon was somehow reduced to two dimensions only: to him the flat surface of the mirror was an entire world, from which he could never break free unless released by an outside agency. The whole thing was mad and nightmarish. For an instant he al-most pitied the shambling, scarlet horror locked in the surface of the ebon glass for dim, unimaginable aeons…

A groan of mute suffering from the young swordsman at his side awoke Thongor from these dark thoughts. Ald Turmis, too, was imprisoned—and his prison was his own living flesh, slowly, inch by inch, petrifying into solid stone. A doom darker and more terrible even than that of the enslaved Demon Prince.

It was time for Thongor to act. He had not moved since the Ptarthan wizard had sent the strange beam of azure radiance sweeping over him and his companion.

Secure in his high place, throned in the midst of his magical forces at the nexus of two universes, Athmar Phong little dreamed that the young barbarian was not rendered helpless from the eerie power of the immobilizing ray. But now Thongor swung into action.

He reached out and laid his hand upon the shoulder of Ald Turmis—the hand that held the all-potent Shield of Cathloda. The flesh of his comrade was harsh, dry, rough and cold to his touch. The surface of the young Zangabali's skin felt strangely granular. But the nullifying powers of the protective amulet were enormous—strong enough to whelm the spell of the blue ray, aye, and far stronger, as would soon be seen.

Ald Turmis cried out as the amulet touched his hardening flesh. A tingle of weird force swept through his body, like the shuddering electric force of lightning. Through every cell and organ, every gland and muscle and tissue of his body it swept, and the spell of Athmar Phong ebbed and died before it. The young swordsman, suddenly freed from the effects of the spell, staggered and fell to one knee, gasping with relief.

On the sparkling crystal throne, Athmar Phong froze with utter astonishment.

Thongor tossed back his unshorn mane and roared with laughter. "Now, wizard—if swords cannot battle against sorcery, we will see what happens when I pit magic against magic!" And before the wizard could move or think, Thongor whipped back his mighty arm—and hurled the all-potent amulet straight at the black mirror of Zaffar.

It flew, glittering, through the dawn-lit air. Straight as an arrow to its mark it sped, and when it touched the invisible forces that wove a viewless shield about the wizard's throne of power, great spells were broken. Canceled energies flashed through the spectrum of visible light. A terrific flash of eye-searing radiance lit the hall like some supernal sun.

Tears pouring from his blinded eyes, Athmar Phong screamed terribly, high and shrill like an animal in pain. He lurched unsteadily to his feet, pawing at his eyes.

Hurled with the irresistible strength of Thongor's mighty arm, the Shield of Cathloda flew through the flashing energy field—and crashed full into the black mirror. The mirror came apart in a dark flash of released forces—it shattered to grains of black dust.

For a single instant, as age-old spells were broken, tremendous energy was released. A seething ball of black flame surged about the crystal throne. The silver pedestal, at the very node and nexus of the canceled binding forces, flashed with intolerable heat. It glowed crimson, then canary, then blinding white. It slumped, crumbling slowly, like the shaft of a waxen candle suddenly thrust into the heart of a roaring furnace. Glowing rivulets of molten metal flowed over the topmost tier of the dais like serpents of liquid flame.

One blazing rivulet crawled between the staggering legs of the blinded, howling wizard. His glistening, black cloak went up in a puff of fire. Suddenly sheathed from throat to heel in a sheet of crackling flame, the wizard screeched and fell flopping and writhing to the steps. He rolled down them and crashed against the stone paving of the hall, crushing out the flames beneath his heavy weight. Panting, his flesh blistered and blackened, he staggered to his knees, sobbing with agony and naked fury.

But neither Thongor nor Ald Turmis could spare a glance for the dethroned sorcerer. Their gaze was riveted with horrible fascination at that which stood above the dais. For the Shield of Cathloda had severed the seven thousand spells which had bound the Demon Prince within the depths of the enchanted glass.

Now Aqquoonkagua was free.

12

Flames of Hell

Up out of the whirling cloud of black flame towered and grew a titanic shape of terror. It was crimson, and covered with crawling fire; bestial of shape, hulking and monstrous. It had great sloping shoulders like some mighty ape, from which long arms swung, arms that ended in great three-clawed paws, that also smoldered and smoked as if molded out of red-hot iron.

Up and up it went until it loomed forty feet above the stone pavement. Flames slithered across its shaggy skin; the fiery red light that beat up from it was dazzling. The room swirled with smoke. Blistering heat like the breath of an open furnace went baking across the hall in waves. Soot blackened the walls and hung thick in the air.

Roaring, raging, the crimson thing stood free after long, weary centuries of time. It had no neck. A heavy-jawed, apelike head swung between the burly shoulders. One huge eye blazed with fires of madness under beetling brows. The fanged maw gaped and slavered. One great paw closed into a fist and came smashing down on the soot-blackened, overturned throne. It burst to fragments and was ground to dust under the weight of the blow. The other paw reached down for Athmar Phong.

Naked, the wizard's heavy body sprawled panting at the foot of the dais. Blind and horribly burnt, the Ptarthan sorcerer somehow knew or guessed what was about to happen. Like a huge, fat slug writhing under the gardener's hoe, he squalled and wriggled on the hot paving as the titanic, flaming hand came down upon him. Waves of heat beat from the grasping paw, crisping flesh and withering cloth to ash. The demon's hand was huge as the wizard's body, and the three mighty claws were big as smouldering logs. The searing heat of the demon's flesh smote him first, and he kicked and screamed. Then the hand came down upon him and snatched him up.

Thongor had seen much of battle and death and suffering, but never before had he heard such a cry wrung from mortal lips as that which now went ringing through the hall. A hoarse, terrible bellow of ultimate agony and unutterable despair—the sort of cry that rips the lining of the human throat.

The naked wizard flopped and wriggled on the flaming palm of the demon's hand. Then the burning claws closed over him slowly—tightened—and the screams were cut off. The sickening stench of broiling human flesh filled the great hall. Ald Turmis gagged and spat; Thongor's own gorge rose at the nauseating smell.

Bearing the smoking corpse of Athmar Phong in one great paw, the roaring, raging demon burst up through the dome of dawn-lit crystal and was gone—back to whatever ultracosmic hell the blasphemous rituals of the thaumaturge Zaffar had conjured it from, ages ago.

The broken dome collapsed, strewing the soot-smeared pavement with shattered wreckage. Mighty stone pillars, shoved askew by the demon's skyward passage, toppled slowly, shaking the wizard's house to its foundations as they came crashing down. Black cracks zigzagged through the fabric of the walls. The house was coming down upon their heads.

Thongor grabbed Ald Turmis by the shoulder, shouting through the roar of wreckage. They ran across the buckling stone flags for the yawning blackness of the secret panel, which still stood open. Thongor snatched up their cloaks and harnesses as they sprinted for freedom.

The terrific heat of the demon's crimson body had touched to flame the tapestries and hangings in the hall. Overturned benches and fallen beams blazed like oil-soaked torches. The ruined hall was transformed into a thundering inferno within mere instants.

The two warriors plunged into the black door and vanished from view. Down the secret passageways they went. Room after room, as they passed, was bursting into flame. It was weird to see solid marble burn, and metal, and crystal, too. The fires that blazed within the demon's body were the fires of some ultracosmic inferno—hotter than any flames of man's knowledge. The terrible hellfire burned through stone walls and floors, consuming everything in its path like a ravenous dragon.

And thus it was that doom came down upon the house of Athmar Phong and he was never again seen by the eyes of men.

13

A New Day Dawns

The morning breeze blew fresh and clean from the great Gulf of Patanga, and the tang of the wet salt sea was upon it. They drew deep lungfuls of cold, fresh air with hearty zest after the stench of the burning house and the reeking slime of the subterranean passage. It was good to be alive, and free, watching the sun come up over the shoulder of the world. All things looked pure and clean and new in the clear, strong light, and the horrors of the night were over and done. Thongor drank deep of cold red wine and stretched out his weary legs with a grunt of satisfaction.

They had found the secret door in the pits, the door that led to the branching ways of the subterranean network of tunnels beneath the city, and for a time they had followed the yellow Yan Hu characters that marked the way back to the Temple of Seven Gods. But Thongor had not survived this long in the Land of Peril—as the *Scarlet Edda* named all these realms of the devil-haunted Southlands—without evolving a strong and canny sense of survival. Why return empty-handed to the gaunt, scheming priest? He would pay nothing for a task undone—and Kaman Thuu would not be very happy to learn the black mirror was now destroyed for all time. Instead, the barbarian recalled what the priest had said about Shan Yom glyphs with which side tunnels were blazoned in scarlet, glowing pigment. Hence he and Ald Turmis had taken this route, and come out in an empty alleyway beside the seafront where tall ships rode at anchor, waiting on the morning tide.

The two youths were filthy, hungry and exhausted from the trials of their night in the house of hell. But it would have been unlike Thongor to have come forth empty-handed from the wizard's house; so he had lingered for a moment in one of the lower chambers to snatch up a gem-covered ornament or two with which he and Ald Turmis had purchased themselves a hearty breakfast in the quayside tavern called The Sailor's Haven.

Across the rooftops of the city, a pillar of oily black smoke stood against the pure morning skies. Blue and scarlet flames flickered through it strangely. The house of Athmar Phong was burnt to ashes and all his terrible sorceries were dust, aye, and the loathsome, mewling hybrids of his blasphemous experiments in life-making had gone to rest at last and were freed forever from the torment of living. But still the rubble burned.

"Where now?" Thongor grunted to his companion.

Ald Turmis emptied the last drop of wine from their third bottle and sat back with a sigh of repletion. "The gods know, friend," he said. "But one thing at least is certain: it would be unhealthy for the two of us to remain here in Zangabal for long. Kaman Thuu has long arms and many cunning fingers. And he will not like this night's black business, you may set a wager on that!"

"I know," Thongor grunted lazily. "I have a mind to see the gates of Zangabal close shut behind my back, and to strike out for another city. I have good reasons for avoiding Shembis, where I am not enamoured of the Sark, Arzang Pome. What about this Thurdis, the Dragon City across the Gulf, of which you spoke earlier?"

"Well, why not?" said Ald Turmis. "Phal Thurid, Sark of Thurdis, arms himself for conquest and I have heard he enlists a mighty host of warriors. Surely there is a place among his warriors for your mighty broadsword, and my rapier. Shall we try our fortunes in the ranks of the mercenaries? There is a merchant galley flies the Dragon of Thurdis at the ninth quay. They sail with the early morning tide, and if you have any gold left after purchasing this magnificent feast of which I can eat not a single bite more, perhaps we can buy passage to Thurdis. Shall we go together for a while, Thongor, and see what Fate has in store for us?"

Thongor stretched lazily, like a great cat. His black cloak was slung about his bare, bronze shoulders, and a gold coin or two still nested in the pocket-pouch of his warrior's harness. He ached to shake the dust of Zangabal from his heels, and to feel the gulf-wind blow fresh and clean in his face, and to explore the winding ways of a new city for a time.

"Well, why not?" he growled, and it was decided.

And thus were the feet of Thongor set upon the path that would lead him in the fullness of time to a destiny stranger and more glorious than that of other men…

ABOUT THE CONTRIBUTORS

LIN CARTER (1930-1988) was one of the most prolific proponents of sword & sorcery, and his work in promoting and expanding Robert E. Howard's "Conan" series helped introduce the genre to countless millions of fans. He is also the creator not only of Thongor, his own best-selling fantasy hero, but of numerous other series which have delighted legions of fans over the decades. His "Green Star," "Terra Magicka," "World's End," and "Callisto" books have long proved themselves popular favorites. Wildside Press has reprinted many of Carter's best-known works in recent years.

ROBERT M. PRICE (born July 7, 1954) has written a significant amount of articles and short fiction. He edited and wrote regularly for the excellent *Crypt of Cthulhu* magazine and also edits and writes for the extensive Chaosium, Inc. Mythos books, inspired by the work of H.P. Lovecraft and arguably the most exhaustive compilation of Mythos related fiction published anywhere in the (known) universe. His critical, thoroughly researched articles, mainly on Mythos fiction, have appeared regularly since 1981. His is also the author of a book-length study on Lin Carter's fiction.

ADRIAN COLE (born July 22, 1949) has had 21 fantasy novels published, beginning with *The Dream Lords* trilogy in 1975. Other such works include the *Omaran Saga*, the *Star Requiem* books and more recently, from Cosmos Press, *Storm Over Atlantis*. He has also had two young adult novels published, *Moorstones* and *The Sleep of Giants*, set on Dartmoor and in the South West of England, his home.

Wildside Press has recently published *Oblivion Hand*, the first volume in a trilogy of books about the dark fantasy character, the Voidal. One of the stories from that book, *First Make Them Mad* was runner up for the British Fantasy Award.

www.ingramcontent.com/pod-product-compliance
Lightning Source LLC
Chambersburg PA
CBHW020321260626
47156CB00004B/1314